Sleigh BELLES

JANICE HANNA

Belles & Whistles

Sleigh BELLES

summerside
PRESS™

Summerside Press™
Minneapolis 55337
www.summersidepress.com

Sleigh Belles

Scripture references are from the following sources: The Holy Bible, King James Version (KJV).

The author is represented by MacGregor Literary Inc., Hillsboro, Oregon.

Cover design by Peter Gloege, Lookout Design, Inc.
www.lookoutdesign.com

Interior design by Müllerhaus Publishing Group
www.mullerhaus.net

Summerside Press™ is an inspirational publisher offering fresh, irresistible books to uplift the heart and engage the mind.

Printed in USA.

DEDICATION

To Eleanor Clark, one of the strongest women I have ever known.
And to my Montana grandbabies. Nina misses you.

For which cause we faint not;
but though our outward man perish,
yet the inward man is renewed day by day.
For our light affliction,
which is but for a moment,
worketh for us a far more exceeding and
eternal weight of glory;
while we look not at the things which are seen,
but at the things which are not seen:
for the things which are seen are temporal;
but the things which are not seen are eternal.

2 Corinthians 4:16–18 KJV

ONE

Women of America, awaken! Do not close your eyes to injustice and inequality one moment longer. We call on you to unite in soul and spirit. Separated in thoughts and ideals, we falter. Together, we overcome our fears, our obstacles, and those who would dissuade us from such a mighty cause as the one set before us. Women's suffrage is more than a passing fancy. Yes, there are still sisters—young and old—who have not yet latched onto the vision. We pray they will be won so that, together, we might make a difference in our lifetime. May history record our efforts! When we work as one, anything is possible.

—Ellie Cannady, editor of *The Modern Suffragette*

* * * * *

October 1916,
SAVANNAH, Georgia

"I'LL TELL YOU WHAT WE'RE going to do." Alanna Lessing fought to get her emotions under control as she turned to face her younger sister. "We're going to get on a train and go to Montana and talk some sense into Margaret. If that husband of hers is half the man she says he is, he will bring her back home to Savannah where she belongs."

"What if she won't come?" Sixteen-year-old Tessa twisted a strand of her long, dark hair around her finger and plopped down on the edge of the bed. "Then what?"

Alanna took several steps in Tessa's beautifully decorated bedroom, her hands now trembling. "Then we'll hog-tie her and bring her back ourselves. I'm not above such efforts to save my own sister."

Tessa paled and released the hold on her hair. "But…she's with child."

"Hmm. True." Alanna paused to consider that and willed the knots in her stomach to dissipate. After taking Margaret's delicate condition into consideration, she thought through her impulsive plan. "I don't know what in the world Brett Jacobs was thinking, carrying a fragile Southern woman off to the wilds of Montana. How and why she went along with him is a mystery."

"It's no mystery." Tessa rose and sashayed across the room as if dancing with an invisible partner. "They're in love. And love—at least the kind I read about in novels—makes you do strange and unpredictable things."

"Clearly." Why else would their impulsive older sister leave home, family, and everything she'd ever cared about to travel to the godforsaken wilderness of Montana—a place riddled with rustic men and women with peculiar ideologies?

Tessa sighed. "If I fell in love with a man as handsome as Brett Jacobs, I would move halfway across the world to be with him. And I wouldn't look back, no matter what." In her usual impish fashion, Tessa twirled around, her dark curls bobbing about her shoulders. She stopped and crossed her arms over her chest, as if to give herself a hug. "Ah, love!" As she tumbled backward onto her large four-poster bed, she let out a little giggle.

Alanna released a slow breath then stated her case. "Love or not, this is a practical matter. With Margaret in the family way, Brett will have to come to his senses. She needs to be here, in Savannah, where she can get the proper care for herself and the child. And what sort of upbringing will that baby have, growing up in the wild? Coming back to civilization—proper civilization—is the only option. Surely Brett and Margaret can see that."

A strange shiver ran through her as she thought about Margaret's impending role as a mother. What changes had occurred in such a short time.

"I wonder what kind of mother she will make." Tessa's brow knitted. "It's difficult to picture, isn't it? She's always been so... so..."

"Feisty."

"Yes." Tessa rose and crossed the room to the dressing table, where she examined her reflection in the mirror. "I'm feisty too. That's what Papa says, anyway." She gave her cheeks a pinch and grinned as they turned a rosy hue.

Alanna patted her younger sister on the arm. "One feisty woman in the Lessing family is enough, I daresay. Besides, I think we're dealing with a bit more where Margaret is concerned. After reading her most recent letter, I'm convinced that those...those... suffragettes have gotten hold of her."

"Ooh, what makes you say that?" Tessa's eyes widened.

"She intimated as much in her letters. I'm surprised you

haven't taken note of it. They've filled her head with all sorts of nonsense about women's rights. That's why she's unwilling to come back to the South. Likely she thinks we're old-fashioned."

"Heavens. I'm not the tiniest bit old-fashioned." Another giggle erupted and Tessa reached for a powder puff, which she dabbed on her nose and chin, sending tiny wisps of pink, powdery dust flittering through the air.

Alanna took the organdy-covered summer hat she'd been holding and slipped it onto her head. Leaning in to take a look in the mirror, she fussed with its wide brim as she spoke. "We must be intelligent in our approach to this situation, Tessa. More so than ever before. We are fighting a battle unlike any we've ever faced as the gentler sex. This suffragette movement…"

"What about it?"

Alanna shook her head, overcome with emotion as she spoke to both of their reflections. "It will be the death of gentility, if we're not careful. And now those fool-hearted females have gotten their hooks into Margaret. I fear she's been won over to their way of thinking." Alanna swallowed hard as she tried to imagine Margaret marching with rough-hewn placard in hand, fighting for women's rights. She backed away from the mirror and tightened the wide sash at her waist. "Doesn't make a lick of sense to me."

"Ooh, it does to me." Tessa whirled around, a thoughtful expression on her face. "I might be a Southern girl at heart, but I want to make a difference in the world. How will I ever do that if I'm not given the opportunity to share my opinion publicly like the fellas do?"

A flicker of apprehension coursed through Alanna, and she

felt her cheeks grow hot. She paced a few steps toward the door to regain her composure then turned back to face Tessa. "I've already lost one sister to this absurdity. I'll not lose another. There are a thousand ways you can make a difference without making a fool of yourself in the process."

"Oh, I've never minded making a fool of myself." Tessa tossed her head back, sending her hair into a state of disarray, and laughed. "You, of all people, should know that."

Alanna fought the temptation to respond with, *True*. Instead, she forged ahead, stating her case. "Those women in that suffragette movement are bringing shame to all of womanhood. Why, they're nothing more than a spectacle for men to gawk at and newspaper reporters to take advantage of."

"On this point, we can agree to disagree." A grin softened Tessa's expression and the twinkle in her eyes spoke of mischief. "But I promise to remain open-minded if you will do the same."

She gazed intensely at Alanna, who squirmed. "I will only open my mind to the truth. Of that you can be quite sure," she responded. "You know what the Bible says about truth, don't you?"

Tessa's smile faded and her brow creased. "That we should strive to walk in it?"

"Well, certainly, but it also says the truth will set us free. That is my prayer, little sister. Those women are completely misled. They need a heavy dose of life-changing truth, the kind that will set them free from their progressive way of thinking."

"Isn't that the point?" Tessa spun in a circle, her arms extended. "Being set free? Isn't that what women are striving for?"

Alanna sighed. "Yes, but—"

"Then we both agree!" Tessa clasped her hands together then made quick work of tidying up the white French coverlet on her bed. "So, what are we waiting for? Let's go talk to Mama and Papa about scheduling the trip."

"I've already spoken to Mama. She is beside herself with anguish over Margaret's situation. No doubt she will race us to the station to be the first to board the train. And I have no doubt she's already planned out the speech she will give once we arrive in Montana. Surely she can persuade Brett to bring Margaret back home where she belongs. But first we must convince Papa to let us go. You know how skittish he is about letting us travel without him."

"You don't imagine he will want to go too?" Tessa smoothed out the remaining wrinkles on her bed and fussed with the lacy pillows.

"No. He's just started a new semester at the university. His students need him. And this trip—should we make it—will take us away from Savannah for several weeks. Possibly even months, should we decide to stay until the babe is old enough to travel."

"A trip to the Wild West." Tessa's eyes sparkled. "Do you think we'll see real cowboys like the one in the painting in Papa's study? And Indians too?"

Icy fear twisted around Alanna's heart, and she shuddered. "We have a strong enough foe in the suffragettes. I'd rather face Indians, to be quite honest."

Tessa wrinkled her nose, her splattering of freckles becoming more pronounced. "But you didn't answer my question about the cowboys. You know that painting in Father's study?

The one of the rugged young man with broad shoulders who's roping cattle and riding horses across the open plain—doesn't that sound romantic?"

"I'm sure it makes for a lovely picture...something to gaze upon. But the reality of a cold, difficult winter in Montana, surrounded by smelly cows and hard-hearted women with no respect for gentility and tradition? No thank you." Alanna fanned herself with her hand. "The very idea makes me feel sick to my stomach. So, to answer your question, I'm not looking forward to the cowboys or the roughshod women with outlandish ideas. This trip will be for business only."

"Business?"

"Yes." Alanna gave her reflection one last look in the mirror. "We'll be about the business of rescuing a sister in need and bringing her back to a place where women are women and cowboys hang on the wall painted in oil."

"How you phrase things, Alanna. If I had a cowboy, I wouldn't frame him and hang him on the wall. I'd kiss him square on the mouth." Tessa leaned forward and gave her reflection a pucker, leaving the imprint of lips on the mirror.

"Tessa Lessing, take that back! Why, if Mama heard you say such a thing, she would reach for the bar of lye to wash out your mouth."

Tessa released a girlish giggle. "I'm nearly seventeen, Lana. She hasn't threatened to wash out my mouth for years. Besides, I'm convinced even Mama would be swept off her feet by a handsome fella in a Stetson with a gun strapped to his side."

"What's this about a handsome fella with a gun?" their father's voice sounded from the doorway.

Alanna turned and gave him a nod. "Papa, I'm glad you're here. There's something very important we need to discuss."

He gave her a pensive look and ran his fingers over his mustache. "Hopefully it does not involve a gun."

"Indeed, it does not."

Alanna's plan did, however, involve a bit of wheedling. If she could coax Papa into letting the females in his family take a little journey without him, the rest of the plan would come together with ease. She and Mama and Tessa would spend a few months in the godforsaken wilderness of Montana—long enough for Margaret to have the baby and get rested up—and then they would convince Brett to return home to Savannah, where they all belonged.

Lord willing. In the meantime, from the look of consternation on Papa's face, it would appear that Alanna had a lot of convincing to do.

TWO

I wish I had a nickel for every time I've heard the phrase, "Women are the weaker sex." Indeed, I would be a rich woman, at least by this world's standards. Women, are we—as these naysayers claim—weak? We, who bear children, slave over hot stoves, tend crops in perilous weather, and care for the needs of our families at every turn? We, who link arms and hearts with other sisters to bring justice where there is no justice? Others would call us weak? I think not. In fact I've never seen such strength. All the more, now that we are working in tandem to prove our position. Before long, they will see just how strong we really are.

—Ellie Cannady, editor of *The Modern Suffragette*

* * * * *

October 1916,
Missoula, Montana

TANNER JACOBS LEANED BACK AGAINST the fence post and gazed

across the vast expanse of acreage on the south end of his family's Montana ranch. Off in the distance, the Bitterroot mountain range rose up before him in all its triumphant glory. Ribbons of color layered the mountains—wintery white on top and varying shades of brown and tan below. He found himself lost in the view, the snowcapped peaks drawing him away to an imaginative place, as always.

After a long day's work with the cattle, his dog rested at his feet, panting from her labors. Tanner flexed the muscles in his upper arms, equally as glad to be done with his work for the day. He released a slow breath and took in the sunset. Brilliant reds, golds, and oranges streaked across the near-evening sky in a wondrous display, with a tiniest hint of purple framing it all. Truly, nothing could spoil this moment.

Well, almost nothing.

"You're avoiding the question, Tanner." His younger sister's voice came from behind him for the second time in a row, a reminder that she didn't plan to go down without a fight. He turned to face her and tried not to laugh at the overly serious look on her face. Katie always hated it when he made light of her conversations. Best to play along with her…again.

"What would you like me to say?" He stuck a piece of straw into his mouth and gave it a thoughtful chew as he took in his younger sister's sour expression.

Katie's eyes narrowed, and an escaping curl—the pale yellow of a field of grain—fell over her forehead. "Say that I'm right, that women deserve the right to own property and to vote, not just in Wyoming or Montana, but across this vast nation. I've stood here in silence for a good five minutes waiting for you to respond to my question about equality for women, and yet you continue to ignore me. Nothing ever changes, does it?"

"On the contrary. I would say you've changed a great deal over the last couple of years." He reached for his hat and slipped it on before tossing the piece of straw, ready to be done with this conversation. When would his thickheaded sister get it into her skull? He would never sidle up to the idea of women's equality, no matter how many arguments ensued.

"Surely you don't want me to agree with your notions just to bring this uneasy conversation to an end," he said. "Even you wouldn't wish that."

"Well, I..." Her gaze shifted to the ground. Then she looked back up at him with a sly grin. "Maybe I do." Her eyelashes took to fluttering, and her cheeks turned a shade darker than the roses planted in Mama's front garden.

Tanner groaned as he watched her manipulative ways. "I find it humorous that you're using your womanly wiles to convince a man that you're not the weaker sex. Ironic."

Katie paled and planted tight fists on her hips. "What did you say?"

"I said you're the weaker—"

"I heard you!" She turned on her heel and marched across the pasture. After a few steps, she stopped in her tracks and looked back at him with burning reproach in her eyes. "And for your information, there's nothing weak about me. I'm tougher than most of the fellas I know."

"Guess no one could argue with that. And you're twice as

mean too." He quirked a brow and did his best not to laugh.

"You—you—you…" Katie couldn't seem to finish the sentence. Instead, she pointed herself in the direction of the house once again. After a few more steps, she turned again. "You're such a…such a…man!" She pummeled him with the words like stones, but he managed to remain unharmed. In fact, he found it all rather humorous.

"That I am." He tipped his hat and gave a little bow. "You would do well to remember that, little sister. There are so few real men left in the world, after all. Now that our women have decided to wear the pants in the family, the menfolk are all out shopping for corsets to stiffen their backbones."

"Ugh!" She yanked her dark wool skirt and twisted about, nearly stepping into a cow patty. A funny little hop and skip followed—not at all dainty, but she did manage to avoid ruining her shoe. At the last moment, she turned back. "And just for your information, girls don't wear corsets much anymore. Those medieval devices were antiquated death traps, probably designed by some man wanting to keep his woman from spreading her wings."

"Well, go on and fly, little sister," he said with the wave of a hand. "You've been squawking like a bird long enough. Might as well take to the skies."

She took off toward the house, and Tanner doubled over in laughter—for a couple of minutes, anyway. After a few seconds of reflection, his common sense returned and he straightened. Katie's outlandish reaction was funny, no doubt about it. But her point was not. Neither was her passion or her inability to keep a single thought inside her head. All this hogwash about equality for women was enough to ruffle a fella's feathers. What would it take to squelch this idea that women should be on equal footing with men in the political arena?

He paused to think about his older brother, Brett, who was happily married and expecting a child in just a few short months. "Now there's a real man for you," Tanner mused to the dog resting at his feet. "He knows how to keep his wife in her place." Snowball responded with the wag of a tail.

Not that Margaret was the subservient sort. No, even the once-gentle belle from Savannah had latched onto this idea that all women should be allowed to own land and vote like the Montana suffragettes. Of course, they had his sister to thank for that. Katie and those friends of hers had stirred up a hornet's nest among the young women in Missoula. And if they didn't stop her, before long she'd do real damage.

He turned his gaze to the skies once again, noticing that the brilliant colors of the sunset had slipped off behind wispy clouds.

His good mood...well, it seemed to have disappeared right along with them.

* * * * *

AFTER A WEEK OF SHIFTING from one train to the next, Alanna grew to regret her impulsive decision to make the cross-country journey to Montana. As the days progressed, she battled her emotions as well as the usual troubles associated with long journeys—weariness and stiff joints at the top of the list. By the time they arrived in Colorado, however, her spirits lifted. The change in scenery brought about a shift in her attitude. She'd never seen anything so beautiful.

"Girls!" Mama leaned close to the Pullman car's window and gazed outside. "Come and look at this."

Alanna joined her mother and gasped aloud as she took in the view. "Breathtaking," she whispered. Indeed, the clear blue sky contrasted beautifully with the mountains, which stretched to incredible heights.

"I don't believe it." Tessa pointed to the snowcapped mountain peaks in the distance. "I've read about this in books, of course, but to see it in person? Snow? In October, no less."

"Yes." Practicality took over. Alanna turned away from the view so as not to distract herself. "One more reason for concern. It's bitterly cold in the Northwest at this time of year. I cannot believe that would be good for Margaret in her condition. And what of that poor baby, arriving in the bleak midwinter?" She shuddered, just thinking about it.

Mama shook her head. "Why, in Savannah, we're scarcely beyond our summer season. Inconceivable."

"I, for one, am not looking forward to the cold. It wreaks havoc on one's hair." Alanna fussed with her silky tresses and sighed—loudly, for effect.

"Why must we always look at the negative when we're surrounded on every side by such glorious sights?" Tessa pressed her nose against the window. "I think this is by far the prettiest thing I've ever seen. Now I know why Margaret is so happy in the mountains."

"Missoula is technically a valley." Alanna pulled the curtains closed. "Now, is anyone else hungry? I'm starved."

"Me too." Tessa rubbed her hands together. "You know me.

I'm always hungry."

Alanna fought the temptation to add, *And it's showing in your waistline.* No point in upsetting her. Still, Tessa would have to work hard to maintain her figure once they returned home.

Mama reached for her scarf and sighed. "I'll bet I've put on five pounds since we left Savannah. There's been little to do on this trip but eat."

"I know. Isn't it wonderful?" Tessa rubbed her belly. "I've become quite the expert at it."

"I suppose we've all got to be good at something." Alanna gave her sister a warm hug. "But it is lunchtime, and roast beef sounds lovely."

"Indeed. They have wonderful beef in this part of the country. You can't deny that." Tessa grabbed Alanna's hand, and they headed outside the privacy of their compartment en route to the dining car.

As they made their way down the aisle, the stench of body odor greeted them along with varying smells from a variety of unfamiliar foods. Many of the other passengers traveled in the regular train cars, many doing their best to sleep sitting up. Alanna didn't envy them. In fact, she felt rather bad for most, especially the mothers and children. They passed by a couple of older men playing cards and a woman with four small children—three of them bickering and the fourth bawling. Tessa stopped to tickle the little one under the chin, which slowed her cries.

"Here you go, baby girl." Tessa reached into her bag and came out with a slice of bread, no doubt from today's breakfast. "See if that doesn't cheer you up."

The youngster took it and began to nibble, the tears now gone. Alanna fought to keep her hand from her nose as she smelled the stench of a dirty diaper. How could one endure such odors? Had the mother grown so accustomed to it that she didn't notice?

"Thank you so much." The mother looked at her with weary eyes. "I'm grateful."

"Happy to be of service," Tessa said with a lilt in her voice. "I'll be back later with whatever dessert I can abscond in the dining car. Then all will be well."

Gratitude resonated in the woman's eyes.

Alanna resisted the urge to hurry her sister along. Really, with Tessa's soft heart leading the way, a trip to the dining car could take double the usual time. This, Alanna had learned the hard way. Still, there was something to be said for her younger sister's tenderness toward strangers. She truly had the gift of compassion, no doubt about it. Perhaps next time she could choose less smelly people to extend a hand to. One could hope, anyway.

As they passed through the next car, newsboys and other vendors made their way up the center aisle, shouting the latest headlines and hawking their wares. Nearly anything one longed for could be purchased—ice water, books with tattered pages, stale sandwiches, two-day-old newspapers…. Alanna found it all rather intriguing. Apparently so did Tessa, who found one of the newsboys charming enough to stop and chat with.

"Tessa, we're going to starve at this rate," Alanna said.

"Hardly!" Tessa rubbed her belly again in an unladylike fashion and laughed. "I could live off the fat of the land for a good week, at the very least."

Mama looked aghast at Tessa's outburst in front of the boys but didn't say a word. A proper Southern lady would never enter into such candid conversation about her weight. Not in public, anyway.

By the time they arrived in the dining car and took their seats, Alanna's hunger had almost gotten the better of her, especially with the ever-present sound of silverware clinking at every table. And when the roast beef arrived, hot and covered in scrumptious gravy, she fought the temptation to dive in at the speed Tessa managed. Only after several slow bites did the hunger pangs cease. And by the time they reached dessert—lovely slices of tasty apple pie—Alanna was finally ready to talk business with her mother and sister.

She leaned back in her chair and did her best to avoid the beautiful view outside the window, lest it deter her from the matter at hand. "Ladies, it's been a nice trip, but we've been remiss in discussing the one thing most important to this mission. We've got to cook up a plan of action regarding Margaret and Brett."

"And the baby, of course." Tessa removed her pie from the plate and wrapped it in her napkin then eyed Mama's plate.

Mama took a nibble of a cinnamon-coated baked apple slice and looked Alanna's way. "What do you have in mind, Lana?"

"Nothing yet. But the Bible says that the plans of men—and women—fail for lack of knowledge. If we're going to convince Margaret and Brett that they need to come back home to Savannah, we need to be strategic. We've got to think like...like..."

"Like men?" Tessa reached for her fork, which she directed toward Mama's plate.

Alanna shrugged. "It is true that men are often more strategic in their approach to life than women."

"Not the women I know." Mama's eyes twinkled with

unexpected mischief. "Trust me when I say that the ladies in my circle know how to get what they want. I can assure you, there is a great deal of strategy involved." She dabbed at her lips with a napkin and leaned back in her chair.

"Well, the sort of strategy I'm referring to is appealing to Brett's common sense. And his pocketbook."

"His pocketbook?" Fine lines appeared on Tessa's forehead as she took a bite of Mama's apple pie. "But he's doing well for himself on the ranch, isn't he? I don't believe money has been an issue."

"Perhaps, but every man wants to improve his current situation. It will be our job to convince him that he can make a better living in Savannah."

"Doing what, though?" Mama took a bite of the pie.

"Easy. We'll ask Papa to give Brett a job at the university. Papa's very well loved there, and he should be able to open the door for Brett to teach. He has his degree, after all. He should be using it for the good of others."

"Yes, but will Brett enjoy working in a university setting?" Mama asked. "He's always been the sort who's fascinated with the out-of-doors. I can't imagine him cooped up inside a university. Doesn't seem like a good fit to me."

"Hmm." Alanna released a slow breath, her gaze shifting once again out of the window.

Tessa took another bite of Mama's pie then spoke with a full mouth. "If you were really using your noodle, you would find him a job doing something he loved—give him an opportunity he can't resist. Now that's strategy."

"An opportunity he can't resist." Alanna squinted against the blinding glare of sunlight streaming through the window. "Yes.

You're right, Tessa."

"Say that again." Tessa made a production out of swallowing her bite of pie.

"Say what?"

"That I'm right. I hear it so rarely."

Alanna laughed. "Well, I don't mind saying it again. You're right. We need to present him with the perfect opportunity. What say we all put our pretty little heads together and come up with just the right job—something he can't possibly resist?"

"Just like I can't resist this apple pie." Tessa jabbed her fork into Mama's pie and consumed another bite, a look of sheer bliss coming over her.

Instead of scolding her younger sister, Alanna forced her attentions to the matter at hand. Soon enough they would see that same look of bliss on Brett's face—when they presented him with the opportunity of a lifetime.

After a pause she sat straight up in the chair. "Oh, I have it! It's the perfect idea."

"What's that?" Mama placed her napkin in her lap and leaned a bit closer.

"Papa told me just two weeks ago that the university is starting a new agricultural program. An entire department focused on farming, animals, and such."

A smile lit Mama's face. "I love it!"

"Yes, indeed." Alanna fought the temptation to giggle. "And if we work our magic over the next few months, Brett and Margaret will grow to love the idea too."

One could hope, anyway.

THREE

Women, do not lose heart, even when those around you disagree with your philosophies. For years, it has been thus. Women have faced opposition at every turn. Look at the great heroines who traveled this road before us. Contemplate the struggle of Frances Wright, a bold Scottish woman who arrived in our great country nearly one hundred years ago. Her lectures on the topic of women's suffrage were extensive and quite bold for her day. We can—and should—be just as bold. Opposition will come. You can count on it. It only serves to make us stronger, from the inside out.

—Ellie Cannady, editor of *The Modern Suffragette*

* * * * *

ALANNA GLANCED OUT THROUGH THE train window as the city of Missoula came into view. In every direction—to the north, south, east, and west, she saw mountain ranges iced over with glistening white snow. The town sat low—a luscious valley in the midst of it all. The whole thing reminded her of the biblical towns of old, surrounded on every side. Only, in this case, man-made walls had not been built to keep out the enemy. No, the Lord Himself had constructed ranges of mountains as a fortress to shield Missoula from harm. Fascinating.

She could not deny the town's beauty. Still, she would not allow herself to be swayed—by the scenery, the vast expanse of blue skies, or the look of excitement in her younger sister's eyes— as the train neared the Missoula station.

Tessa pulled her gaze away from the window. "It's as if everything just sort of...merges...here."

"Indeed." Mama slid on her gloves as she glanced at the scene before them. "It's lovely. Not at all what I pictured."

"Me either." Tessa sighed. "It's ten thousand times better, in fact."

"Let's remember why we're here, ladies." Alanna gave them both a solid look. "We're about our Father's business."

"Father?" Tessa shrugged. "No doubt he would love it here too. He's always been fond of beautiful landscapes. And I can't help but think he would enjoy that wide-open sky, as well. I can almost imagine him living here and being quite happy."

"I was referring to our heavenly Father," Alanna said. "Looking to Him for guidance is key, particularly when surrounded by temptation. Did He not give us the story of the prodigal son in need of a homecoming? We must keep that story in mind as we do our best to convince Brett and Margaret that they should come back home to Savannah."

Tessa wrinkled her nose, her eyes narrowing. "I'm not sure that story really applies in this case, Lana. After all, the prodigal was, well, a prodigal. Margaret is a good girl."

"With a good head on her shoulders," Mama chimed in.

"But one who has been swayed by love to leave home, hearth, and family to come to this godforsaken…" Alanna looked out the window once again, completely captivated by the beauty. "This…place."

"Doesn't look godforsaken to me." Tessa rose and reached for her hat. "If anything, I would say that the fingerprints of the Almighty are all over this place. When I look out there, I feel as if I could practically touch Him." She released a breath against the glass, leaving a foggy circle, which she wiped away with her hand.

Alanna sighed. "Beautiful or not, we have a bigger plan."

"Bigger than that?" Tessa pointed to the majestic mountains off in the distance.

"Well, bigger in the grand scheme of things."

Alanna would have said more, but the squeal of brakes sounded as the train jerked its way into the station. The car jolted with such force that she had to steady herself against the wall to keep from tumbling headfirst into the glass window.

"That soot." Mama raised her voice to be heard above the brakes. She pointed at the black cloud rising outside the window as the brakes continue to scream their displeasure. "I'll never get used to it. I daresay I've eaten it for breakfast, lunch, and dinner for days now."

"It will be worth it as soon as we see Margaret." Tessa scrambled in her usual unladylike way to gather her belongings. "I can't believe we're here at last."

"Lord be praised. I'm so ready to see my girl again." Mama looked as if she might faint.

Alanna glanced through the window one last time as the

noise fell to a tolerable level. Her gaze landed on her brother-in-law. "Mama, look!"

"Brett looks more rugged than I remembered," Tessa said. "And I don't recall seeing him in denims before, do you?"

"Of course not." Alanna reached for her gloves. "No self-respecting Southern man would be seen in public wearing such rustic attire."

"Still he looks different in other ways too."

"He's quite…hairy," their mother observed.

"Ooh, I think the beard suits him, don't you?" Tessa used the sleeve of her dress to wipe the window. "I would imagine it's very fitting for the surroundings."

"I prefer a clean-shaven man, myself," Alanna countered. "If the Good Lord had wanted man to have hair on his face, He would have…" *Hmm.* She stopped before finishing. "Anyway, a cultured man wears, at most, a mustache. Nothing more."

"All this chatter about Brett, and we've not talked a whit about Margaret." Alanna's mother pressed in close to the girls to have a look. "I do hope he's brought her along. Then again, in her condition, she might not be able to venture out—" Mama stopped cold as a very expectant Margaret came into view. "Oh, my baby!"

"Hardly!" Alanna laughed as she gazed at her older sister's changed physique. "Your baby is having a baby."

Mama's lashes brimmed with moisture. "And I've come just in time to be of help to her. That's the real reason for my coming, of course. I'd love to see Margaret and Brett back in Savannah, but these first few weeks have to be about her. Are we in agreement on this one point?"

"One hundred percent," Alanna said. She didn't have time to say more because the porter arrived to fetch their bags and help them disembark. Moments later, with a swirl of black soot surrounding them, the Lessing women made their way from the train.

Alanna took one look at Margaret and began to cry. Indeed, she had not adequately prepared herself for seeing her older sister up close in her expectant state. Margaret's dress—a solid brown-wool number with no trim or collar—hugged her rounded midsection. In the South, a woman would scarcely be seen in public in such a condition, especially in such a drab frock. Margaret, on the other hand, seemed perfectly at ease while dressed in such plain attire in a public setting. And very happy to show off her rounded belly, which she rubbed.

Mama, of course, got first dibs at throwing her arms around Margaret's neck. Tessa came next, forcing her way into the line. Finally, the moment arrived. Wrapped in Margaret's warm embrace, Alanna wept for the sister she had missed the past two years.

"Is it really you?" she whispered. "I'm afraid I'm seeing a phantom."

"A rather wide-girthed phantom." Margaret rubbed her expanded midsection again and laughed.

"Just the right size and shape for a woman in your position. And you're beautiful. Absolutely glowing, in fact. Just as all mothers-to-be should be." *Though I wouldn't be caught dead in that drab brown dress. Have they no pretty fabrics in Missoula?* Alanna felt a chill and pulled her ruffled coat a bit tighter.

"Here is the primary reason for the happiness you see on my face." Margaret gestured to Brett, who joined them for an embrace. Alanna laid aside her feelings of frustration at Brett for taking her sister away. Right now, all that mattered was seeing them again and sharing in a joyous reunion.

For some, the joy was more overwhelming than others. Off to the side, Mama continued to weep. "Don't mind me." She reached into her beaded reticule for a lace-trimmed embroidered hankie then dabbed at her eyes. "These are tears of joy, trust me. I feel as if I'm seeing you for the first time. And, indeed, perhaps I am." She took Margaret by the hand and then stepped back to examine her from head to toe. "I can hardly believe it's you."

"It's me. I'm the same Margaret Lessing—er, Jacobs—from Sunny Savannah."

"Seems impossible to me," Mama whispered.

No, this was certainly not the sister who had left Georgia two years ago. She had transformed in a multiplicity of ways—everything from hairstyle to clothing. Why, even the way she spoke had changed.

"Your voice sounds different." Creases appeared around Tessa's eyes as she frowned slightly.

"Really?" Margaret paused and offered a little shrug. "I hadn't noticed. It's not deliberate, I can assure you. Must've just happened gradually."

"You sound so…Western."

"Western? What does that sound like?" This time the voice—a male voice—came from behind Brett and Margaret.

Alanna tried not to gape as a handsome stranger stepped

into view. His broad shoulders filled the coat he wore. Her gaze traveled up to a face bronzed by wind and sun. The firm set of his chin suggested a stubborn streak and the half smile, a hint of cockiness. She could not look away, no matter how hard she tried. Something about him seemed…familiar. He bore a striking resemblance to someone she had seen before, though she could not figure out who or where. Still, the likeness nearly took the breath out of her.

"Where are my manners?" Margaret gestured for the man to join them. "Everyone, this is Tanner, Brett's younger brother. His ranch is just a few miles from ours. We'll pass it on the way home."

The handsome stranger's eyes twinkled with mischief as he offered a fast, "How do you do?"

"Fine, thank you." Tessa eased into the spot next to him, her eyelashes picking up speed. "And you?"

"Fine and dandy."

He was a dandy, all right, but not the sort she was used to. His compelling blue eyes, the masculine features, the confident set of his wide shoulders…all these things served to disarm her at once.

Apparently she wasn't the only one affected. Poor Tessa stood with her mouth wide-open until Alanna nudged her. "Stay focused, little sister," she whispered.

"Oh, I'm focused, all right." Tessa's lips curved up in an impish grin. "Never more so."

Alanna did her best not to sigh aloud at this proclamation, but she could smell trouble coming a mile away. If this handsome cowboy didn't keep his distance, Tessa would fall head over heels in love before nightfall. Alanna would have none of it. She'd already lost one sister to Montana. She wouldn't lose another.

* * * * *

TANNER FOUND HIMSELF TONGUE-TIED AS he took in the genteel young woman standing before him. What the younger sister lacked in manners, the older one—what was her name, again? Alanna?—more than made up for.

In all his life he'd never seen such a beauty. A wealth of thick dark hair hung in long graceful curls over her shoulders, captivating him at once. What really drew him in, though, was that exquisite face—so much like a painting that he found himself wondering what colors one would use to capture it. A perfect oval, it spoke of both delicacy and strength, from the arched brow to the full, rosy lips.

His gaze traveled to her attire. The frilly green coat would never keep her warm during a Montana winter, but the belt showed off a small waist and curvy physique. Not that he should be paying mind to such things. A better man would've kept his eyes on the scenery, not the woman's figure. Still, one couldn't help but appreciate a masterpiece, and this woman certainly qualified.

Tanner cleared his throat and gazed off in the distance, determined not to gawk.

For a moment, anyway. Then he slanted his gaze her way once again.

Alanna took a couple of steps, walking with stiff dignity, then tripped over one of the smaller bags. He reached for her arm. "Careful, miss."

Her cheeks flushed, and her long, dark lashes took to fluttering. The whole thing reminded him of a scene in a book he'd read as a boy in school. Was this Southern belle acting, or did she always come across as a breakable china doll?

Not that he minded one bit. Oh no. In fact, he had a sudden affinity for china dolls, particularly those with big green eyes and dark, upswept curls framing a beautiful face. Throw in flushed cheeks, and he wanted to sweep that doll across the room in a friendly little waltz.

Again the lashes fluttered. Did she have something in her eyes?

"You all right?" he asked.

"Well, *yay*–us. Why–*ev*–uh do you ask?"

Her exaggerated manner of speaking held him spellbound. It reminded him for all the world of the day he'd first met Margaret. Not that Margaret stretched her vowels these days. No, sir. They'd weaned that nonsense right out of her. Women in Montana didn't have time for extra syllables. They spent far too much time working.

He turned to Margaret's mother—the one who looked about ready to drop—and gestured to her luggage. "I'll get those for you."

She nodded then patted her brow with the back of a gloved hand. "Thank you, young *may*–un. That would be *luv*–lee."

Looked as if they all struggled from the same speech malady. He stifled a laugh and focused on the bags. For whatever reason, Alanna didn't look as if she found his gesture lovely at all. This, he could ascertain from the glare she shot his way. Had he done something to upset her?

"W–what?" he asked, suddenly feeling more than a little intimidated.

She gave him a pensive look, her eyes narrowing to slits as she punctuated the word, "*Ma*'am."

"Beg pardon?" He released his hold on the bags and raked his fingers through his hair.

"*Ma*'am." She brushed some wrinkles out of her skirt. "That's what young *me*-un say when they're speakin' to a *woe*-man. They call her '*ma*'am.' You neglected to do so just now, but I daresay this is one more injustice we shall have to en–*doo*-uh, now that we're out of the South."

"Yes, *ma*'am." He did his best to mimic the word but apparently fell short, judging from the pained look on her face.

"Not younger women such as my–*say*-ulf," she drawled. "My *muh*-thuh. You should refer to her as '*ma*'am.'"

"Ah." He paused, suddenly unwilling to say anything at all for fear of being corrected once again. "I just figured I'd call her 'Mrs. Lessing.'"

Thank goodness the younger sister laughed, which seemed to break the ice. Still, he had a feeling Alanna would be a different story altogether. If looks could kill, she would've murdered him already, all for calling her mother *Mrs. Lessing*. What was wrong with that? Not enough syllables, perhaps?

Tanner picked up the bags and took several steps. Seconds later, he felt a slap on his back and turned to see his older brother's smiling face. "You have a lot to learn about women from the South, little brother." Brett's chuckle reverberated through the air.

"No doubt. They're…different." Tanner's gaze shifted back to Alanna, who'd started fussing about the cool weather.

"That they are." Brett took to laughing aloud. "That they are."

FOUR

Ladies, if you want to join the cause for women's suffrage, why not come to the beautiful state of Montana? Here, you can meet face-to-face with our nation's first-ever congresswoman, Jeanette Rankin, who hails from Missoula. Surrounded by nature at its finest, you can link arms with strong women of the Northwest who have a passion for women's causes. Lest you think we are behind the times, think again. Our rugged surroundings have strengthened us and caused us to appreciate both our backbones and our future. Join us if you dare.

—Ellie Cannady, editor of *The Modern Suffragette*

* * * * *

AS THEY CLIMBED INTO THE backseat of Brett's Ford, Alanna fought to keep her focus on the mountains in the distance. Doing so proved to be a bit of a challenge, what with the broad-shouldered cowboy hefting the bags into the trunk of the vehicle. It took every ounce of strength not to turn around and gawk at his rugged physique. As he lugged the largest of Mama's bags, the muscles rippling under his white shirt quickened her pulse. He carried himself with a commanding air—not really haughty, but self-confident. A girl could go a long way on a sight like that.

Still, a Southern lady would never be caught dead staring at a fella, handsome or not. Think about it, certainly. Do it? Never.

She turned to look at the scenery. Seconds later, the cowboy walked directly past her, distracting her all over again. Still, she could not be held accountable. Not when he walked smack-dab in front of her.

Tessa let out a little whistle as she climbed into the car. "We've died and gone to cowboy heaven. This is my reward for being so well-behaved all my life."

"Hardly." Mama also climbed in and then took the spot beside her.

Tessa's eyes fluttered closed, and she sighed. "I would like to capture Tanner's image and keep it forever embedded on the insides of my eyelids. That way, when I'm sound asleep, I will still see him."

Mama tugged at her gloves, finally wriggling them off. "I believe we've seen that face before. He looks just like the cowboy in the portrait in your papa's study, don't you think?"

"There are some similarities, I suppose." Alanna turned to catch a glimpse of Tanner to compare, but he'd disappeared from sight.

"Ooh." Tessa's eyes widened. "All shockingly handsome cowboys must look the same, whether one paints them in oil or has the privilege of seeing them firsthand. Makes me wonder why we waited so long to come to Montana." A girlish giggle followed.

"Shush." Alanna put her finger to her lips as she caught a glimpse of him rounding the back side of the touring car. "He's coming."

She remained silent as the young man climbed into the driver's seat. Alanna glanced out the window, taking in the view, then shifted her gaze to Margaret as she too joined them in the backseat. "Squeeze in, everybody. There is more of me than ever before." Her happy smile reminded Alanna of their real reason for coming to Montana. Cowboy distractions aside, she focused on her older sister, giving her hand a loving squeeze.

Brett took his spot up front in the passenger seat, and they were on their way. Alanna drank in the beauty around her—mostly the landscape, but a wee bit of the back of Tanner's head, as well. He did have lovely hair—so thick and wavy. A luminous buttercup-yellow, it stood in stark contrast to his deep tan. She fought the overwhelming desire to reach out and run her fingers through it.

Heavens. Perish the thought. He's a total stranger to me.

Not that she was accustomed to running her fingers through a fella's hair, anyway. Must be something about the state of Montana that had tipped her moral compass off its center. Why, she never had scandalous thoughts like that back in Savannah.

Alanna gestured out the window at the mountain range in the distance, ready to focus on something other than the cowboy's features. "I've never seen anything quite like this."

"Isn't it beautiful, Lana?" Margaret squeezed her arm. "Every morning I wake up and gaze at that mountain range and think about how blessed I am to be living in a place of such beauty."

"It is very pretty." Tessa closed her eyes and drew in a breath. "And the air is so fresh. It's very…crisp."

Tanner laughed and turned back to face them, revealing two well-placed dimples. "That's because we're so close to the mountains and they're capped with snow. It's great for the lungs. The fresh air is, I mean."

"I just can't get over it, though." Tessa looked completely mesmerized by the very idea. "Snow, in October."

He gave her a little smile. "Just wait a month or so, and you will likely see much more of it on the ground, not just the mountaintops."

Alanna shivered, just thinking about it. Suddenly the idea of staying put in the rigid cold held little appeal. What was she thinking, bringing her mother and Tessa all this way—only to turn them into blocks of ice?

Oh, yes. To save a beloved sister from a fate worse than death. For that, she would endure the cold. She breathed in deeply and made up her mind to be strong even if the weather did not cooperate.

Please, Lord, let it cooperate.

Her thoughts shifted to sunny Savannah, to the town she loved. How she pined for the tropical breeze that picked up the salty scent of the Atlantic and floated through her bedroom window. She could almost envision it now. If not for the ripples of sunlight streaming off the white peaks in the distance, anyway.

Alanna focused on the small group of people. Tilting her head to one side, she stole a look at Tanner's profile. Something about him still captivated her. Perhaps it was the strong cheekbones and the inherent strength in the set of his jaw. She appreciated a man of strength.

Meeting him almost made the trip tolerable. And something about the way he talked about Montana made her appreciate him even more…to a point, anyway.

"All the seasons here are beautiful," Tanner said as he pointed the vehicle down a long, winding road. "And they're so distinct."

"Oh, yes." Margaret sighed. "I remember my first summer here. I saw countless fields of flowers. White bear grass. Yellow evening stars. Blue hyacinth. Purple fairyslippers. Pink bitterroot." On she went, describing her favorite Montana flowers. "Of course, you'll see all these if you stay till the spring. Then you'll know that I'm not exaggerating."

"My favorite part of Missoula is the vast expanse of land." Tanner took his hands off the steering wheel—which almost caused poor Mama to lose her breath—and pointed to the range in the distance. "You can stand atop the mountains and gaze down at acres that go on for miles."

"Sounds lovely." Mama smoothed her skirts and leaned back against the seat, her eyes fluttering closed.

Tanner continued to ramble about their surroundings, now carrying on with a hint of boastfulness. "If you think that's nice, just wait until you see the herds of elk, lumbering along, or a baby fawn resting in the tall grasses in the late afternoon."

"I can honestly say we've never seen elk in Savannah," Alanna's mother said.

"Heavens, no." Alanna fussed with her gloves. "I can't even

imagine it. Of course, Savannah is quite genteel, so animals are rarely seen."

"Except for our neighbor's cat, of course," Tessa chimed in. "But he's not part of a herd, though Papa insists he's more trouble than a dozen yapping canines."

Everyone got a laugh out of that except Mama, who offered up a weak smile and looked wearier than ever.

"Maybe one day I will visit the South," Tanner said. "Tell me what I'll find there."

"What you'll find in the South, or in Savannah in particular?" Alanna asked.

"You choose." He turned and gave her what appeared to be a little wink.

Fresh!

Well, two could play at this game. "I choose Savannah, of course." She paused. "Everything in Savannah is pretty much the opposite of here. Where you have cold weather, ours is luscious and warm, wrapping one in a summery cocoon. Where you have mountains, our terrain is flat. But there's nothing dull about our area. Why, we're—"

"Oh, look at that, will you?" Tanner pointed through his open window at the sky above.

"What is it, Tanner?" Brett leaned out of the passenger window, likely to have a better look.

"Didn't mean to interrupt, but look at the patch of sky over the Bitterroot Range. It's prettier than any painting." Tanner glanced back at the ladies and grinned. "Montana boasts the biggest sky in the country, you see."

"Biggest sky?" Tessa pursed her lips and appeared to be thinking. "I always thought the sky was the same size everywhere."

"Nope." Tanner chuckled. "It's bigger here, trust me. And look at those colors, will you? Brilliant blue. The clouds are like the wisps of fur on Snowball."

"Snowball?" Tessa's asked.

"Our dog. She's an Eskimo."

"An Eskimo?" Alanna and Tessa spoke in unison.

Tanner laughed. "That's the breed. She's as white as those clouds and nearly as fluffy." He gazed off in the distance again, his voice intensifying. "Aren't they magnificent? It's as if they've been instructed to hang there in shimmering white to contrast the deep emerald of the evergreens below. Of course, the evergreens fade to white in the winter, like everything else. But even then we have varying shades of white. You've never seen anything like it."

Alanna cleared her throat, ready to remind him that she had been speaking. "Well, if you think that's pretty, I wish you could see some of our plantation homes back in Savannah. And the gardens are magnificent. There was even a write-up in the paper about our local garden society."

"A write-up in the paper?" Tanner chuckled. Amusement flickered in the eyes that met hers as he turned. "Is that how a fella is supposed to know what's good to look at? They think folks aren't clever enough to figure it out for themselves?" Before she could respond, he pointed back out at the mountains. "Now, there's something worth discovering on your own."

Alanna chose not to respond.

Tessa sighed as she leaned through the open back-seat window.

"You'd be hard-pressed to tell where the mountains leave off and the clouds begin."

Ready to change the direction of the conversation before this handsome cowboy gave Tessa one more reason to want to stay in Montana, Alanna cleared her throat. "Well, that's lovely, but—"

Tanner glanced back over his shoulder at her. "Not to one-up you, but the kinds of things I'm talking about are God-made, not man-made. You're talking about houses and gardens, things folks have paid to construct. I'm talking about something that rises far above all that."

"Yes, well…"

"Honestly, have you ever seen such a vivid contrast of colors as on that mountain range up there?" He turned the car onto a small, bumpy road. "It boggles the mind how the Lord must've done it. All these mountains, and then, quite unexpectedly, a river cuts through everything. And not just any river, either—one that winds and weaves like a needle. I tell you, there's nothing like it."

"Well, actually, in Savannah—"

"The rivers here twist and turn with rushing waters moving so fast that the fish elude you, no matter how tempting the bait. The way I see it, this was all placed here to stir our imagination." His eyes sparkled as he glanced her way before looking back to the road. "I can honestly say that the Lord planted me right here, in the heart of Montana, in much the same way that he planted deer by streams of water. It's the most spiritual place on earth, one that draws folks to the very heart of God."

Alanna grew silent, unsure how to compete with such high praise of the state in which she now found herself. For, while

Savannah held her heart, it had not captured her imagination to quite this extent. Tanner was absolutely smitten. No doubt the man would never marry. What woman could ever compare with the love of his life—Montana?

She remained silent for the rest of the drive, listening as the others turned the conversation to the weather. When they arrived at the ranch, she could hardly believe the vast expanse of land in front of them.

Alanna glanced Margaret's way. "All of this…"—she gestured to the many acres spreading out before them—"belongs to you?"

"There's much more than this. Brett's portion of the family land is nearly sixty acres. His parents still live on the larger patch of land with Tanner and Katie."

"Larger than sixty acres?" Tessa looked stumped by this idea. "Makes our yard back home look teensy-tiny."

"Actually, our patch of land, as you call it, is a full acre." Alanna pressed her white gloves back on, determined not to be bested.

"A full acre, eh?" Tanner turned back and gave her another wink, which sent her heart fluttering. "Better not go outside without a map, then. You might get lost."

She did her best not to groan aloud. This fella certainly left her feeling discombobulated.

Tanner pulled the car to a stop and they got out. By now, the exhaustion from the past several days gripped her. Alanna could hardly wait to get inside and take a long, hot bath. Hopefully that would ease her aching joints and muscles. Did houses in Montana have indoor plumbing? She took a closer look at the large, rambling, beautifully constructed log home and felt sure it did. In fact, it would appear that her sister had not gone without any of the usual creature comforts during her stay in Montana. Everything seemed very…civilized. Surprisingly so.

As Alanna straightened her skirt, a beautiful young woman with long blond hair came rushing toward them from where she'd been standing on the front porch. She was followed by a large dog as white as the snow on the mountains and as fluffy as the clouds overhead.

The woman's face lit with the prettiest smile as she practically threw herself into Mama's arms, and her blue eyes sparkled with obvious delight. "I can't believe you're here at last. All of you." She released her hold on Mama and reached for Alanna. Now finding herself in a tight embrace, Alanna listened as the stranger carried on. "And you're Alanna. I see the resemblance, of course, though your hair is certainly curlier than Margaret's, as she's often told me. Why, it's beautiful—the color of a starless night sky. What a lovely dark hue."

"Thank you." *I think.*

"It fits your light skin tone. No doubt about it. Have you always had curls?"

"From the time I was a youngster. I didn't care much for them as a little girl, but now that I'm older and my hair has grown out, the curls are my pride and joy." She released a little sigh. "Though I suppose it's wrong to be prideful about such things."

"Oh, I don't know about that," the young woman said. "I think it's quite fashionable."

"Thank you. But with so many women bobbing their hair

these days, I do wonder if it will stay in fashion for long."

"You will find that women in Missoula don't pay as much attention to the latest hairstyles and such." The young woman's messy golden tresses shimmered under the afternoon sun. "We're too busy to fuss, most of the time."

"We stay pretty busy in the South too," Alanna said. "It seems women are always going from one party or charity event to another."

The girl grinned and brushed a wayward hair from her face. "We really are worlds apart. Up here, women are rushing from tending babies to running for political office to plowing the land." The talkative stranger shifted her attentions to Tessa, her smile broadening. "And you're Tessa."

"I am." Tessa grinned, perhaps taken by the girl's enthusiastic welcome.

The vivacious blonde grabbed Tessa by the hand, an unquenchable warmth spilling from her vivacious eyes. "You're sixteen. I'm barely eighteen, myself. We're going to be best friends. True sisters. I can feel it." She put her hand to her heart. "Right here."

"In case anyone's wondering, this is our kid sister, Katie." Brett laughed as he reached for the bags. "She's very shy, as you can see."

"And never seems to have anything to say, poor girl," Tanner threw in.

"Hush now, Tanner. You don't have to go out of your way to vex me on such a special day as this." Katie stuck out her tongue, and he laughed then went to work at unloading the bags.

The outline of his broad shoulders strained against his shirt fabric as he hefted Mama's largest piece of luggage. Alanna did her best not to stare. Still, she could hardly fathom such a muscular fella. Most of the boys back home were...well...boys. Compared to this cowboy, anyway.

Margaret led Mama and Tessa inside, but Alanna remained, with Katie—in part to have a closer look at the cowboy and in part to offer a hand. *If* she could accomplish both at the same time. Right now Tanner held her full attention. And judging from the shy smile on his face, she held his as well.

What was a Southern belle to do? Why, drink up every moment, of course.

FIVE

Ladies, I cannot stress the importance of coming together as one. Far too many times I have seen well-meaning women pitted as foes, each determined that she is more right than the other. May it never be! We learn from one another, in good times and in bad. We grow as a result of studying our differences, not our similarities. When faced with someone who seems to oppose your point of view, I would encourage you to respond graciously. Truly, there's nothing more unseemly than a female cat ready to use her claws on a sister or a friend.

—Ellie Cannady, editor of *The Modern Suffragette*

* * * * *

THE MEN MADE QUICK WORK of retrieving the bags from the car and delivering them to the house, the dog following back and forth on their heels. Katie kept chattering like a baby bird in need of feeding. "You're just going to love Montana," she trilled. "Everything about it."

Oh, dear. Not another Montana enthusiast. Still, it would be easier to play along than to engage a total stranger in an argument. Besides, Alanna could scarcely disagree, what with her new surroundings being so breathtaking and all.

"Thank you. It's certainly lovelier than I expected." Alanna paused and took another sweeping glance at her surroundings. Truly, it did surpass anything she might have imagined. "Actually, I'm not sure what I had anticipated, but it wasn't this."

Katie's face lit in a smile, her blue eyes now twinkling. "Well, you've landed in the closest spot to heaven, and we're happy to have you. Just call me Saint Peter. I will usher you through the pearly gates."

"She's hardly a saint," Tanner quipped as he drew near. As he moved in the direction of the house, he sang out in rousing chorus, "'Oh, when the saints go marching in, oh, when the saints go marching in, Lord, I want to be in that number, when the saints go marching in!'" His voice faded as he disappeared inside the house.

Katie rolled her eyes. "Brothers. They're more trouble than they're worth."

"I wouldn't know. The Lord only ever blessed me with sisters." Alanna shifted her overnight bag to the other arm, relieved when Tanner reappeared on the porch and offered to take it from her. "Thank you kindly. I'm in your debt." She gave him a warm smile. "I was fixin' to drop that."

"Fixin' to?" Katie doubled over, her giggles ringing out. "That's the cutest thing I've ever heard!"

Alanna paused, unsure of what to say next. "You think I'm cute?"

Katie got control of herself and stood aright. "The quaint way you speak."

"Quaint?" Alanna shrugged. "What are you referring to?"

"You said you were *fixin'* to drop it."

"Well, I was. Only now I'm not." Whatever was this girl up to? Making fun of her, perhaps?

"Yes." Katie clasped her hands together at her chest. "But I've never heard it put quite that way before. Simply charming."

"Your brother was kind enough to take it from me before calamity befell me."

"Yes, but when he did, you told him that you would be in his debt." Katie's giggles morphed into an unladylike snort. "Honestly? Are you just saying that to make me laugh, or did you really mean it?"

"Mean it?" Alanna couldn't quite figure out why this girl found it all so irritatingly humorous.

"Yes. If you're in his debt, then we must discuss the interest rate. You need to get the best possible deal." Katie slapped her knee and cackled.

"See?" Tanner rolled his eyes. "I told you she was no saint." Alanna watched as he flashed a warning look his sister's way, but the girl didn't seem to notice. Only when he cleared his throat did she calm herself.

"Y'all just go right on with all that silliness." Alanna offered a wave of the hand. "I need to get inside. Mama didn't fare well during the final leg of the trip. She's tuckered out and likely needs my assistance."

"Tuckered out?"

From the sound of Katie's voice, she still poked fun, though Alanna couldn't figure out why. "Well, yes. Mama has a weak constitution."

Katie looked perplexed. "Weak constitution? Is she ill?"

"No. She's just...fragile."

With a shake of her head, Katie appeared to dismiss the idea. "Must be a Southern expression."

"I beg your pardon?"

Katie shrugged then reached for a couple of the larger bags. "Up here, women aren't delicate flowers. They don't take to their beds with a headache or swoonings. They work from sunup till sundown. Never heard a one of 'em use the words *weak constitution* before. Just a new phrase to me, I suppose. I can only imagine it's something you folks say in the South. Up here women are tougher than a ten-cent steak."

Heat rose to Alanna's cheeks as she contemplated the young woman's harsh words. Not to mention her poor manners. Who would greet a total stranger—a visitor, no less—with such unkindness? And how dare she imply that Mama wasn't weak in constitution? Why, she didn't even know Mama! Alanna glanced toward the house, wishing Tessa or Margaret had stayed here to lend their support. Surely they could attest to the fact that Mama needed extra tending to at times.

Tanner flashed his sister another look. "Katie..."

"What?" Katie's eyes widened. "I'm not trying to be offensive, Tanner." The young woman turned her attention back to Alanna, squaring her shoulders as she manhandled one of Alanna's bags. "In Montana, women are hearty oaks, strong and deeply rooted.

Not much topples us. We'll fight to the finish."

"Hmm. So I see." *And what I see makes me not care for you one whit. So...there.*

"Yep, women up here are different." Katie struggled to take a couple of steps toward the house, nearly dropping the bag in the process. Tanner reached down with a grunt to grab it and strode up the steps to the porch.

"Clearly." Alanna bit her lip to keep from saying more, though her anger nearly got the best of her.

"After all, this is the twentieth century." Now Katie's eyes narrowed as if in warning.

What in the world had this girl wound up tighter than Papa's gold watch? Alanna took a deep breath before responding. "Well, of course."

"It's just that so many women across this great nation haven't made the jump to the new century as our Montana sisters have done. I'm praying you're not one of those who's lagging behind." As she said the word "behind," Katie popped Alanna on the backside.

Alanna jumped and hollered, "I beg your pardon!"

"Just teasing." Katie's brows arched. "Seeing what you're made of."

Trying not to look too wounded, Alanna rubbed her bottom to ease the pain of the smack. "I'm made of pretty strong stuff, thank you, but I have no clue what you mean when you say 'lagging behind.' Doesn't sound terribly flattering."

"Your customs and manners and such. I'm hoping you're not one of those antiquated thinkers." Katie took a few brusque steps toward the large ranch house. "We're awfully progressive here in Montana."

With awfully *being the key word.*

Alanna felt her cheeks grow hot. How dare this girl—this rugged, unladylike girl—challenge her on things she knew nothing about?

Still, a proper Southern woman would never respond with ugly words. Best to choose her next few sentences carefully. Alanna spoke evenly as she followed in Katie's footsteps toward the house. "Social graces are very much a part of who we are in the South and will, I hope, stand the test of time. Let the rest of the country choose their own paths; we in the South will remain chivalrous and genteel no matter the century."

Katie erupted into laughter. She dropped the bag she carried then slung her arm around Alanna's shoulders. "I adore you, Alanna Lessing. I truly do. You're the best entertainment I've had in ages!"

Alanna shrugged out of Katie's embrace, her mood veering south. "If you mean to tease me, I'll go inside now."

Katie's eyes widened and her lashes dampened. "No, please don't. I'm sorry if I upset you. It's going to take me awhile to figure you out, that's all. I hope you won't take my silly comments personally."

"How can I avoid it?"

"Just ignore me. That's what Tanner does."

"Oh?"

"Yes." Katie rolled her eyes. "My brother doesn't listen to half of what I say, particularly when I get to talking about women's rights.

Well, that and my stance on the war. I'm an adamant pacifist, you see."

"You could have fooled me." Alanna clamped a hand over her mouth, realizing she'd spoken her thoughts aloud. "Oops."

Katie laughed again. "Point well-taken, point well-taken. I claim to be a pacifist but do tend to get riled up on occasion. Perhaps I should have been more specific: I am opposed to war in its usual fashions. This belief doesn't sit well with Tanner."

"Really?"

"Yes. He volunteers at Fort Missoula, you know. No doubt he will be the first to enlist, should our country..." Katie's words faded away and her eyes misted over. "Anyway, he's not keen on my ideas."

Alanna felt the breath go out of her as she contemplated the fact that Tanner might end up going to battle. She watched him from a distance as he worked. "Does he have his heart set on going, should the need arise?"

"He does." Katie shook her head. "But I'm praying and believing that the Lord will change his mind."

"The Lord's mind or Tanner's mind?"

A ripple of laughter rose from Katie as she reached for the remaining bag once again. "Well, I'm pretty sure where the Lord stands on this. He longs for all men to live in peace, as the Bible says. It's my brother who needs to change."

"I see."

Only, she didn't. Not really. And what did Katie mean about the Lord being on her side? Why, one could cite dozens—no, hundreds—of Scriptures about folks going to war. Even God got upset once in a while. At least in the pages of her very Southern Bible.

Katie gave Alanna a pensive look. "Just promise me one thing: don't go trying to change Margaret back to that namby-pamby she was when she arrived in Montana."

A chill ran down Alanna's spine, but it had nothing to do with the weather. "I beg your pardon?"

"I've spent nearly two years enlightening her to our ways. I fear all my work could unravel in a few days if she's persuaded otherwise."

Alanna's cheeks heated up again. "My sister is strong, to be sure. And she's opinionated, though not as vocal as some." Here, she paused and gave Katie a pensive look. "But I can assure you, she still carries the heart of a Southerner even though she's miles from home. You can take the girl out of Savannah, but you cannot—and I repeat, *cannot*—take Savannah out of the girl."

Alanna pivoted on her heel, away from the ghastly young woman, and took quick steps toward the house. Just yards away, her anger in full bloom, she tripped over her bag and fell flat on her face, exposing both her temper and her backside to the state of Montana.

* * * * *

As Tanner rushed to Alanna's side to extend a hand, he could almost read the thoughts tumbling through her head. She looked as intimidated by his sister as most folks were—even the locals—when they first encountered her.

He helped the beautiful Southern belle to her feet, observing the rosy glow in her cheeks. They were the color of hollyhocks blooming in the springtime. If tumbling turned her face that magnificent color, he'd have to trip her more often.

Thank goodness, Katie decided to go inside the house to visit with the others. Tanner lingered behind to make sure Alanna wasn't bruised—mentally or otherwise.

"You all right?"

"*Yay*–us." She brushed the dirt from her skirt and sighed. "Just hum–*il*–iated, is all. First you make fun of my speech, and now this."

He gathered his wits about him to respond. "Please don't let Katie bother you."

"Too late."

Tanner offered Alanna his arm, and she took it. He took advantage of the opportunity to share his thoughts. "To be honest, I'm grateful to finally find someone who agrees with me."

"Agrees with you?" A hopeful flicker lit her face.

"Yes. I have a feeling we're both of the same opinion where the suffrage movement is concerned."

"*Are* we now?" A beautiful smile turned up the edges of her mouth. "Well, I *dare*–say that's a mighty fine thing. Perhaps once I've rested we can compare notes. I know why *I'm* opposed, but it would be good to hear from other like-minded souls."

He paused before answering. "I've stated my opinion on this before and almost lost my head over it. Just don't let Katie know I've told you this."

"Never, as long as I live."

He paused and gave her a thoughtful look. "I've long felt that a man's place was to lead his family. The Bible is clear on this, in fact. With women rising up in such militant fashion, a man could get pushed to the rear and lose all sense of authority in the home and the workplace."

"So, your only *re*-al concern about the suffrage movement is that men will lose some sort of respect in the process?"

"Ah. Well, this is a genuine concern. But, as I said, it's one I rarely voice, because so many in these parts feel differently." He thought of changing the direction of the conversation but decided to get one more thought in prior to doing so. "I'm not saying women are less than men. Let's make that clear."

"Yes, let's." Her eyes sparked with mischief as she drew so near, he could smell her perfume.

"I, um..." For whatever reason, as he gazed into this belle's beautiful green eyes, he couldn't seem to collect his thoughts. She'd cast some sort of spell on him, perhaps a sprinkling of Southern fairy dust and genteel charm combined.

One thing was for sure—he couldn't seem to resist it. He would fight for his country, if need be, but he couldn't seem to fight the weakness in his knees as he gazed upon the face of the loveliest belle ever to grace the town of Missoula.

SIX

Ladies, today I am reminded of the words of Jeannette Rankin, our country's first female congresswoman and Montana's most famous suffragist. Her speech to the state legislature just three years ago opened the door for Montana's women to vote. In that passionate address, she poured out her heart and appealed to naysayers with her compelling words: "We are asking for the same principle for which men gladly gave their lives in the Revolutionary War. Taxation without representation is tyranny." Jeanette, you were right then, and we continue to thank you now for your tireless efforts on behalf of the women of Montana. You are a true sister and friend to the suffrage movement.

—Ellie Cannady, editor of *The Modern Suffragette*

* * * * *

ON THE MORNING AFTER THEY arrived in Missoula, Alanna rose earlier than Mama and Tessa. After washing up and dressing for the day, she made her way downstairs to the oversized kitchen, where she found Margaret seated at the table with a solemn look on her face.

Alanna's heart quickened at once. "Margaret? Is everything all right?"

Her sister looked up, eyes brimming with tears, which she brushed away. "Yes. I mean, no." She choked back a sob. "I'm sorry, Lana. I've just received word that a good friend, Ellie Cannady, is fading fast. She's been ill for some time—the doctor calls it lupus, I believe—but she has managed to pull through every time. This time her lungs are affected, and I fear the worst. I rarely get down in the dumps, but my faith is low this morning."

"Well, that's understandable, considering the circumstances. I'm so sorry to hear about your friend."

"It's just tragic. My heart is broken." Margaret rose and tended to a skillet filled with scrambled eggs. She scooped a large helping onto a plate along with a piece of toast and a couple of thick slices of bacon before passing it off to Alanna, whose mouth watered, just thinking about how hungry she was. She would have to guard her appetite, or her fine dresses would soon be tight in the middle.

She took the jar of huckleberry jam Margaret offered and spread it liberally on her toast. "Are you very close?"

"Yes." Margaret dabbed at her eyes. "She's the most wonderful woman you'd ever care to meet. She's the editor of *The Modern Suffragette*, a newspaper that offers support and encouragement to women in these parts."

"Ah. Well, no wonder I've never heard of her. I seriously doubt we can get that paper in Savannah." She took a bite of the toast, the sweet jam slippery on her tongue. *Mmm.*

Margaret took a seat at the table and nibbled at her eggs. "Oh, you might be surprised. She and Congresswoman Rankin travel in the same circles, which means her writings are known from Montana all the way to Washington DC. She's quite prolific, you know. And she's a woman I've come to admire on many levels. I still have a lot to learn from her, which is one reason this is all so distressing."

"I'm sorry she's ill." Alanna managed the words but secretly wondered when her sister had grown so attached to such a person. Could it be Margaret had already been won over to the suffragette's way of thinking? Alanna nibbled on her toast, distracted by her worries.

Margaret put her fork down and sighed. "Poor Ellie is in worse shape than any of us imagined. The doctor has been to see her this morning and has sent word that she might not make it more than a week or two. I'm simply beside myself. Why, to think I just spent time with her." Margaret seemed to perk up a bit. "I daresay women will come from all over the state when the news goes out that she's passed. You've never met a gal so well-loved."

"Must be quite a spitfire."

"Indeed."

Alanna reflected on her sister's words before broaching the subject on her mind. "Can I ask a question of you, Margaret? I do hope you won't take it the wrong way."

"What sort of question?" Margaret pushed her plate away and leaned back in her chair.

"You seem…different somehow. Are you the same sister I once knew?"

Margaret's laughter resonated across the room. "What did you picture in your head before arriving?"

Alanna offered a weak smile. "Well, I knew you were with child, of course, so I felt sure you would be physically changed. Though I didn't expect you to look quite so vibrant and strong."

Margaret sat up straight in the chair, a confident look on her face. "I've never felt as resilient. Glad it shows on the outside as well as the inside. I'm not the slightest bit interested in taking to my bed just because I'm with child. You can thank my Montana sisters for that."

"I see." Alanna stared at her sister, more confused than ever. "I look at you now and wonder if you're the girl who left Savannah just two years ago."

"I'm still Margaret, through and through. Just because I'm expecting a child doesn't mean I'm fundamentally changed." She ran her slender fingers across her rounded midsection and smiled. "Well, some parts are more changed than others."

Alanna shook her head. "I am referring to the change in your beliefs."

"My...beliefs?" Margaret looked stunned at this statement. "I am as strong in my faith as ever. Nothing has changed there. If anything, I've come to rely on the Lord even more than before. Up here, in such rugged territory, our faith sees us through many hardships I'd only read about in books or newspaper articles."

"I'm sorry, Margaret." Alanna reached out a hand to touch her sister's arm and was more than a little taken aback by the rough, scratchy fabric of her sleeve. "I didn't mean to imply that your faith has waned. Not at all. When I say the word *beliefs*, I refer to ideology.

I don't recall your being such a strong supporter of women's rights when you lived in Savannah. From my conversation with Brett's sister, it's clear she is."

"I'm sorry if she came across as brusque. Katie often speaks without thinking."

"I can take care of myself. I'm just concerned that she has... well, has she rubbed off on you, perhaps?"

"Possibly. A little." Margaret's expression brightened. "But there's more to it than that, Lana. Up here, women's issues aren't a matter of prestige. It's not about bragging rights. It's a matter of life and death. If women didn't have the right to maintain their property and any funds acquired during the marriage, they would wither and die. I couldn't bear to watch that. That's why I've linked arms with the suffrage movement. We've made progress in the Northwest, certainly, but there's much more road ahead to travel before the battle is won across this great country of ours."

"You've already won the right to vote." *And please don't ask my opinion on that.* "What more could you ask for?"

Margaret shook her head then leaned back in her chair once again. "My sweet sister, you really have no idea, do you?"

"I—I guess not."

"Here in Montana, life is different. Issues for women are different, as I said. Why, I could tell you stories of women who risked their reputations and their livelihood to take a stand for what they felt was right."

"Oh?"

"Yes. I knew nothing of such women when I moved here, but I've been a ready learner. Do you know the story of Esther Strasburger?"

"Can't say as I do." Alanna studied her eggs, wishing she could change the direction of this conversation.

"She taught in one of our local schools several years ago but wasn't allowed to vote in school elections. To be able to do so was critical to her career. You can imagine how winning the vote in 1914 changed her life. And the lives of all Montana women, actually." Margaret's eyes took on a new shine. "I mean, just think about it, Lana. Though she wasn't much older than we are now, Esther Strasburger was finally able to support herself. What a battle to be won for single women across this great state."

"Hmm."

"That's why I'm so passionate about winning that same right for women in every state. We have watched women young and old being pressed down, unable to earn the proper income or support themselves as need be. But no longer. It shouldn't matter if a woman lives in New York or Texas or Wyoming; she should have the same rights. Don't you agree?"

"Well, I guess I'll have to think about that one. I'm still not convinced."

"You might think differently if this hit a little closer to home."

"What do you mean?"

"If something happened to Papa—God forbid—would our family's property still belong to Mama?"

"I—I never thought about it."

"You should. If you and Mama and Tessa are the only ones left on that property, you would want it to be protected, would you not?"

Alanna rose and paced the kitchen, finally looking her sister in the eyes. "I never really stopped to think about it like that before, to be honest."

"Here's my point, and it's only something I've recently come to understand: widows can retain the rights to their land. But the only reason they can—the only reason women are given any property rights at all—is because our female predecessors took a stand on their behalf. Otherwise, thousands of women and children would be living on the streets right now. Now women and children are protected. They receive the property by default. And if Mama, for example, received an inheritance of some adjoining acreage from, say, her brother, she could keep that too. It would be her property."

Alanna pivoted on her heel, feeling a little stirred up by this conversation. "Why did you have to go and make this about Mama?"

"That's the point. When it's 'the great unknown,' when we're talking about other people, other places, it's easy to stand against them. But when it hits home—when it's your mama or my sister— it's much tougher. I'm just saying that the things I didn't understand before are now a bit clearer. And because they're clearer, my thoughts are shifting."

"Well, don't let them shift too much. Promise me you will always still be my sweet Savannah sister."

"Sounds like I'm missing a doozy of a conversation in here." Tessa's voice sounded from the bottom of the stairway. "And it smells yummy, to boot. Bacon?"

"Yes. And scrambled eggs." Margaret's expression softened. "Have you seen Mama? Is she coming down?"

"You know Mama. She's got a weak—"

"Constitution. Yes, I know." Margaret rose, rubbed her extended belly, and made her way over to the stove, where she heaped bacon and eggs onto a fresh plate for Tessa. "Have a seat. I'll bring this over. Then I'll get busy on these dishes before Mama comes down."

Tessa, for once, did as she was told. Likely because there was food involved. She'd no sooner taken her first bite than a knock sounded on the door.

"Wonder who that could be this time of morning." Margaret rose and made her way to the door, returning moments later with a very repentant-looking Katie. At once Alanna cringed. Would she really have to endure the young woman's teasing so early in the morning? Wasn't yesterday's how-do-you-do enough?

Katie approached, her eyes to the ground. She spent a couple of seconds in silence then blurted out an unexpected message. "Alanna, I—I, well, I need to apologize for how I spoke to you yesterday."

"Oh?" Alanna continued to nibble at her toast, determined not to let Katie see the surprise in her eyes.

"Yes." The young woman sighed as she plopped down into the chair next to Alanna. "What I said was deplorable. Tanner really put me in my place last night on the ride home."

"He did?" Alanna couldn't help but smile at that news. So, the handsome cowboy had come to her rescue. Maybe there was a little Southern gentleman inside of him after all.

Katie nodded. "He really gave me what for." She took Alanna's hand. "Please say you'll forgive me. So many times my mouth runs away like a train barreling down a mountain. And I confess, it has derailed me more than once."

Alanna, determined to respond as any good Southern girl would do, wrapped Katie in a warm sisterly embrace. "All is forgiven. Now, come and join us for breakfast."

Katie smiled, but only for a moment. Just as quickly, her eyes misted over. "I don't know if I'm up to eating this morning, to be honest. I'm so distressed over the news about Ellie Cannady." Her gaze shifted to Margaret. "Have you heard?"

"Yes. Brett saw the doctor early this morning on his way back from Ellie's place. So sad."

Katie rose and took a few steps toward the stove. Reaching for a plate, she heaped it with scrambled eggs and bacon. "We must do something special to lift her spirits. I'm not sure what, exactly, but I'll think of something. I'm loaded with ideas."

"That she is." Tanner's voice rang out. Alanna turned to see him standing in the doorway with his hat in hands. "She's come up with at least ten or more on the drive over here—most of which involved *me* in some form or fashion. She tends to wear me out with her ideas."

Katie laughed. "He's a good sport, though. Always listens so patiently as I ramble."

Tanner took a few long strides into the kitchen, a half smile lighting his face. "Very nearly lost my patience this morning, I'll have you know."

"And why is that?" Alanna gazed into his beautiful blue eyes as he drew near, intrigued by the overgrowth of stubble. Had he forgotten to shave, perhaps, or did all cowboys look this scruffy?

"All this hoopla about the roles of men and women. It's grating on me." His gaze shifted to the stove.

"Here, let me fix you a plate, Tanner." Margaret rose, but he shook his head.

"No. I mean, yes, I'll have some food, but I'll fix it myself. No point in your getting up."

"See there?" Katie pointed at him, in an accusing fashion. "You say you're not in favor of liberating women from their confining roles and yet you choose to wait on yourself."

He looked boggled by this statement. "I was just trying to be courteous." With a shrug, he reached for the plate. "Didn't mean to make an issue out of it."

Alanna continued to watch as he loaded his plate. She couldn't help but allow her gaze to linger on his broad shoulders. As he leaned over the stove to spoon the eggs, a swath of wavy hair fell casually on his forehead. She found herself riveted to it. And him.

"Alanna?"

"Hmm?" She glanced at Tessa, who gave her a curious look.

"Would you pass the jam, please?"

"Sure." She pushed it her sister's way then snuck a second glance at Tanner. He stood tall and lean and definitely muscular. Those denims suited him, though she couldn't imagine any of the fellas back home turning up in them at a soiree. And that plaid shirt would be laughed out of the cotillion. Still, as Tanner turned back to face her, she had to admit the truth—he looked good. Mighty good. Scruffy or not.

When he took the seat next to her, she could scarcely concentrate on her food. Thank goodness he seemed content to do the talking, so she didn't have to.

"Ladies, I don't wish to quarrel. You've won the right to vote. I'll give it to you, willingly. Just humor me when it comes to the various roles of men and women. I'll go out and tend to the cattle. You stay home and tend to the young'uns."

Katie let out a gasp. "I cannot believe you just said that."

"What?" He spoke around a mouthful of eggs in an ungentle-manly way. "You enjoy tending cattle?"

"That's not my point. You know very well I can't abide cows."

"Neither can they abide you, Cattle Kate." He laughed at his own words, and Katie turned red in the face.

"How many times have I told you not to call me that?"

"So, you're not fond of cattle, and you have no inclination to care for children." Tanner lathered a piece of bread with a heaping mound of huckleberry jam. "What else are you opposed to? Oh, wait. I remember now. Men. You're opposed to men." He took a bite of the bread, and a look of contentment came over him at once.

"Oh, not me." Tessa give him a giddy stare before dissolving into fitful giggles.

"You know perfectly well I'm not opposed to men." Katie shook her head, anger flashing in her eyes. "When I find the right one—the one who will stand with me and offer support for the causes I care about—I will marry him in an instant. But in the meantime, there's work to do. Perceptions must change, or my daughters and granddaughters won't stand a chance. The idea of bringing a baby girl into the world right now gives me the shivers."

"Maybe God will give you sons, then." Tanner gave a brusque nod and swiped a napkin across his mouth—missing a spot of jam, which remained on his upper lip. "Either way, I don't like to quarrel. But I think we can agree on one thing. If you read the Word of God, you know that men and women were not created by God to play the same roles. Men are men and women are women."

Katie rose and paced the room. "I've never advocated the idea of reversing roles. That's not what this is about. If you saw my heart, you would see that my beliefs are really not much different from your own. I believe that women can—and should—enjoy wonderful lives as wives, mothers, and caregivers. But I also believe that women have intelligent minds and strong bodies and much to contribute outside of the home. They are bright and witty and clever."

"But Tanner's right about what the Bible says," Alanna chimed in. "On that point, I must agree."

"Thank you." Tanner gave her a wink before taking another bite of his food. Another dab with his napkin and the jam disappeared from his lip.

Still, Alanna could hardly bear the embarrassment. Had he really winked at her again? And in front of the others?

Katie looked at her in a way that made her feel traitorous. "I believe men are prone to take such Scriptures out of context. And they completely ignore other passages regarding the stronger women of faith. Do you know the story of Deborah, the prophetess? The men of her day saw her as an authority figure. I'm not saying we're all Deborahs. That's not what I mean to imply. I'm just saying that we have biblical examples of women who were mightily used by God to speak with authority." She squared her shoulders. "That's what I want to be—a Deborah. For my generation."

"My goodness." Alanna fanned herself. "Just yesterday Margaret told me that she feels like Ruth because Ruth trusted

God to lead her to a strange new land. And you want to be like Deborah. I wonder who's next."

"Me." Tessa's voice rang out. "I want to be like Martha. She's the one who wanted to make sure everyone got fed, right?" Tessa shoved another spoonful of eggs into her mouth.

"I want to be like Hannah," Mama said as she entered the room. "She's one of my favorite women in the Bible. She cared enough about her son to dedicate him to the Lord and then trusted the Lord with his care. That's much harder than it looks, I must admit."

"So which woman in the Bible are you most like, Alanna?" Tanner asked.

She paused to think it through. "I would have to say Pharaoh's daughter."

"That's an odd choice," Mama said as she eased her way down into a chair. "How ever did you come up with her?"

"Because she saw someone facing a perilous situation and stepped in to save the day. She rescued Moses from certain death."

"And you plan to rescue people?" Katie looked intrigued by this news.

"I do." If only they knew. She would rescue her sister from these crazy Montana suffragettes and take her back to Savannah where she belonged.

Eventually.

Right now, however, Alanna was content to go on nibbling toast with huckleberry jam and drinking in the image of a like-minded Montana cowboy with very broad shoulders. Broad enough to carry the conversation for both of them.

SEVEN

Many strong women of our day wonder if they can merge romance with a strong backbone. It is possible, though one must choose their mate with great care. Many a man has worn down the weary suffragette, molding her into the image of someone she scarcely recognizes in the end. Ladies, it is our place, our time, to stand firm, even when romantic notions threaten to topple us. Love, yes. Concede, no.

—Ellie Cannady, editor of *The Modern Suffragette*

* * * * *

THE NEXT FEW WEEKS IN Missoula flew by. Though Alanna hated to admit it to anyone, including herself, the town continued to grow on her. So did its inhabitants. One in particular.

Not that she would give any serious thought to a fella like Tanner. Oh no. With plans to return to Savannah, she could hardly entertain the notion of finding a beau on the opposite side of the country.

Of course, Tanner wouldn't be the sort of man she would be drawn to, anyway. Heavens, no. Why, he was her opposite in nearly every respect. Where he loved Montana, she loved Savannah. Where he wore rugged clothes, she preferred lace and frills. Where he spoke of cattle and feed stores, she spoke of cotillions and fine department stores.

There were a few things they shared in common, of course. Their faith, for instance, as well as their views on the suffrage movement. Knowing she had someone on her side in that argument made the ongoing debate with Katie and Margaret more tolerable.

Still, in spite of the fact that he was easy on the eyes, she found his teasing a bit much to take and his never-ending speeches about Montana's beauty taxing. Worst of all, he seemed determined to poke fun at her way of speaking. Not that she had ever taken note of her speech before, but now she found herself choosing her words more carefully in his presence so he wouldn't pester her. But even that seemed to humor him.

So when they found themselves alone on Margaret's front porch on a chilly Saturday afternoon, Alanna was hard-pressed to keep her wits about her.

And all the more when he gazed at her with those teasing eyes.

"Want to be a liberated woman, Alanna?" He wiggled his brows.

"Whatever do you mean?"

"You can help me tend to the horses and cows. Brett's gone to town for the day, and I told him I'd look in on Prissy. She's in foal."

"Prissy?"

"His favorite heifer. She's due to deliver soon."

Alanna felt heat creep up her face. "And you require my help?'

He rose and extended his hand. "Well, not your help, perhaps, but the pleasure of your company."

She stood, still feeling rather unsure of herself. Did Tanner really wish her to traipse across the yard to that dirty, smelly barn? What in the world was he thinking?

Still, as she gazed into his hopeful eyes, she couldn't very well say no, now could she? She followed on his heels, wondering where the journey would take her.

* * * * *

TANNER COULDN'T BELIEVE HIS GOOD fortune. The Southern belle was ready to enter his world—the world of cows, horses, barns, and sweet-smelling bales of hay. Hopefully she could manage it.

All along the way, she grumbled. About the uneven ground. The stench. The cackling of the chickens. The gnats on the cows. Even the dirt on Snowball's thick coat. You'd think she'd never been in a barn or seen a dirty dog before.

Then again, maybe she hadn't.

He went to the stall to check on Prissy and offer her food. Alanna continued to chatter—and he countered her a couple of times, making fun of her speech. This seemed to stop her cold. She swept a hair off her face and stood her ground, now silent.

Shame washed over him; he'd obviously hurt her feelings. "I'm sorry, Alanna. Looks like we can't be around each other without sparks flying." Tanner clamped his mouth shut at this point, wishing he'd phrased it another way.

"Ah." Alanna's cheeks flushed. "I didn't *re*–alize."

"Sure you did. We've been sparring partners from the beginning—teasing back and forth—and I've been determined to figure out why I spend so much time goading you about the way you talk. We're on the same team, after all."

"Same team?"

"Well, sure. We've got similar beliefs—everything from spiritual to practical."

"You know nothing of what I find *prac*–tical." She gave him a quizzical look. "Have you ever been to the South, Tanner?"

"Went with my brother to Colorado once."

The most delightful giggle erupted. "You think Colorado is the South?"

"Well, it's south of here. Isn't that what matters?"

"You simply have no i–*de*–a. Why, the true South is the most charming place, filled with young women who pay attention to customs and decorum and young men who play the role of the gentleman with such ease that one realizes he is not putting on airs, he is simply being himself. In Savannah, we have truly turned the roles of the sexes"—here she blushed—"into an art form."

"Well, then, it would seem I have much to learn."

"Indeed, you do."

"Let's start right away." Tanner couldn't hide the smile that followed as he came up with his best idea thus far. "You can be my teacher."

"Your teacher?"

"Yes." Oh, what fun this would be! "Here's my first question about ladies from the South. Why do they call you belles?"

"Ah." Alanna fingered a loose tendril of hair along her cheek. "A young lady is seen as the belle of the ball if she's charming. And beautiful, of course, but I never claimed to be a great beauty." She wrinkled her nose.

"If I were you, I'd start claiming it."

She looked a bit flustered but managed a quiet, "Thank you."

"So, let me get this straight. A Southern belle is a charming and beautiful young woman from the South."

"Well, yes, but there's more to it than that. The ladies of the South are con–*si*–derably different from the women I've met here."

"A clear understatement on your part."

"Perhaps. Ladies in the South have different concerns. We don't bother much with politics 'n' such. We leave that to the men."

"I like Southern belles already." *One in particular.*

"We focus much of our time on social graces."

"Social graces?" He regarded her with amusement.

"Yes." After a pause, she let out a little squeal then patted his arm, her green eyes swimming in mischief. "That's it! I'll teach you proper Southern social graces. I'll turn you into a gentleman."

"Gee, thanks."

A giggle followed. "I mean, a *re*–al *Sou*–thern gentleman. That way, should you *ev*–uh visit the South, you will fit right in."

"Somehow I doubt I'll fit right in." He pulled off his hat and raked his fingers through his hair. "Not sure as I'd want to."

"Still, we can pretend. So, in order to accomplish that, I will teach you all of the finer graces."

"You want to turn me into a girl?"

"No, of course not!" She put her hands on her hips. "I am only hoping to show you that a gentleman *must* refine his etiquette skills."

"Skills? Such as?"

"Well, such as sharing the conver–*sa*–tion—something you have yet to learn, I should add. Letting everyone involved take a turn."

He gave her a quizzical look. "And you are skilled at this, are you?"

"I—I…" She paused, a hint of chagrin in her expression. "Well, I'm an ongoing learner, of course."

"Of course. What else?"

"Never use shockin' language, particularly in front of the ladies."

"That will not be an issue, I assure you."

"You should also know that it's improper to ask about the cost of something when you are in a social setting. This is very important."

"I see." He rose and paced the room. "Well, now, that one might be a bit of a problem."

"Oh?"

"Yes." As he faced her, lines of concentration deepened along his brows and under his eyes. "Let's say I need to know the price of a certain cow my neighbor is selling. How am I to know unless I ask?"

"There is a time and a place for such business. A party is not that time."

"I see." He pursed his lips, deep in thought. "So, if my friend happens to mention his cow at the party, am I to ignore him?"

"However did we shift the conversation to talkin' about cows?" She released the most delightful little sigh, clearly exasperated with his bantering. All the more reason to continue.

"Happens all the time in Montana." He gave her another wink.

"Yes, well, this leads me to my next point. When one is at a party, one must listen carefully and respectfully to others. And please do not wink."

"So, let me understand this correctly—if my friend speaks to me about his cow, I must be respectful but not ask the price? Is that it? And I'm not allowed to wink at him?"

Alanna groaned. "The greater point is that you want to keep things light. No arguing in a social setting. Nothing to stir the waters. Always respond with a gracious word. Do you see?"

"So, if he tells me that his cow is prettier than my cow, I can't argue the point, even if I happen to own the prettiest heifer in the valley—which I do, by the way. She's much prettier than Prissy here."

Alanna plopped down onto a bale of hay, clearly exasperated. "Honestly, we *ne*-vuh speak of cows in Savannah. I have no idea why we're discussing them today unless, perhaps, you've some hidden meanin'."

"No hidden meaning. I just happen to like my cows. You can't fault a fella for liking his cows, can you?"

"As long as he doesn't carry on about them in a social setting, no." She paused. "Now, that reminds me, you must never correct your friend's etiquette, grammar, or behavior in public."

"Like you're doing now."

She crossed her arms at her chest and glared at him. "We're not in public."

"I beg to differ." He pointed to Prissy and the other heifers. They stood a distance away, nibbling on straw.

"Well, I—"

He laughed. "You go right on correcting me, Lana. I don't mind a bit."

"*A*–lanna." She punctuated her name. "Now, one more thing to contend with. If you're going to compliment someone, your compliment must be sincere."

"Have I mentioned that your hair is prettier than my palomino's mane? Casey's a fine horse, but your hair beats his a hundred times over."

She groaned and closed her eyes. "I can see that I have a *lot* of work to do."

"Indeed. This could take days, but I don't mind. I have plenty of time on my hands, once my morning chores are done at the ranch. I will be your apt pupil." He took the spot next to her on the bale of hay, and Snowball curled up at their feet, muddy tail wagging.

"No doubt. I can see that I will have my hands *ver*–y full."

She gave him a closer look, and he found himself embarrassed by her lingering gaze on his shoulders.

"Do you mind if I ask what you're doing?"

She startled to attention. "Oh. I, um—well, I'm measurin' you for a suit."

"Excuse me?"

"I'm doing some calcu–*la*–tions in my head. I believe you're about the same size as my father, only your shoulders are *broad*–uh." She put her hand to her mouth and her face reddened. "Not that I've been paying particular attention to your shoulders, a'course."

"Of course." He paused to think through what she'd said.

"Do you mind if I ask why you're trying to envision me in a suit?"

"Because my sister is about to celebrate a very special birthday and Margaret is hostin' a fine party, complete with a dozen guests and a grand meal in the dining room. You will have to dress nicely for the event."

"I have a Sunday suit, thank you just the same."

"I've seen your Sunday suit. Last Sunday in fact. But…well, I hope you don't mind my sayin' this…"

"I have a feeling you're bound and determined to say it anyway."

"Hmm." She paused. For a moment. "Anyway, there's a new sort of fashion that the fellas back home are wearing. It's quite formal."

"I despise it already."

She slapped him on the arm. "Pay attention."

"Striking a fella in the arm like that serves as a mighty big distraction from the conversation at hand."

When her face contorted, she looked cuter than ever. "If you would pay attention, I wouldn't have to strike you."

"If you would let me wear my Sunday suit, I wouldn't have to pay attention."

She shook her head, her eyes fluttering shut. He resisted the urge to grab her and plant a kiss on those beautiful lips. No telling what she might do. If she slapped him for not paying attention, she'd probably take a shovel to him for a stolen kiss.

Alanna dove into a lengthy description of men's suits, but he tired of it quickly, especially when she got to the pleated trousers. He released a lingering groan, followed by, "Is fashion such a serious consideration in the South? Really?"

"Yes, it's critical. Why, a lady would *ne*–vuh show up for a social function in anything less than her finest. And a party—especially a fancy one—is the perfect place for a fella to show off his latest suit."

"If I show up at Tessa's birthday party wearing the kind of suit you've described, I'll be laughed out of the county. Besides, it's too late in the season for frills. Winter snows are coming soon, in case you haven't noticed. Look at those skies up there."

"Snow?" She turned to face him. "So soon?"

"Soon?" He laughed. "It's nigh on to Thanksgiving—just a few more weeks. We often have snow by the holidays."

She glanced up and shrugged. "What does that have to do with your clothing?"

"Everything. You've never felt cold like you'll feel it here in the valley. It's not the right time of year to be buying anything but long johns."

She paled at the mention of undergarments. "Regardless, I still think you need a new suit, and there's no point in waitin' till spring. And as for what the other fellas will say about it, they'll be jealous, I assure you."

He wasn't so sure about that, but he was sure of one thing—if this beautiful china doll wanted to dress him up and prance him around in front of the whole town of Missoula, he'd let her do it. And if she kept gazing into his eyes with such a radiant smile on her face, he might just lose his heart in the process.

EIGHT

Many women confuse strength with external power. I submit to you that strength rises from the inside, from the very core of our being. If we are strengthened from within, we can stand firm even when the unexpected storms of life begin to blow. Many women are secretly weak on the inside, playacting at strength in front of others who are looking on. They falter in their attempts to stand strong when external forces rise against them. May it not be so. Gird yourselves, ladies. Storms will come. I can attest to that, having walked through more than my share, of late. But if you're strong on the inside, you will stand firm.

—Ellie Cannady, editor of *The Modern Suffragette*

* * * * *

THE FOLLOWING SATURDAY MORNING, ALANNA awoke chilled to the bone. She shivered and pulled the quilt up to her chin. Next to her, Tessa continued to doze. Burrowing under the covers, Alanna got as close to her sister as she could without waking her, in the hopes of warming up.

Unfortunately, that did not happen. Minutes later Alanna rose from the bed, her teeth chattering. She pulled on her housecoat and took a few tentative steps toward the window. Streaks of early morning sunlight flitted in through the window, but what she saw sparkling beneath that sunlight caused her to lose her breath. Outside, everything was covered in a fresh white blanket of crystallized snow. The shimmers of early morning light reflected off the ground, nearly blinding her.

Alanna could hardly breathe. Sure, she'd seen snow off in the distance as they had traveled. And, yes, the mountain ranges surrounding Missoula were capped in the stuff. But up close? Snow so fresh you could practically taste it? Never!

"Tessa!" she called. "Tessa, wake up!"

Her younger sister rolled over in the bed and yawned then reached to pull the quilt up over her shoulder. "C–cold!"

"There's a reason for that. Come look."

"No." Tessa huddled under the covers, her teeth now chattering.

"You have to see this. I promise you won't be disappointed." Alanna pointed outside to the picture-postcard scene.

Tessa rose, grumbling all the way. "I don't know what's so important that you have to get me out of bed. I was having the loveliest dream about a certain handsome cowboy." She gave Alanna a little wink.

"Never mind all that. Just come look."

Tessa wrapped herself in the quilt and took a few steps in her direction. "What is it?"

"Look." The word came out as a whisper. Alanna pointed off

in the distance to the large field just beyond the side yard. "Have you ever seen anything like it?" She turned her gaze away from the window to glance at her sister.

Tessa stood motionless in what appeared to be stunned silence, her eyes wide and mouth rounded to a perfect O. "Oh, Lana!" She came closer and wiped her palm against the window, but the glass didn't clear despite her rubbing. "It's coming down in sheets."

"Or would that be blankets?" Alanna giggled. "Whatever it is, it's beautiful." Her gaze drifted up to the heavens, to the heavy, white sky. Somewhere up there the Lord had orchestrated all of this, just as He'd orchestrated the warm sunny days in Savannah.

"It's exquisite." Tessa raced for the bed and reached for her slippers. "And the sooner I can get out there to feel it for myself, the better."

"Don't forget to put on your warmest clothes. You're going to catch your death, otherwise."

"I'll be fine, Alanna. Why is it you always find the need to ruin my good time?"

This stopped Alanna from adding, "And don't forget your coat." Instead, she offered up a shrug.

Tessa, in her usual fashion, rushed to dress and didn't even bother with a coat. No doubt she would turn up later with a head cold. Nothing Alanna could do about that. If her little sister chose to put her health in danger, so be it.

Alanna took care to dress warmly and then grabbed her heavy coat. She slung it over her arm and made her way downstairs, where she found Margaret in the kitchen, making pancakes.

"Have you seen—?"

"If you're looking for Tessa, she headed outside to play in the snow."

"Ah. I might like to take a walk out there, myself."

"Be careful, Alanna. The walkway is iced over. Guard your step and keep an eye out for Tanner, will you?"

"Tanner?" For whatever reason, her heart leaped at the mention of his name.

"Yes. He's bringing over some sugar. We were running low and I didn't want Brett to have to make a trip into town in such bad weather. Mama and I plan to make cookies today. Lots and lots of them. And we're baking a cake for the party too."

"Very gentlemanly of Tanner to bring by the sugar." *Perhaps my lessons are working already.*

"Yes, well, that's not out of character for him, you will learn. He's definitely one of the kindest people I've ever known. And polite too."

"Oh, very." Alanna shrugged on her coat then opened the door that led from the kitchen to the backyard. "I'll be back shortly, no doubt." She took just a couple of steps out onto the porch before her teeth began to chatter. No sooner did she realize she'd left her gloves inside than a familiar voice came from behind her. She turned to discover Brett walking her way.

"Enjoying our weather?" He flashed a boyish grin, and she noticed the frozen mist on his beard.

Alanna shivered, her fingers now feeling a bit numb. "It's beautiful, but I don't believe I could live like this."

"Oh, you get used to it. Just ask Margaret. That first winter she shivered nonstop, but these days she scarcely notices the cold. Besides, there are some wonderful things you can do in wintery weather. Take sleigh rides, for instance. And ice-skating."

"Ice-skating?"

"Yes." His eyes sparkled. "Ever tried it? Soaring across the ice, free as a bird, with the winter winds whipping through your hair and the afternoon sunshine bright on your face. Wonderful fun."

"I doubt that." Alanna tried to imagine herself slipping and sliding across the ice but could not. Her mind clouded over as she thought about her poor sister, having to acclimate to such intense weather conditions. The more she thought about it—the more she pondered Margaret's sacrifices—the more frustrated she got. Finally unable to hold her feelings inside, Alanna turned Brett's way, ready to speak her mind.

"Admit it."

"Admit what?" Brett stamped his feet on the porch and snow fell off in clumps. He glanced back up at Alanna, his brow furrowed.

She folded her arms over her chest, determination setting in. "This was never Margaret's dream. It was yours. You're a dreamer. You always have been."

"There's nothing wrong with being a dreamer, Lana."

"Please don't call me that. Having a nickname as a child was fine, but I'm grown now."

He shoved his hands into his coat pockets and leaned against the side of the house. "Then surely you're old enough to understand that Margaret is here of her own free will. She married me knowing that I planned to come to Montana to raise cattle and be near my family. She loves it here."

Alanna shivered, regret sweeping over her. Why had she started this conversation out-of-doors, in the bitter cold? "I'm not sure *love* is the correct word. She's swept away by the beautiful surroundings, true, but I wouldn't go so far as to say she's happy here."

"What do you mean?" Creases formed on his brow. "Has she hinted at some sort of unhappiness?"

"No, but I can see it in her eyes." Alanna drew in a deep breath, and the cold air sent a shock of pain into her chest. "S–she's d–downcast much of the time."

With the wave of a hand, Brett appeared to dismiss her concerns. "Ah. I'm sure that has something to do with the weather. She often gets a bit blue in the wintertime."

"All the more reason to bring her back to the South, where it's warm."

"Is that what this is about, Lana?" He sighed then said, "Alanna."

"Coming back home just makes sense. There's nothing for you here, Brett. Nothing long-term, anyway."

He shook his head and reached for the doorknob. "You're wrong about that. I find everything I need in Montana. If you would give it a shot, you would find a few things here to enjoy, yourself." He disappeared inside the house in a huff and Alanna felt her shoulders slump forward as defeat set in. Why, oh why, had she chosen today to bring up the subject? Hadn't she agreed to wait until the proper time to share her thoughts?

She lifted her hands to blow on them, hoping the pain in her fingers would cease. Instead, her breath seemed to cloud the air between her mouth and her hands. Fascinating. This served to distract her from the obvious problem.

"Are you all right?" A familiar voice sounded from behind her. She turned to find Tanner standing close enough to reach out and touch her. "W–where did you come from?"

"Ah, the age-old question. From what my mother tells me, the stork left me in the vegetable garden." The laughter that followed warmed Alanna's heart, if not her hands. He shifted the bags of sugar from one arm to another.

"I–I've never felt c–c–cold like this before." Her teeth took to chattering once again. "Hurts a–all the w–way to the b–bone."

"Guess I'm just used to it, but we'd better get you inside."

"I came out to look for—" Just then, Tessa breezed by them, bumping Tanner in the shoulder as she passed and almost knocking the bags of sugar from his arms.

"Oops. Sorry, Tanner. Must not have been looking where I was going."

"Mm-hmm." Alanna fought the desire to roll her eyes. Tessa knew exactly where she was going and what she was doing.

"Coming in?" Tessa held the door open and gave Tanner a sweet smile.

He turned back to look at Alanna, who nodded, every part of her body now trembling from the cold.

They stepped inside, and she remained in her coat, still shaking. Tanner walked to the counter on the far side of the room and put the bags of sugar down then greeted Margaret, who gave him a hug.

"I just love the snow!" Tessa exclaimed. "It's absolutely divine."

"It took me some time to get used to it, to be quite honest," Margaret said. "That first winter I didn't stop shivering until the snow thawed. But I hardly notice it now."

So Brett said.

Alanna's fingers and toes cried out in tingling pain. Whatever could be causing such a reaction to the cold?

"Now I've learned how to dress myself so that I'm prepared." Margaret paused from stirring the pancake batter. I can't wear my fancy shoes and dresses like I did back home, but that's all right. I've gotten used to it. I just make sure I wear several layers of clothing to keep warm. And gloves, of course." She gave Alanna a funny look.

"Warm hands, warm heart." Tanner poured himself a cup of coffee then took a seat at the table. "That's what my mama always says."

"Actually, I think it's more important to keep the feet warm," Margaret said. "I've learned that when my feet are warm, the rest of my body follows suit. That's why we keep a warm brick at the foot of the bed at night, so that our toes are toasty." A smile followed. "Brett is the sweetest husband in the world. He always thinks of little things like that to take good care of me, especially now that we have a little one on the way." She ran her hand across her belly and smiled.

Alanna was silent until the tingling subsided in her fingers. She thought through her earlier conversation with Brett before adding to the conversation. "I can't quite figure you out, Margaret," she said at last.

"What do you mean?"

"You're strong and independent, ready to change the country and the lives of women from shore to shore. But you melt like butter whenever Brett's name is mentioned."

"Is that all?" Margaret grinned. "Well, loving my husband doesn't make me weak. Just the opposite, in fact. His love strengthens me from the inside out. It gives me courage and makes me think I'm capable of anything I set my heart and mind to."

"That's what the love of a good man will do." Tanner gave a brusque nod then took a hefty swig of his coffee.

While she found his remark humorous, Alanna did not say so. Indeed, she found herself distracted by Margaret's comments about Brett. They seemed contradictory to her sister's stance on women's rights, at least to Alanna's way of thinking. How could she be so enamored with a man one minute and so set on women being freed from their proverbial yokes the next? Nothing about this made sense. Why couldn't Margaret make up her mind? Either she linked arms with the suffragettes or she sang the praises of the man she loved.

"I suppose I'm just confused." Alanna shrugged, ready to be done with this conversation and ready to feel her toes once more.

"Maybe you're thinking too hard." Margaret's grin lit the room. "Honestly, I don't spend my days thinking about my independence or the lack thereof. Not when I have a husband as wonderful as Brett. My beliefs haven't changed. I still believe what the Bible says about men and women. I'm not trying to rewrite the greatest love story of all time. I mention this only because you seem concerned."

She went off on a tangent, listing several of her favorite Bible stories. Alanna tried to stay focused but found her thoughts flittering away. If what Margaret said was true—if loving a good man really could strengthen you from the inside out—then, perhaps, what she needed was a good man.

* * * * *

TANNER TRUDGED HIS WAY PAST mounds of newly banked snow, headed to the barn. His boots left slushy prints along the way. In spite of the cold, he felt warmed from spending time with Alanna. Well, until those last few moments when she and Margaret held that awkward conversation.

No point in worrying about that right now. He was a man on a mission, after all, responding to a request from the ladies: find Brett. Ask him to come inside for breakfast.

Tanner stepped inside the barn and brushed the snow from his shoulders. "Brett?" He called out his brother's name but heard no answer. He tried again. Still nothing.

Tanner made his way toward the stalls, where he checked on Prissy, who was huddled against several bales of hay.

"Mornin', girl. How are you today?"

He half expected her to respond. Instead, she huddled low next to several of the other heifers.

Tanner stepped beside her and patted her on the back. "Don't blame you. It's always warmer in a herd."

For whatever reason, the words put him in mind of Katie and those women friends of hers. Whenever they got together, they sure could get things heated up. Not that he was comparing them to cattle, but one thought had certainly stirred the other.

"Little brother, you out here talking to the cows again?"

Tanner turned and grinned when he saw his brother. "Margaret said I'd find you out here. It's time for breakfast."

"Looks like you showed up just in time." Brett's gaze narrowed. "Kind of like yesterday morning. And the morning before that."

A strange uneasiness settled over him. "Have I overstayed my welcome or something?"

"Nope. That's not my point. I think you're coming for something far more exciting than breakfast, that's all."

Tanner opened his mouth to respond, but since he couldn't think of anything intelligent to say, he closed it again.

"Yep. Just what I thought." Brett's expression—half smile, half smirk—shared his feelings on the matter. "You're smitten, aren't you?"

"Smitten?" Tanner snorted. "Since when do you use words like *smitten*?"

"Since I married a woman from the South. And don't laugh, little brother. If that sister of hers gets her clutches in you, you'll say things like that too. Those Southern belles have a way of turning a man's heart—and life—upside down." Brett went to work tending to Prissy. He gave the cow a gentle pat on the backside then turned to face Tanner head-on.

"Oh, well, I..."

"Looks like it's already started." Brett grinned. "No need to stutter. I understand completely. At least you're still able to speak. You might remember that I went mute for a couple of weeks after falling in love with Margaret."

"Don't be ridiculous," Tanner blurted out. "Besides, I have a perfectly good reason for being here. Margaret asked me to bring over some sugar for the coffee. Don't you remember? We had this conversation last night just as I left for home."

"And the night before that, she asked you to bring flour for a cake."

"Right."

"And the night before that, she asked you to bring eggs."

"Well, yes."

"Starting to see a pattern here? Either the women love to bake or they're after something else entirely." Brett laughed. "Don't get me wrong, Tanner. I'm happy to have you stop by as often as you like. But I hope you're smart enough to see that you're being played like Pa's fiddle. These girls know who they want to rope and how to go about it."

Tanner sighed. "You make me sound like a rodeo bull."

"Maybe you are. I think they're lookin' to see how long they can hang onto the possibilities of winning you over before you buck 'em off. Or vice versa. I hate to tell you this, but these so-called "genteel" women are all about the chase. Just think of 'em like you would a hunter on the trail of a moose."

"That would make me the moose."

"Or the moose's rear end." Brent chuckled. "But who am I to talk? I'm happily married to the prettiest gal in the county."

"Hmm." Tanner paused to absorb his brother's words, realizing they weren't exactly true. Margaret was a handsome woman, no doubt about it. But no one beat Alanna when it came to true beauty.

He offered up a lame shrug. "Anyway, we're wanted inside. It's time to eat. And, between you and me, I'm starved. So if it's all the same to you, I'd like to forget about this conversation and just go have breakfast."

Thank goodness, Brett went along with the idea. Moments later, Tanner found himself seated at the spacious breakfast table with the ladies gathered 'round—eating fluffy pancakes coated in sticky maple syrup, talking about the first snowfall of the season...and gazing with great longing into the prettiest green eyes this side of the Rockies.

Yep, the ladies might be playing him like Pa's fiddle, but right now the music sounded mighty sweet.

NINE

Women often ask me where I stand when it comes to the role of the sexes. No doubt I will receive a few letters from disgruntled readers if I state my truest feelings, but I will take the risk and do so anyway. Unlike many, I do not hold any grudges against men. Most are wonderful, thoughtful people. There are a few rotten apples in the barrel, of course, but I've met nearly as many women who've soured at equal rate. Instead of blaming or trying to shape men into our image, I've discovered that a little love goes a long, long way. As my mama used to say, "You can catch more flies with honey than vinegar."

—Ellie Cannady—editor of The *Modern Suffragette*

* * * * *

TANNER LOVED A BIG STACK of pancakes as much as the next fella but had a hard time swallowing them at breakfast that morning. It had nothing to do with the taste. No, sir. In spite of her liberated leanings, Margaret cooked up a fluffy pancake, for sure. No, his distraction had more to do with the beautiful Southern belle seated to his right, the one with the girlish lilt to her voice and gorgeous dark, curly hair that tumbled over graceful shoulders.

More than once Brett glanced his way as if to say, "I see what you're toying with, brother, and it's no use. She's headed back to Savannah in a few short months." Once Brett even pretended to play a fiddle and erupted into laughter afterward. This seemed to capture the attention of the ladies, who looked perplexed.

Tanner understood his meaning, of course but couldn't seem to help himself. The temptation was mighty strong. He did his best to focus on everyone at the table, but his gaze kept shifting back to one. Not that she seemed to mind. The fluttering of eyelashes and the heightened hue of her cheeks let him know that she enjoyed his attentions. At least, she appeared to.

After breakfast, Brett headed into town for some supplies, which left Tanner alone with the ladies. As they cleared the table and started the task of washing the dishes, he excused himself and headed to the living room to read the newspaper. As much as he loved hearing about the latest fashions in women's clothing, the headlines drew him even more. With the country on the verge of war—and his own friends at Fort Missoula facing possible enlistment—he'd better stay focused.

Sure enough, the headline—MISSOULANS HOPE FOR THE BEST BUT BRACE FOR THE WORST—caught him by the throat. He read the article half-terrified, half-ready to sign up right here, right now. He would don a uniform, no problem. And he'd be a good fighter too. If they'd take him. He grumbled inwardly as he thought about Doc Keller's recent news that Tanner's heart had been weakened by a childhood bout with scarlet fever. No one else needed to know. It certainly hadn't limited him thus far, had it? Surely the doctor wouldn't hold that against him. To do so would be devastating.

Only when a familiar gentle voice wooed him out of his ponderings did Tanner look up. Alanna's concerned expression caused him to fold the paper and lay it on top of the coffee table.

"What are you readin' there?" She reached behind her to untie her apron strings as she drew near. "You looked so *ser*–ious."

"Ah." He rose and shook his head. "Nothing to worry your pretty little head about."

"Tanner doesn't think women need concern themselves with the news." Katie rolled her eyes as she entered the room behind Alanna. Plopping down onto the sofa next to him, she reached for the paper, her mouth stretching into an *O* as she scoured the headline. After a moment, she tossed the newspaper back onto the coffee table and shrugged. "Maybe he's right."

Tanner chuckled. "Did you just say I was right?" When she nodded, he added, "Circle this date on the calendar. No one's ever going to believe it!"

At that point, as always, she slugged him. He would've feigned offense—or pain, even—but with Alanna looking on, he'd better act the part of a real man. A gentleman, no less.

The Southern beauty took a seat across from them, tiny creases forming between her eyes. "What's happenin'? What did I miss?"

Determined to keep things light, Tanner rose and reached for his hat. "I think the more important question would be, 'What's happening in the barn?' I'd better go check on Prissy. Won't be long now, you know." He gave Alanna a quick glance.

"Want to give me a hand, or was last time enough to make you shy away forever?"

"Well, I suppose I could come along just for fun." Her cheeks flushed the prettiest shade of pink. "I'm not afraid of a little ol' cow."

"Me neither. But Katie is."

"You're afraid of cows?" Alanna's eyes widened. "Really?"

Katie shook her head. "I would rather not discuss it, thank you."

"Yep, Cattle Kate here is terrified of a little ol' cow. But that's a story for another day."

"Since when have you been interested in cattle?" Margaret quirked a brow as she entered the room.

Alanna handed her the apron she'd been holding. "It's something to do to pass the time. And you never know—I might acquire some skills that will be useful back home." A hint of a smile turned up the edges of those beautiful lips.

"Doubtful." Margaret chuckled. "But go on with you. Don't let me hold you back."

"Well, c'mon, then." Tanner gave her a nod and turned on his heels toward the door, hoping against hope she'd follow.

She did.

After donning their coats, he opened the back door and she quickly led the way across the lawn to the barn, shivering all the way.

"Is it always this cold in November?" She blew out foggy breaths, smiling all the while.

"Yep."

"It's f–f–freezing!"

Her teeth took to chattering and he almost regretted asking

her to join him. Almost. Alanna shivered once again and he used the excuse to slip his arm around her shoulder. "There now." He gave her a sympathetic smile. "You didn't really have to come with me to the barn, especially in this weather. I was just teasing."

"I know." She trembled beneath his touch, and he pulled her closer. "But I figured we could use this time for more lessons."

"Lessons?" He paused, a bit confused, but then realized what she meant. "Ah. Manners and such."

"Yes." Alanna paused as he opened the door of the barn. "My sister's party is comin' sooner than you think. I'm determined to turn you into a proper Southern gentleman before it's too late."

"Too late?" He couldn't help the laugh that followed. "You make it sound like the end of the world."

"Well, not the end of the *lit*–eral world, of course, but a lack of social graces can bring about the end of a person's *so*–cial world, at least in the circles I travel."

"If I were in your shoes, I'd be looking for wider circles." He winked, and again her cheeks flushed.

She tagged along on his heels as he made his way inside. "At any rate, we need to get busy, because there's not much time left."

"Can I tend to an expectant cow and learn my manners all at the same time?" he asked. "Brett's counting on me to keep an eye on Prissy since he's gone into town for more supplies."

"I suppose, though I've never taught under such un–*us*-ual circumstances."

"Ah. So you're in the habit of transforming men into your image, then?"

"My image?" She looked aghast at this idea. "Certainly not. I… well, I don't want you to think you're not perfect just as you are."

"Perfect." He erupted in laughter. "Hardly."

"Well, you know what I mean. I'm simply here to add the icin' to the cake. It's plenty sweet as it is." At this proclamation, she clamped a hand over her mouth and her eyes grew wide.

"Well, now, I've been called sweet—by my mama, mostly—but I've never had a girl compare me to a cake. Which flavor would I be? Vanilla or chocolate?"

She shook her head, still looking mortified as she pulled her hand down, revealing a very red face. "Can you just forget I said that?"

"Not if I live to be a hundred." He gave her a wink and her gaze shifted. "I plan to remind myself every day for the rest of my life."

She cast her gaze to the floor, clearly embarrassed. Not that he minded one little bit. Seeing her in such a vulnerable position felt good. Mighty good.

Tanner walked over to Prissy and rubbed her expanded belly. He turned back to Alanna, who still looked out of sorts.

"Want to pick up where we left off before?" She lifted her gaze from the floor and glanced his way. "I believe we were talking about the importance of table manners and such."

He groaned. "Do I have to?"

"Well, no. Of course not." Her eyelashes took to fluttering. "I will certainly understand if you choose not to listen to what I have to share. But with the party coming up in just a few days, we haven't much time."

"Then I am all ears." He wiggled them, just to make her laugh. It worked.

She dove into a lengthy dissertation about the importance of properly folded napkins, a conversation that would've been completely lost on him had it not come from the prettiest Southern belle he'd ever seen. He continued to tend to Prissy and the other cows then brushed his hands on his jeans. At once he saw the look of consternation coming from Alanna and offered a little shrug.

"I'm all finished out here, if you want to go inside."

"I would love that." A genuine smile followed. "Do you mind if we visit in the parlor? There's a fireplace in there. I'm chilled to the bone."

Sitting by the fire with Alanna sounded like the ideal way to spend a snowy morning, so Tanner followed her all the way to the house.

* * * * *

Alanna settled onto the sofa and, after washing up, Tanner started to take the spot next to her. She shooed him away, determined to keep her distance. No telling what sort of spell those beautiful eyes of his would put her under.

She gestured to a wingback chair. "If you don't mind, please sit there."

"But I don't want to sit there." A pout curled down the edges of his lips.

"Lesson number one: don't argue." She punctuated the words for effect.

"Well, there goes half my conversation. What else?"

"Let's see..." She pulled a folded piece of paper out of her pocket. "I've put together a list." Indeed. She'd stayed up half the night working on it and could hardly wait to dive in.

"Really? A list?" He dropped into the chair, looking more

than a little stunned. "Don't you think you're taking this a mite too seriously?"

"Never. We have a lot of work to do before the party." She paused and glanced at the paper in her hand. "Now, we've covered most of the rules of etiquette for dining, but I think I forgot to mention that you should always speak with the persons on both your right and your left when seated at the dinner table."

"What if the pastor's wife is seated on my right?"

Alanna wrinkled her nose. "I'm sorry, but I don't understand your question. Do you not wish to speak to her?"

"It's not that. She's deaf in her left ear. Seems a bit inconsiderate to sit on that side of her, don't you think?"

Alanna sighed. "I don't think you're taking these lessons very seriously at all."

He raised his hands, as if to concede. "I am, I am. What else?

"There are the obvious things, of course. You should always say 'please' and 'thank you.'"

He rose from his chair and reached to take her hand. "Which reminds me—I haven't taken the time to adequately thank you for teaching me all of this." With a gentlemanly flair, he swept her hand to his lips and gave it a kiss.

Alanna started at his unexpected display of affection and found herself caught off guard. "Well, you are most welcome. Now, may I have my hand back?"

"If you must." He sighed and released the hold on her hand so quickly that it fell to her side. "What else, oh noble teacher?"

"It's important to write a thank-you note when someone has offered you a gift."

"I shall start composing my note right now, then." He took

several steps toward Brett's desk then opened the drawer and reached for a pen. That done, he took a seat. Dramatically, he began to pen his words, speaking them aloud as he wrote. "My dearest Alanna—"

"Wait. You're writing the note to me?"

"Well, of course." He glanced her way, with an all-too-serious expression on his face. "You've given me the gift of Southern hospitality. I need to repay the favor." He returned his gaze to the page. "My dearest Alanna…"

She rose from the sofa and took several steps in his direction, her heart now thumping wildly. "*Dearest* might be a bit much, since we're newly acquainted and all."

"Yes, but I feel as if I've known you forever."

"Same here." The words just slipped out, but they were true. She'd only just met him a short time ago, and yet it seemed they'd been friends for years. The sparring sort, anyway.

A devilish grin lit Tanner's face. "Then you will allow me the kind endearment?"

She pulled a chair close and sat next to him. "I suppose. But there's really no time for a thank-you note just now. We're in the middle of a lesson."

"True." He wadded up the paper and tossed it at a nearby trash can. It missed by a good six inches.

Alanna referred to her list, which now trembled in her hand. "Now, speaking of things to be written, have you responded yet to the invitation to my sister's party?" She lifted her gaze to him once again.

He shrugged. "I told Brett we'd be there. Even promised to provide the beef. Just had my best Hereford slaughtered for the occasion."

Alanna groaned. "Yes, but did you offer a proper RSVP?"

"RSV–what?"

"RSVP. It means *'répondez, s'il vous plaît.'" Honestly, he doesn't know what RSVP means? Where has he been living—under a rock?*

"Well, shoot." He rose and paced the room. "If I have to bring one of those along with the beef, I guess I can't come."

She sighed. "It's not something you bring to the party. It's something you send ahead."

"Like a side dish?"

Alanna groaned, ready to be done with this. "RSVP means 'Respond if you please.' I'm referring to a little note that you send to let the person know you're coming. Let's write one right now so that Margaret knows you're coming to the party."

The exasperation in his eyes was clear. "Like I said, I told Brett in person. I'm bringing the beef, remember?"

"Yes, but in the South a verbal response would never suffice for a party. A guest always sends a written acceptance. Unless they can't come, of course, in which case they send their regrets."

"I'm starting to regret agreeing to these lessons." He folded his arms at his chest. "Didn't have a clue it would be so complicated to go to dinner at my own brother's house. I've been here hundreds of times before and never RPSDed or nuthin' like that."

"RSVP—oh, never mind." Alanna folded the paper and slipped it into her pocket. "I suppose it's not really necessary between family members. Though, you're not specifically related to the birthday girl."

"Perhaps I could be. Marry me?"

His words knocked the breath out of her. "I—I beg your pardon?"

He laughed. "Just slipped out. Not sure why. But we both know you'll never marry the likes of me. You'll end up with a true Southern gentleman who knows how to speak to all the folks at the table and send his regrets when he can't attend every little shindig."

Alanna couldn't seem to collect her thoughts but finally managed a few shaky words. "I do have my heart set on a man who cares for such things, certainly." She paused, determined to change the direction of the conversation and yet strangely flattered that he'd just proposed marriage to her.

He sat up and squared his shoulders. "Very well, then. I shall learn to care about them."

The twinkle in his eyes let her know that he planned to do no such thing. Still, she couldn't help but smile at his words. Whether he went along with her teachings or not, one thing was very, very clear—this Montana cowboy was a force to be reckoned with. And if she didn't watch her heart, he might very well ride off with it while she sat idly by, babbling about table manners.

TEN

Some women spend their days fussing with the latest hairstyle or fashion. While I am not opposed, in theory, to a woman looking her best, I find far more value in a woman who is beautiful on the inside. You can outwardly adorn yourselves all you like, ladies, but do not use your beauty, or your lack thereof, as a basis for your value. Neither should you try to outdo one another in dress or style. The next time you're in a social setting, do not judge what those around you are—or aren't—wearing. Remember, the outward appearance is fleeting. Truth, justice, honesty, love...these are life's true adornments.

—Ellie Cannady, editor of *The Modern Suffragette*

* * * * *

ON THE AFTERNOON OF TESSA's birthday, Alanna dressed in her finest emerald-green satin party dress, one she had strategically chosen to match her eyes. Though she couldn't explain why, her nerves presented a particular problem. Given all the social functions she had attended over the years, what was it about this one birthday party that left her nerves in a jumbled mess?

Ah yes.

The cowboy.

The near stranger who'd asked her to marry him.

Alanna still felt completely unnerved whenever he came around, and this feeling did not lessen on the day of the party. She held back a smile when he entered the room with Katie and his parents in tow. Greeting them with decorum and a true dose of Southern hospitality seemed the best way to break the ice, since they'd never met. Best to make a good impression.

"Mrs. Jacobs, Mr. Jacobs." Alanna extended her hand, using her best manners and most convincing voice. "At long last we meet."

"You must be Alanna." His mother reached for her hand and gave it a warm squeeze. "We've heard so much about you from Margaret."

Alanna gave a little nod. "And I've heard such wonderful things about you, Mr. and Mrs. Jacobs. I simply have to learn how to bake those ranger cookies Tanner brought over the other day. I don't believe I've ever tasted anything quite like them. Did I taste pecans, or were those walnuts?"

"Well, for pity's sake." Mrs. Jacobs paused to give her an embarrassed smile. "That's the kindest thing anyone's said to me in a month of Sundays." She leaned in to whisper, "And those were pecans, by the way, though a woman rarely divulges her cooking secrets, especially when the reverend's wife is around. She fancies herself the finest cook in Missoula County."

Alanna did her best not to laugh aloud. "Your secret is safe with me, I can assure you. And I have no doubt that her cookies pale in comparison."

"Thank you, sweet girl." Mrs. Jacobs gave her a warm embrace and then shrugged off her heavy winter coat. "Perhaps you would enjoy learning? I could certainly teach you how to bake. It's one of the few things I do well."

Tanner took the coats from his family—even Katie—and hung them up on the coatrack. Alanna kept a watchful eye on him, impressed by his kindness.

She turned her attention back to the woman in front of her. "I would love that, Mrs. Jacobs, though I would imagine you do many things well. You've done a fine job of raising Brett, Tanner, and Katie, after all." *Well, Brett and Tanner, anyway.* Alanna kept a forced smile plastered on her face, hoping her thoughts about Katie's zealous nature wouldn't betray her.

"Perfect. We'll set up a time to make some Christmas goodies. Snickerdoodles, peanut brittle, divinity, and several others to boot. Oh, we'll have a grand time."

Alanna's mouth watered. "Sounds scrumptious."

"They are, if I do say so myself. I'm very much at home in the kitchen. Just ask anyone."

Katie rolled her eyes and mumbled something under her breath about the need to get women out of the kitchen and into the Capitol building. Tanner flashed her a warning look, and she disappeared into the parlor with the others.

"It smells quite good in here," Mr. Jacobs said. "Like roast beef."

"Yes. And Margaret has whipped up the loveliest mashed sweet potatoes as a side dish."

"I do believe she's added nutmeg to those potatoes." Mrs.

Jacobs sniffed the air. "Possibly ginger, as well. I can always guess the spices in every dish."

"It's a gift," Tanner chimed in. "No matter where we go, Mama always guesses the spices."

"Yes. And I can tell we're having pumpkin pie for dessert. It's as plain as the nose on my face."

"You're quite good at this," Alanna admitted. *But it's pumpkin bread, not pie.*

"Thank you." A broad smile lit the older woman's face. "Now, where's that little sister of yours? We've come to celebrate her birthday, but we've not met her yet."

"Let me introduce you both to my mother first." Alanna looked around the room, hoping to see her mother nearby. "If you don't mind."

"Mind?" Mr. Jacobs dismissed that idea. "Why, she probably wonders why we haven't come by to introduce ourselves sooner."

"We owe your mother an apology for our tardiness," Mrs. Jacobs explained. "We've been out of town visiting my younger sister in Helena. She's been down with the flu and needed assistance with the children."

"My mother will certainly understand." Upon finding her mother, Alanna made quick work of the introductions. Mama seemed very much at ease with the Jacobses. Within minutes Mama and Mrs. Jacobs appeared to be fast friends.

"Well, that pretty much settles it."

Alanna turned as she heard Tanner's voice in her ear. She found herself face-to-face—er, face-to-broad-shoulders—with the man who'd captured her thoughts so often of late. Glancing up at him, she managed a smile.

"Settles what?"

"Our families have bonded. Settles the issue once and for all."

"Which issue?" Alanna paused for a glance in the front hall mirror. After smoothing back a loose curl, she turned and looked Tanner's way.

"The issue of whether or not my parents will approve of you. Looks like they do already. For this, I am extremely grateful. And relieved, to be quite honest."

"Relieved? I have no idea what you're talking about. Why would they need to approve of me?" Alanna fixed her hands on her hips and raised her chin with a cool stare in his direction. "Why should I have to win their approval? And what would it matter if they disapproved of me, anyway?"

"Mm-mm-mm." He reached to brush a wayward hair out of her face, which sent a delightful little shiver through her.

"W–what?"

"You've broken one of your own rules, Alanna Lessing." He leaned in so close to whisper that his breath felt warm against her cheek. "No public arguments in a social setting. Didn't we go over this? I believe it was number seventeen on your list."

She felt her face grow warm, and a slow breath followed. "Yes. Indeed." Her right eye began to twitch. Odd. Finding herself bumfuzzled, she fought for words. "Speaking of breaking the rules, you've come into the house with your hat on. I believe we covered that as well."

"Ah." He reached up to pull it off and slung it onto the hat rack. "So we have, little missy. So we have."

She fought the temptation to groan as she pressed a fingertip against her twitching eye. "I'm just saying that a real gentleman never wears his hat inside, remember?"

"Yes, and a real lady would never have the audacity to wear a gown that so beautifully matches the color of her eyes. It is completely inappropriate, particularly in a setting such as this."

She pulled her hand down, startled by his words. "Whoever told you such a thing?"

"I'm pretty sure I read it in a book somewhere. It's far too distracting for the menfolk who pay attention to such nonsense. Not that I'm the sort to notice. But I'll have to keep that in mind if my parents agree to let me marry you. Mama might hold that one itty-bitty thing against you. She doesn't like to see her boys distracted by beautiful women. Unless, of course, they plan to marry. But we have already established that you will never agree to marry me. Right?"

Alanna's heart skipped to double time, matching the pace of her right eye. "I don't have a clue what you're talking about. I wouldn't marry you if…" She clamped her mouth shut before saying something she might regret.

Still, she couldn't figure out why he would say such a thing. To tease her, no doubt. But all joking aside, why did anyone in his family have to approve of her? Was he really trying to say that she wouldn't measure up?

Before she had a chance to ask, he moved with exaggerated grace and flair across the room—putting on far too many airs for his own good—and sidled up next to Tessa. The two entered into a lively conversation, one that left Tessa all giggles.

Alanna kept an eagle eye on her younger sister—using the non-twitching eye, of course. Tessa took to flirting with the skill of a stage actress.

Frustrated, Alanna plopped onto the sofa in an unladylike

manner, not giving one whit what anyone thought about it. She squeezed her eyes shut to stop the twitching. "You might be seventeen, little sister, but you've got a long way to go before you're a grown woman."

The words were whispered, but obviously not quietly enough. Mama slipped into the chair beside her and sighed. "She's at again, isn't she?"

"Yes. But I'm about to put a stop to her ridiculous behavior."

Alanna rose, but Mama's firm hand on her arm caused her to sit once again. "Let her be, Lana. This is her birthday. A little harmless flirtation on one's birthday never hurt anything."

"Harmless?" Alanna's temper rose as she watched her younger sister giggle with exaggerated delight. "She's anything but."

"I daresay you're protesting a bit too much, daughter." Mama's eyes lit with a faint glint of humor. "Could it be the one you're upset with isn't Tessa at all?"

Alanna reached for her fan and waved it, hoping to change the direction of the conversation. "Mama, I really don't think this is the time or the place...."

"Posh." Her mother whispered the rest. "Maybe you're more concerned that a certain young man is paying her too much attention. Is that it?"

The words stung, but Alanna would not admit it, not even to herself. The strange sensation in her eye came to a halt as she released a lingering sigh.

"That's just silly, Mama. You, of all people, must know that I would never latch onto a man from this part of the country. Why, to do so would be..."

"Complicated?"

"Of course. But more than that, it would be foolish. I have no intention of staying in Montana. We've come to rescue Margaret and take her home again after the baby's born. That is truly my only mission."

"And an admirable one, at that. Though I'm sure Brett would be far happier in Savannah if his brother and sister would join him." Mama rose and gave Alanna a little wink then sashayed across the room.

In that moment, a world of possibilities opened up to Alanna. Yes, indeed. Convincing Brett to move to Savannah would be much easier, should his brother join them. Why, with Tanner learning the proper social graces, he would fit right in.

Of course, there was the issue of Katie. Would she want to tag along? That one presented quite the pickle. Hard as she tried, Alanna couldn't imagine the outspoken young woman settling well in Savannah. What a ruckus she would cause with those women's rights speeches of hers! The very idea made Alanna nervous. So nervous, in fact, that she quickly set her mind about the task of figuring out a different plan, one that would leave Katie in Montana where she belonged.

Seconds later, Margaret announced that dinner was ready in the dining room. Tanner moved in Alanna's direction with a mortified look on his face.

"What's wrong?" she asked.

He leaned close to respond in a hoarse whisper, "What happens if I get into the dining room and forget what to do?"

She patted his hand to offer gentle reassurance. "I will be right here to help you."

"I'm counting on it." He looped his arm through hers.

"Otherwise I don't know what might happen." He turned and gazed at her with such intensity that she lost herself in his beautiful eyes. "Any final instructions before we head in there?"

"You make it sound like you're about to have your last meal before the execution."

"Maybe I am."

Alanna did her best not to roll her eyes. Instead, she opted to straighten his tie. "Since you asked, there are a couple of things I could mention. For instance, you should always rise when a lady approaches the table."

"Seems like a terrible waste of time when a fella could be enjoying the vittles." He placed his hand on top of hers, which sent a little tingle coursing through her fingers.

"Still, it's the proper thing to do." She nudged his hand away and continued fussing with his tie, finally getting it straight. He put his hand on her shoulder and gazed into her eyes, perhaps for a moment too long. She released her hold on his tie when she noticed the pastor's wife looking her way with some degree of curiosity.

Tanner chuckled. "With all the women at this party, I'll be up and down more often than a gopher coming out of his hole."

Alanna groaned. "Kindly refrain from talking about gophers. And pigs. And cows. This is an animal-free event."

"Not entirely. Not if you plan on eating the steak, anyway. It's 100 percent Montana beef. That was my favorite Hereford." He sighed. "Jack. We called him Jack. May he rest in peace."

She squeezed her eyes shut then popped them open again. "You know what I mean. There are no *live* animals at this event."

Tanner did not look convinced. "Not sure I'd agree with

that, either. Have you seen the way the pastor's son is eyeing your little sister?"

"Tessa?" Alanna sighed. "Well, naturally, I could count on you to keep a watchful eye on my sister. I noticed you paid her a great deal of attention earlier." She didn't mean for the words to come out with such a bite, but once they were released, she could hardly take them back.

Tanner looked genuinely stunned. "Not at all. I only spoke a few kind words about her birthday. Best wishes and all that. Just as you taught me to do. Being gentlemanly—nothing more."

"Hmm." Alanna looked across the room at Tessa, who flirted with the pastor's son—a gawky-looking fellow with a shock of red hair and freckles covering every square inch of his face.

Methinks you try too hard, little sister. I see whose attention you're really trying to nab.

As predicted, Tessa's gaze shifted to Tanner, and her eyelashes took to fluttering.

No time to worry about that right now. No, indeed. Alanna would head into the dining room, take the seat next to Tanner, and hope that the lessons she'd taught him would pay off.

* * * * *

WHEN THEY ARRIVED AT THE table, Tanner approached a chair to the right of Mrs. Sullivan, the pastor's wife. Remembering his manners, he pulled out the chair to the right of his for Alanna. "M'lady."

"Hardly." She took a seat and adjusted her skirts. "But I appreciate the gesture."

"Of course." He made a few pleasantries with the pastor's wife, who seemed a bit out of sorts. Something to do with poor digestion. He took a seat to her right, and before long all the others had taken their places, as well.

To his right, Alanna cleared her throat and gestured for him to place his napkin in his lap. He deliberately dropped it, letting it fall to the floor in the space between them. "Oops."

She shook her head as she glanced down at the napkin, which had landed on her shoe. "Honestly."

"Now what?" he whispered.

"Now you fetch it," she spoke through clenched teeth, "and hope that no one is any the wiser."

"Ah."

Tanner leaned down, eventually disappearing under the table. While reaching for his napkin, he allowed his gaze to travel to her shoes and wondered how she managed to walk in something so delicate-looking. He remained fixated on those shoes, wondering where she'd purchased them and—more importantly—why. They were the most impractical things he'd ever laid eyes on. Of course, the ankle attached to them was nice, but a fella probably shouldn't comment on that.

He rose, banging his head on the underside of the table in the process, before placing his napkin on his lap. As he reached for his fork, he felt Alanna's hand cover his.

"Well, now…" He gave her a warm smile as he whispered, "An unexpected pleasure."

She leaned close to respond, her voice low. "No, I simply wanted to tell you something else. Should there not be enough chairs for all of the ladies to sit, you should offer yours. It's the polite thing to do."

He sighed and dropped his fork. "I will astound the locals with my politeness; watch and see. Even if it means I have to stand to eat."

"I'm sure they're already astounded that you removed your hat when you came through the door. From what I've observed, that's a first."

"True."

He leaned back in his chair, grateful that the chatter of those around them continued as the food was served. He was even more grateful that every one of the ladies managed to find a seat.

"Just remember not to talk with your mouth full," Alanna admonished.

"Never."

"And wait until everyone is served before eating."

Just to tease her, he reached over to grab a radish from the vegetable tray in the center of the table and popped it into his mouth.

Alanna slapped his hand. "Wait."

"I am." He spoke around the radish. "Like a pig at a trough." Tanner made a funny little pig snort, which looked to get Alanna more riled up than ever.

"I thought we agreed to leave the animals out of this."

"Oh. Right." He tossed the half-eaten radish onto his plate.

Alanna rolled her eyes as she glanced down at it. "I forgot to mention one thing," she said.

"Just one?"

"Yes. If your dinner knife gets dirty, whatever you do, don't put it on the tablecloth."

"Oh?"

"Yes. Place it along the edge of your plate."

He fussed with his knife, having several ideas percolating at once. Alanna gripped his arm, her eyes growing wide. "Ooh, I thought of one more thing."

"Naturally. But just one, of course."

"Of course."

As she leaned his way, he caught a whiff of her fragrance. *Mmm*. Something floral. It suited her.

"Did you hear me?" Her voice interrupted his thoughts.

"I'm sorry, no." *Smelled you, yes. Heard you, no.*

"I was just saying that a gentleman should help the woman to his right whenever she sits or rises from her seat."

"Well, now, that's a happy problem, since you happen to be seated to my right."

"Careful with your fresh words, or I'll take the chair to your left."

"Impossible," he mumbled to avoid being overheard. "The pastor's wife is already seated there. Remember? She's deaf in her left ear so I deliberately sat to her right to make polite conversation."

"You are catching on." She found it impossible not to return his disarming smile. "Just be sure not to speak of controversial things."

"Controversial?"

"Yes. I understand the reverend's wife is quite adamant on the subject of hymnbooks."

"Hymnbooks?"

"Yes. She is opposed to Margaret's notion that the church needs new ones. So do not mention them."

"Heavens." He worried the edges of his napkin, half tempted to toss it onto the floor one more time just to catch another glimpse of her ankle. In the end, a calmer head prevailed. He would be well served to keep his gaze on those dazzling eyes now flashing with a hint of frustration.

Still, he couldn't resist the temptation to be just a little bit wicked. Jumping in ahead of the others, he took a large bite of roast beef, turned to the pastor's wife with a very full mouth, and said, "Mrs. Sullivan, Alanna here tells me that you're tickled pink about the new hymnbooks Margaret has suggested. I happen to be very fond of the idea, myself."

At once, the heel of Alanna's shoe dug into the top of his right foot. Tanner pulled his foot away, forced a smile, and immediately reconsidered his position on both hymnbooks...and women.

ELEVEN

The modern woman stands her best chance of enjoying the favor of her peers when she is at ease with her beliefs. Remaining calm, cool, and collected is the key to winning folks over even when you feel encompassed by disbelievers. Far too often, passionate suffragettes use social settings to let their tempers—and their tongues—get the better of them. May this never be the case, ladies! A ship is gently turned with a light hand on the rudder. Yank it, and the whole vessel goes under. There's no place like a public forum to watch a well-meaning ship—er, suffragette—drift like lead to the ocean floor.

—Ellie Cannady, editor of *The Modern Suffragette*

* * * * *

TANNER SOMEHOW MADE IT PAST the hymnbook debacle, though he felt sure Alanna would let him have it—with guns blazing—when everyone else went home. With that in mind, he did his best to follow the rest of her silly etiquette rules as the meal progressed. Still, he had a hard time keeping up with it all.

Stand when a lady enters or leaves a room.

This one grew increasingly more difficult as Margaret scurried back and forth from the dining room to the kitchen.

Hold the door for a lady.

This one he found to be equally as complicated, what with there being a door separating the two rooms. After all, there were only so many times a fella could jump up and down during a meal without someone wondering if he were up to something.

He was up to something, of course, and it came down to more than minding his p's and q's. Making a good impression on Alanna was key. Sure, playacting was fun, and teasing her came naturally, but when he gazed into those beautiful green eyes, Tanner almost believed he really could transform into someone she might be proud of.

His thoughts were interrupted by a female voice raised above the others. Katie appeared to be having it out with the pastor, and the others at the table sat in nervous anticipation.

"Pastor, I'm shocked that you don't give more thought to the plight of women." Her tone was velvet but edged with steel.

The pastor choked on his roast beef. After a swig of water and several exaggerated coughs, he finally regained his composure. "Katie, you know that I care very much. Why else would I have agreed to be the overseer at the Missoula County Widows and Orphans Society?"

Katie dabbed her lips with her napkin. "I understand that, but if you really cared about the needs of women, you would be opposed to the war."

Tanner felt his gentlemanly manners slip right out of the window.

He saw his father flash Katie a warning look. For that matter, nearly everyone at the table flashed her warning looks in tandem. Still, she seemed to heed not a one of them. How dare she speak to the pastor that way? Had the girl completely lost all control of her senses?

"It's just like a man to want to fight." Katie took a bite of her potatoes and leaned back in her chair. "Why settle something reasonably when you can go to battle over it?"

Tanner observed the concern in his mother's eyes across the table and knew that he must intervene, even if it went against everything Alanna had taught him about being a gentleman.

"Katie, perhaps this conversation would be better served up with hot coffee and dessert," he said, his smile forced. "Let's leave it till then, shall we?" He hoped she could read the unspoken words in his stern expression, but she appeared not to care.

Katie shrugged. "I don't blame you for trying to change the direction of the conversation, Tanner. It is an awkward subject, for sure, and not one usually discussed at the dinner table."

"Exactly." *So, drop it. Let it go.*

"But I do wonder why it is that men are happiest when they're fighting."

His mood veered sharply to anger. "I know a few girls who excel at it, as well." Tanner placed his dirty knife at the edge of the plate and tried to convince his little sister with his tightened expression that enough was enough. "In fact, some make sport of it. And others suffer at their expense."

She pointed her index finger his direction. "You know what I think?"

No, but I have a feeling you're going to tell me.

"I think that men are afraid to be peaceable because they think their women will stop looking up to them. They're afraid of being seen as weak."

Heat rose and wrapped Tanner's neck like a heavy winter scarf. He argued with himself internally before finally spouting, "That's the most ridiculous thing I've ever heard."

This, of course, caused everyone at the table to look his way. He felt both their pity and their embarrassment at the awkwardness of this situation.

Katie tossed her napkin onto the table, nearly taking down her glass of water in the process. "Well, of course you think it's ridiculous, because it comes from a woman." Her accusing voice seemed to drain all the air out of the room. Or out of his lungs, anyway.

"Oh, really? That's what you think, is it?" The intensity of his voice elevated with each word. "Well, there you go, putting words in my mouth again. I never said any such thing." A thin chill hung on the edge of his words.

To his right, Alanna cleared her throat. She reached over, took his hand, and gave it a squeeze. This served to calm him down for a few seconds, but the blood continued to pound in his temples.

"Now, now, you two." Margaret looked back and forth between them. "Have we forgotten that we're here to celebrate Tessa's birthday? I'm sure this isn't how she wants to spend it."

Tanner released a couple of long breaths, completely embarrassed—both by his sister's words and his reaction. What a bumbling mess he'd made of things. Alanna would likely never forgive him for this. And poor Tessa! What a miserable way to spend her birthday.

"Actually, I'm enjoying this immensely." Tessa leaned forward and put her elbows on top of the table. "I'll never forget this birthday conversation, in fact."

Mrs. Lessing paled. "Neither will any of the rest of us," she commented quietly.

"Yes, well, maybe Tanner was right. It would be better to save this conversation for dessert." Margaret pushed back her chair and took a few steps toward the kitchen before turning around. Her expression brightened, though it looked a bit forced. "I'll just put the coffee on and slice the cake. We can convene in the parlor, if you like."

Tanner hoped this would stop Katie—or at least slow her down a bit—but it did not. Instead, she kept right on yammering, her intensity increasing as she spoke.

"What do you think will happen to women, say, a hundred years from now, if we don't begin to stand up for what we believe in?"

Do not fight with her at the table. Do not fight with her at the table.

"You have nothing to say?" Her eyes narrowed to tiny dark beads. He found the effect to be chilling.

"I say we go into the parlor." Their mother rose and scurried from the room, chattering all the way about the weather.

"Yes, let's." Mrs. Lessing shot out of her chair, followed by the pastor and his wife. Brett and their father followed on their heels. This, of course, left Katie and Tanner alone at the table with Tessa and Alanna. The pastor's son stayed put in his chair, too, likely intrigued by the impending battle.

Then again, he was probably used to Katie's shenanigans. Nothing out of the ordinary...unless you counted the fact that she'd interrupted a perfectly good birthday party to get folks worked up. Now, if only he could find a way to get her calmed down to a reasonable level. Then maybe this party wouldn't go down in history as the worst one ever.

* * * * *

ALANNA LISTENED HALF HORRIFIED AND half intrigued to the conversation going on between Katie and Tanner. To say that she was disappointed with the way the evening had turned out would be an understatement. This was catastrophic.

Poor Tessa! To have her birthday ruined—and with such pointless chatter. Why had Katie broached such a delicate subject at the dinner table? Did she have no manners at all?

Just a few seconds into thinking this, Alanna realized that Katie and Tanner were still arguing. Well, Katie was, anyway. Tanner sat in a slumped position, looking like a whipped puppy.

"You didn't answer my question, Tanner." Katie leaned forward and placed her elbows on the table as she glared at him. "Are you ignoring me?"

"I don't believe that would be possible, Katie." He released a breath and sat up. "You're rather difficult to ignore."

Alanna coughed into her napkin, wishing she could figure out some way to escape the rest of this conversation. She could always feign illness. Her stomach did feel upset, after all.

"I will take that as a compliment." A devilish smile turned up the edges of Katie's lips. "Now, let me repeat my question:

What do you think will happen to women, say, a hundred years from now, if we don't begin to stand up for what we believe in?"

Alanna glanced at Tanner to see how he would respond.

He scooted his chair back and rose. "I'm more concerned about what will happen to them if you do." He placed his napkin on the table. "Now, if you don't mind, I'm going to join the others in the parlor." He took hold of the back of Alanna's seat to pull it back, and she stood, ready to be rid of this room and this conversation.

"Not so fast." Katie met them at the head of the table. "I want to know what you meant by that."

"I'm just saying that women these days seem so hard. Determined."

"Nothing wrong with that."

Alanna could hold her tongue no longer. "No, but traits often get more pronounced as the generations progress. When I think of women a hundred years from now, I wonder if there will be any softness left in them at all. Maybe—if they all win the right to vote now or accept political offices—they will eventually take the place of the men."

"Ludicrous."

Alanna wasn't so sure. "I'm just saying that a little softness and gentility today could lead to more of the same tomorrow. I don't want my daughters and their daughters to trade in their God-given tenderness to become…" She fought for the right word. *You?* Probably not wise. She settled, instead, on "aggressive."

Katie paused, perhaps a bit stumped by Alanna's impassioned speech. Her facial features softened. So did the intensity of her voice.

"I never really thought about it that way, to be honest. I've always looked to the women a hundred years from now as having been freed up from the near slavery of our current position. If women across this nation have the freedom to own property, to vote, to have their say about political things, they won't be hardened by the opportunities. If anything, they can relax and enjoy what should have been theirs all along."

Alanna bit back the argument that threatened to erupt. "It never ceases to amaze me how different we all are."

"Mama used to say that when God made me, He broke the mold." For the first time in several minutes, Katie grinned. An honest, genuine, relaxed grin.

"Funny." Alanna reached over and squeezed her hand, ready to be done with this quarreling. "My mama told me the very same thing."

In that moment, the tension in the room lifted.

"If I promise to keep my conversations to a dull roar, will you meet me halfway?" Katie looked between Alanna and Tanner.

"Meet you halfway?" This time Tanner spoke.

"Yes. I need your help with something."

Tanner shook his head, clearly exasperated. "After an evening like this, when you shamed all of us in front of the pastor and his wife, you ask us for a favor?"

Katie hesitated, finally responding with, "I suppose I see your point, though it's not just me asking. It's all of the Sleigh Belles."

"Sleigh Belles?" Alanna and Tanner spoke the words in unison.

"What are Sleigh Belles?" she asked.

Katie's grin softened her face. "That's what we're calling

ourselves from now on. Ellie and I came up with the name because Tessa's from the South and the word *belles* just makes sense. They thought it would be fun and could make people think."

"That you're a nitwit?" Tanner chimed in, easing the tension a bit more.

Alanna suppressed a laugh, grateful for his sense of humor.

"No, silly." Katie smirked. "Though I've often been accused of that very thing. We got to talking about Margaret and Brett's old sleigh—how fast it moves across the snow. It takes your breath away."

"I still don't see what this has to do with the suffrage movement," Alanna said. "Am I missing something?"

Katie's eyes sparkled as she drew near. "The sleigh glides across rough terrain. Wagon wheels would get stuck in the snow. So would the tires on a car. But a sleigh moves with ease across something that seems impossible to traverse. That's why we're the Sleigh Belles. We're going to cross terrain that most think is impossible. We're going to soar over every obstacle, making new ground for women."

"I see." *Sort of.*

"And that's not all. We're going to locate every sleigh in the county and parade through the center of town next Saturday before the big rally. Jeanette Rankin is speaking, you know. She is opposed to the war, and we are linking arms with her to make our voices heard."

Alanna felt her breath catch in her throat as she anticipated Tanner's next words. Sure enough, he spoke up, his voice firmer than ever.

"Then I daresay she will face opposition from those who feel we should enter the war."

"You can't possibly mean that." Katie crossed her arms and glared at him. "Surely you don't think we should go to battle. What good could come of it?" Tears sprang to her eyes. "You could lose your life, Tanner. I'm not willing to take that chance."

"You know where I stand on this, Katie. Let's not beat a dead horse into the ground."

Alanna's eye began to twitch again. She reached for her fan to cool her burning cheeks. Oh, how she wished they could all just settle down and get along. Were things always this difficult in Montana?

"So, you're holding a rally in the center of town. Why in the world would you embarrass your family by doing such a ridiculous thing so close to Christmas?" Tanner's gaze remained fixed on Katie. "Of all things."

"To draw attention, of course."

"Of course." Tanner plopped down into his chair once again.

Now Tessa joined in, her voice animated. "Every sleigh is going to be done up with bells. Not just one or two bells, mind you, but dozens and dozens. Can you even imagine how much attention we'll draw? Why, folks will be coming out of their businesses to see what all the ruckus is about."

Alanna groaned. "Does Mama know about this?"

"Not yet. But she will. We're going to ask her to help. Katie has put me in charge of looking for sleighs. And bells too. If we can't find enough, we'll need to make some." She turned to face Tanner. "And that's precisely why I need to speak to you, Tanner.

I've thought of the best birthday present ever! I'd like you to make me some sleigh bells as a present."

"Oh no you don't." He put his hands up. "I've already succumbed to a bit of external changing—putting on gentlemanly airs and all that—but I will not, repeat, *not*, be changed on the inside. My convictions are unshakable, especially where the war effort is concerned."

"Don't be such an old grouch, Tanner." Katie rolled her eyes. "We're just asking for bells."

Tessa drew near and put her hand on his shoulder, her smile leading the way. "Katie says you're quite the expert with metalworks."

Alanna watched as his expression visibly softened after hearing her words of flattery.

Oh no you don't, little sister. You will not win him over with your flirtatious ways.

Or maybe she would. Tanner glanced Tessa's way, his frown easing into a hint of a smile.

Tessa continued with her hand on his arm. "Don't you see the symbolism, Tanner? Bells ring out the news that the sleigh is approaching. We suffragettes are ringing out the glorious, blissful news that change is in the air."

"And heaven help the person standing in the way," Katie chimed in.

Alanna found all of this more than she could take. "This has all been great fun for you, I would imagine," she said. "But it's gone too far, Tessa. Mother will never go along with this plan. I cannot imagine for one minute that Margaret is in agreement, either. In spite of her liberated ways, she has a good head on her shoulders.

She would not wish this sort of embarrassment on the family."

"I'm asking Margaret to bake cookies for the event." Tessa rose and removed her hand from Tanner's arm.

"She won't do it. She might be in favor of women getting the vote, but I cannot believe she would go along with these other notions. Why, you heard the president's speech regarding the situation overseas. He believes our country needs to take a stand for democracy."

"We're going to start right here, in Missoula, Montana. I'm taking a stand for what I believe."

"Tessa, I don't mean to state the obvious, but these convictions are borrowed from your new friend." Alanna gestured to Katie, who flinched. "They are not your own."

Worry lines appeared around Tessa's eyes. "They have become my own. And as soon as we return to Savannah, I plan to take up the cause among my friends and relations. Katie says I must."

Another groan escaped. Still, what could she do? With the clanging of two Sleigh Belles pealing madly in her ears, Alanna excused herself to the parlor to join the sensible folk.

TWELVE

Women across this great land have merged their hearts, lives, and voices to accomplish a great goal—for women to hold the God-given rights they deserve. Most recently the National Woman Suffrage Association—a great champion for women on the federal level— has merged with the American Woman Suffrage Association, a group that has long served women through state legislation. Our arms have been strengthened by this delightful union, ladies! To paraphrase a Scripture found in Deuteronomy 32:30, one woman can put a thousand enemies to flight. Two women...ten-thousand! I, for one, have always been in favor of working together, not tearing asunder. This is a biblical principle, after all.

—Ellie Cannady, editor of *The Modern Suffragette*

* * * * *

THE FOLLOWING MORNING ALANNA AWOKE feeling stiff and sore. She'd spent most of the night tuning out Tessa's incessant chatter about the upcoming rally. When she'd finally drifted off to sleep somewhere around three in the morning, her head ached and her eye twitched nonstop.

As the morning sun peeked in through the window, Alanna lay quiet in the bed, begging the Lord to help her figure out a plan to calm things down. Her prayers, though frantic, were heartfelt. If she couldn't manage to get Tessa under control, she might very well lose her to this madness.

Her younger sister stirred, stretched, and muttered a drowsy, "Morning."

"Good morning to you too, sleepyhead." Alanna kept her words light, determined to start this new day on the right foot. "You slept later than usual."

"We deserve it, after the night we had." Tessa sat up in the bed. "Oh, but wasn't it fun? I had the best birthday ever."

Alanna could think of little to say except, "Glad you enjoyed it." Still, she could hardly imagine the other guests felt the same, especially Mama and Mrs. Jacobs. And poor Margaret. How embarrassing, to have such a conversation take place with the pastor and his wife present.

Tessa propped herself up on her pillows and narrowed her gaze. "Now, Alanna, we must talk, sister to sister."

"Oh?" *Didn't you say enough last night to last a lifetime?*

"Yes." Tessa leaned forward. "Tell the truth, now."

"The truth?"

"Yes. Aren't you the one who once told me that the truth would set me free?" Tessa's impish grin turned up the corners of her mouth.

Alanna plumped her pillows and leaned back against them,

pulling up the quilt to shield herself from the cold room. "Well, yes, but I've no idea which truth you're referring to." A little shiver crept along her spine, and she couldn't help the visible shudder that followed.

Tessa put her hands behind her head and narrowed her gaze. "The truth about Tanner Jacobs. You're infatuated with him, aren't you? I can see it in your eyes every time you look at him."

"W–what?" Alanna felt her right eyelid begin to twitch once more. She stared at her sister, not quite believing what she had just heard. "Have you been reading those ridiculous dime novels again?"

"Of course not. The only thing I've been reading is your face. I know you better than anyone else, Lana. You don't flirt with any men back home, but you do with Tanner. It's undeniable."

At this point, heat started in Alanna's neck, rushing up her face and straight to the top of her head. "Take that back," she managed. "I do not."

"I won't take it back. The way you giggle and smile. The way your eyes sparkle. There's no avoiding the obvious. You're drawn to him." Tessa rolled over on the bed and released an exaggerated sigh. "Oh, but who wouldn't be? I told you, he's just like the man in that portrait in Papa's study. Rugged. Handsome. So very charming and witty too." She giggled. "A girl would have to be blind not to notice."

Instead of arguing, Alanna grew quiet and waited for her cheeks to stop burning and her eyelid to calm down. "I won't deny he's something special to look at," she said at last. Unwelcomed heat crept to her cheeks, and she forced back the smile that threatened to betray her.

"Oh, he is. He carries himself with an air of self-confidence. And don't you think he's devilishly handsome?"

"Perhaps, though I'm not sure why you're bringing the devil into it."

"Because the devil has blinded me to the handsomeness of every other man in the state." Tessa released another sigh. "I've never met anyone quite like Tanner Jacobs."

After a brief pause to take in her younger sister's expression, Alanna snapped to attention. "Now, wait a minute. You're too young to be thinking about him in this way."

"I am not."

"That snake charmer has pulled you into his web, as well."

"As well?" Tessa quirked a brow. "So I was right? You're infatuated?"

"That's not what I meant to say, but you're avoiding the question. Do you have a crush on Tanner Jacobs?"

"Well, of course. I thought I made that perfectly plain. And if you're not interested in him, Alanna, then please say so. And stop calling the man of my dreams a snake charmer. He's no such thing."

"He knows just what to say to the ladies to get them to swoon." Alanna shivered and pulled the quilt up to her neck.

"He doesn't have to say anything. That's what's so perfect." Tessa pouted. "I sometimes wish he would say more to me. But he's far too busy trying to go along with this scheme you've cooked up to turn him into a gentleman."

"W–what? Who told you that?"

"His sister. Katie thinks it's a hoot that you're trying to

change him. She's been trying to change him for years, but in the opposite direction. She said he's so confused, he doesn't know if he's coming or going." At this, Tessa erupted in laughter. "Poor fella."

"Poor fella, indeed. I can't believe he told his sister. I've just been working with him...."

"So that he will pay you more attention."

"Absolutely not. So that he will learn how to handle himself in social situations."

"Like last night?" Tiny creases formed around Tessa's eyes. "Because, I'd say you're not doing a very good job. Otherwise he and Katie wouldn't have gotten into it like that."

"It wasn't his fault."

"Ah. And you're defending him." Tessa nodded. "I see. That answers my question, then."

"Your question?"

"Yes. About whether you care for him."

Alanna pushed back the quilt, ignoring the cold, and stepped out of the bed. "I've had just about enough of this. You have no idea what you're talking about, Tessa."

"That's what you always say when I'm right." Tessa climbed out of bed and waltzed across the bedroom with an invisible partner. She stopped in front of the mirror, where she began to fuss with her hair. "But if you're being honest—if you're really not interested in Tanner—I certainly am. I'm seventeen now, you know. A lot of seventeen-year-old girls back in Savannah have beaux Tanner's age. I think Mama would agree to let him court me."

"Wait a minute, Tessa. How did we transition from garnering

his attentions to courting? This isn't a game of Skip to My Lou. Are you telling me that you've really got feelings for this man?"

"He is a man, isn't he?" Tessa giggled. "Oh, he is. Just look at his broad shoulders and muscled arms." Another sigh followed. "None of the boys back in Savannah are like him. Not even one."

"Well, no. Of course not." Alanna paused to let her thoughts wander. Indeed, none of the fellows back home resembled Tanner, physically or otherwise. In fact, she'd never known anyone quite like this rugged cowboy. "I believe that's why he's cast such a spell," she said at last. "He's different."

"Deliciously different." Tessa leaned in close to the mirror and smacked her lips. "Delectably different. But I happen to like different, so if you're not going to claim him, I will." She turned on her heel and headed off to the bathroom.

Alanna took a seat in front of the mirror, gazed at her reflection, and wondered how in the world she could ever get her eye to stop twitching.

* * * * *

"I DON'T KNOW HOW SHE does it." Tanner pulled the cast from the fire and set it to cool.

"Does what?" Brent watched him from a distance, a half smile on his face.

"Katie always manages to talk me into things I don't want to do." He eyed the brass piece, allowing it to cool before releasing it from its cast.

"Like making those bells, you mean?" Brent pointed to the

table where a line of beautiful brass petal bells sat in a perfect row.

"Yeah." Tanner sighed and turned his gaze back to the bells.

"She knows you well, Tanner." Brent chuckled and patted him on the back. "You might disagree with her philosophies, but you still love her unconditionally. And that love gets you roped into doing a few things you don't care to do." He paused and offered a little shrug. "But then again, that's what love always does. Takes you places you didn't know you wanted to go and keeps you from losing your mind once you get there."

Tanner paused to give his older brother a closer look, realizing his words held a double meaning. "What are you saying?"

"Not talking about Katie now." Brent slapped him on the back. "Could be love is taking you to other places besides just bell making."

Tanner focused on the ridge around the middle of the bell and tried to ignore the obvious. No point in denying it, but neither would he address the issue. Not while crafting sleigh bells, anyway.

"Just saying you need to keep your heart and mind open to what the Lord is doing." Brett pointed to the bell. "I've ribbed you about how the ladies are playing you like Pa's fiddle but never really considered the possibility that the Lord might be using them to mold and shape you in some way."

At this, Tanner stopped cold. "Trust me. I've been molded and shaped enough over the past few days. Alanna's got me walking and talking like a dandy. I've played along, but it's getting tiresome."

"You've played along so that you can spend time with her, you mean?"

"Well, sure." Tanner took a chisel and cut the slit across the petal bell, leaving it with a large opening. He gave the ridge around the middle another solid look and double-checked the four holes cast into the lower half of the bell. Satisfied that everything was as it should be, he went to work drilling a hole through the bottom. Eventually, he would attach it to a strap with rivets. Today, however, he needed to stay focused on production.

One hundred sleigh bells. That's what Katie had ordered up. A saner man would've turned her down. But, as always, he had a soft spot for his younger sister, even when she was dead wrong in her principles.

"You think on the things I've said, little brother." Brent gave him another slap on the back, but the look in his eyes spoke of serious intentions. "Maybe it's time to stop joking and start looking at very real possibilities."

Tanner did his best not to wince. Until Brent left the barn. Then he had a lengthy talk with the bells, pouring out his frustrations. On and on he went, sharing his woes with the innocent bells. Only when he heard a familiar voice did his exaggerated conversation come to a halt.

"Tanner?"

He turned to find Alanna and Katie standing behind him, bundled in winter coats and shivering. Clamping his mouth shut, he refused to say a word.

"Just had to see this for myself." Alanna took a few steps toward him, her hands pressed into her pockets. "Katie told me you were out here working on the bells, but I couldn't believe it."

"You can believe it, all right."

She pulled her gloved hands from her pockets, picked up one of the finished ones, examined it closely, then gave him a look of admiration. "These are beautiful. I've never known a soul who made bells before."

Tanner shrugged. "It's something my grandpa taught me years ago. He created the cast. I just mold them according to his specifications then do a bit of tidying up once they're done."

"Tidying up?" She pulled off one of her gloves and ran her finger along the intricate petal-like shapes. "You mean this detailing? It's exquisite."

Tanner squirmed, unsure of what to say. He'd never been very good at accepting flattery, especially not from pretty girls. He'd best divert the attention. "Well, Cattle Kate over there knows how to get me to do what she wants."

"It's a special gift I have." Amusement flickered in Katie's eyes. "From the time I was little, I played on his talents. He's especially good with bells. That's really what prompted this idea in the first place."

"Yep. Cattle Kate and her cow bells. Ironic." He went back to work, doing his best to avoid looking into Alanna's penetrating gaze.

"Why do you keep calling her that?" she asked after a moment.

Katie rolled her eyes then picked up one of the finished bells. "Cattle Kate, you mean? The name is meant to carry a sting, I can assure you. He's poking fun. Taking advantage of a weakness of mine."

"If it's a joke, I've somehow missed the punch line." Alanna looked back and forth at Tanner and Katie. "Is someone going to spill the beans, or do I have to guess?"

Tanner stopped working long enough to give her an inquisitive look. "You mean you've never heard of the real Cattle Kate?"

"No, can't say as I have."

He chuckled. "Well, she's the stuff legends are made of, at least around these parts. She was an outlaw."

"An outlaw?" Alanna paled. "Truly?"

"According to legend anyway," Katie threw in.

Tanner gestured for the girls to sit on the bench across from him. "I'm not altogether sure that's been proven," he said. "But Cattle Kate lived in Wyoming at the time our pa was being raised. He tells the story better than anyone. He says she wasn't charged with a crime but made quite a name for herself performing all sorts of illegal deeds. He named Katie after her, in fact."

Alanna turned to Katie, her eyes widening. "You're named after an outlaw?"

"Yep." Katie chuckled. "Only, I'm scared of cows."

"What?"

"Yep. That's the joke." Tanner laughed so hard he couldn't stand up straight. "Cattle Kate's afraid of the cows."

Katie sighed. "It's true. I'm not partial to them. Haven't been, since one of Brett's Herefords jabbed me in the backside as a kid. Sent me running across the field and straight into my mama's arms. Talk about a wound that took awhile to mend. We don't realize how much we use our backside 'til it's suddenly too sore to use." The girls took to giggling, but Katie grew more serious as she faced Tanner. "Reminds me, too, that I don't know how much I need those who love me until I've been at odds with them."

His heart melted at once. He slipped his arm around Katie and pulled her close, planting a kiss on top of that mop of blond hair. Then he looked at Alanna and sighed. "Now you see how she ropes me into these things. How can I resist a comment like that?"

"I know how to play on his sympathies," Katie said with a wink. "He's crazy about bells."

Alanna sighed as she rolled one of the smaller ones from one hand to another. "Me too. Bells are a vital part of our Christmas celebration back in Savannah."

"Oh?" He gave her a curious look.

"Yes. Our church would ring the bells four times for Christmas. Three times for Easter."

"Interesting. I would think there would be more fanfare for Easter, to be honest. After all, that's when the resurrection is celebrated."

"I'm not sure who came up with the system, but, for as long as I can remember, the bells have pealed four times for Christmas. That's all I know."

"Makes me want to sneak into the bell tower and give that bell an extra ring." Katie grinned. "Why is it I have such a hard time sticking with tradition?"

Tanner chuckled. "Nothing new there."

"Guess I'm something of a rebel." She offered up an overdramatic sigh. "I didn't set out to be, mind you. Just sort of happened."

"Nothing 'just happens,' little sister. We change over time. Nothing to be ashamed of."

"Do you mean that, Tanner? I always thought you were embarrassed by my passion for women's rights."

His heart stirred as he gave his sister another warm hug. "Oh, I've been a little embarrassed at times, but I always get beyond it."

Tanner couldn't help but notice Alanna's eyes sparkling as she looked at them. "This is what I love about your relationship. You can argue one minute and be perfectly at ease the next. I would say the Lord has gone a long way in mending fences between the two of you, which makes me very happy."

"I live to make you happy."

Where the words came from, he could not be sure. Still, as he looked into Alanna's beautiful green eyes, as he pondered the winsome smile on that gorgeous face, Tanner realized he would love to have the opportunity to do just that.

THIRTEEN

Across this great nation, women gather in rallies to spread the word—not about our plight but about our opportunity to progress as women. While I cannot be with my Missoula sisters as they meet in the town square this week, I would like to offer my thanks. Ladies, you have rallied around me as I have borne this illness. You have been my hands, my feet, and my voice. For that, I am eternally grateful. May God grant my darling Sleigh Belles the best possible day as they chime their way through town, proclaiming the message that our time has come at last.

—Ellie Cannady, editor of *The Modern Suffragette*

* * * * *

THE FOLLOWING SATURDAY ALANNA WAITED for Tanner to pick her up in his car for the rally. She had no desire to participate in the event, naturally, but planned to watch from inside the car as the girls jingled their way through town. Mama and Margaret decided to join them as soon as they saw that Mrs. Jacobs had come along for the ride.

Having most of the gang in attendance made Alanna feel a little better about things, though she secretly longed to have some private time with Tanner. Her feelings for him left her feeling strangely unsettled—but in a good way. With each passing day she fought to press them down, reminding herself that she would be leaving Montana at the onset of spring. Still, they would not be squelched. She might as well enjoy them while the opportunity presented itself. Soon enough she would be back in Savannah, away from his teasing and flirting.

With Tanner's assistance, Alanna made her way across the snowy lawn, shivering all the way. With temperatures well below freezing, her back and legs felt stiff. Even walking proved to be a challenge with every joint locked up tight. She finally made it to the vehicle, and Tanner opened the passenger door in the front like a gentleman.

"Mama, don't you want to sit in front?" Alanna asked. Being in back often made her mother feel squeamish.

"Not at all." Her mother chuckled. "Haven't had a bout of carsickness since arriving in Montana. I'm in fine working order."

"Interesting." Alanna suspected that Mama's matchmaking skills were in fine working order, as well, but did not mention it. She wouldn't dare. Instead, she climbed aboard and prayed that her shivering would eventually cease.

As Tanner eased the car out onto the road, Alanna pulled her coat a bit closer.

"Here, use this." He passed a colorful hand-stitched quilt her way. "Brought it just in case."

"T–thank you." Her teeth chattered for a minute or two until the quilt brought the necessary warmth. After a couple minutes of listening to the ladies converse merrily in the backseat, she turned to speak to Tanner privately, lowering her voice so as not to be heard. "I'm stunned Katie talked you into going to the rally, to be quite honest."

He winced. "Well, I really had no choice. Mama needed me to drive. Pa has a calf coming at home." He looked Alanna's way and offered a weak smile. "Besides, I had to come to make sure my little sister doesn't bring shame to the family name."

"Ironic. That's exactly why I'm going." Alanna chuckled. "My sister has been more zealous than usual, of late. To be honest, I've been praying for a snowstorm to sweep in and bring the event to a halt."

"Same here." He gave her an admiring look. "We really are on the same team, aren't we?"

"Yes, though I'm not sure the Almighty has responded to our pleas." She pointed to the clear skies above. "I had rather hoped He would come through with a blizzard."

"Perhaps there's a greater plan at work."

"Oh? Like what?"

"I don't know." He shrugged. "Maybe the Lord wants to show us something through the rally."

Alanna could hardly believe his words. "Please don't tell me you're being won over by these foolish girls."

"Most assuredly not." A boyish grin turned up the corners of his mouth. "To be honest, it's just my pride at work. I can't wait to hear all the bells ringing at once."

"He worked so hard on those," Mrs. Jacobs piped up from

the backseat. "No doubt he wants to hear them in all their glory."

A nod from Tanner followed. "Figured they'd put us in the mood for Christmas. It's only a few weeks away, you know."

"Oh, trust me when I say that Tessa hasn't let me forget." Alanna laughed. "She's given me her list, and I've checked it twice. Though I can honestly say she's been more naughty than nice, especially since we arrived in Montana."

Mama feigned offense at this statement but, in the end, agreed. "She has been a bit on the feisty side since we got here."

Feisty, indeed.

"Speaking of Tessa…" Mama's voice trailed. "I really must look at buying her some new dresses for Christmas. I can't help but notice how she's slimming down."

Alanna nodded. "Yes, I've noticed that her clothes are getting too big for her."

Mama grinned. "I haven't wanted to mention it for fear of drawing attention to the situation, but she has most assuredly dropped a few pounds since we arrived in Montana."

"Not from poor eating, I hope." Mrs. Jacobs chuckled. "I daresay we've cooked up a storm."

"Definitely not from the food. Though, I must say, the way Margaret cooks is healthier, for sure."

"Back in Savannah we deep-fry so many of our meats," Alanna chimed in. "Funny that I've only eaten chicken battered and fried until now. The way Margaret prepares it is delicious."

"And all those fresh vegetables from her garden are wonderful too," Mama added. "I'm just amazed at her green thumb. We never bothered with a garden back home. Makes me want to try."

"I'm so glad, Mama." Alanna smiled, thinking about the changes in both her sister and her mother since arriving in Montana.

"I find that I enjoy physical labor," Mama said. "I think Tessa does too. She and Katie are always off doing something together—and they often walk to get there."

Alanna paused to think it through. "Yes, and Tessa has been working hard on the ranch, as well. Brett told me that she offered to help him brand the cattle."

"She did what?" Mama's eyes widened.

"She helped with the branding. Brett told me all about it. She worked really hard, Mama. Rounding up the cattle and keeping them steady during the branding is quite a process. Brett said she handled it well."

In spite of the cold, Mama took to fanning herself. "My little Tessa, branding cattle! Can you guess what the other girls at the finishing school would say if they knew?" A few seconds later, Mama's laughter filled the vehicle. "Oh, how I wish I'd been there. I'll bet that little girl of mine was quite a sight to see."

"No doubt." Alanna could only imagine.

They arrived in town minutes later, and she found herself mesmerized by the size of the crowd that had already gathered in the town square. Tanner pulled the car up in front of a local art gallery and checked his watch. "Looks like they'll be starting any minute now. We made it just in time."

"I don't know what those girls were thinking, planning this on such a cold day." Mrs. Jacobs shook her head. "But that's Katie for you. She's always had an impulsive streak."

"Looks like our daughters have a lot in common, then," Mama said.

Alanna turned around to give her a pensive look. "Not all your daughters, Mama. I'm not the least bit impulsive."

"That's true. You're as solid as a rock, Alanna. Never wavering."

Something about the way she said "solid as a rock" felt a bit more like an insult than a compliment, but Alanna chose not to react. Instead, she turned her gaze to the street, wondering when her impulsive sister would parade across town in a bell-ladened sleigh for all to see. And hear.

Tanner cracked the window, and a couple of minutes later the peal of bells rang out, along with voices raised in song, off in the distance. A familiar song, no less. "'Jingle bells, jingle bells, jingle all the way!'"

For a moment, Alanna almost joined in. Almost. Then she put the pieces together in her head. "They've turned 'Jingle Bells' into their theme song?"

Tanner slapped himself in the head. "Figures. What will they come up with next?"

The women's voices rang out louder as they drew closer. "'Oh, what fun it is to ride in a one-horse open sleigh!'"

"Well, it is almost Christmas." Mama said from the backseat. "I think they're being resourceful. And it is a perfect match for the Sleigh Belles theme, you must admit."

"Really? You agree with them, Mama?" Alanna strained to see past the crowd in front of the car, wondering when the sleighs would appear.

"Honey, please don't misunderstand," her mother said. "I don't believe in going against what the Bible says about men and women. I certainly think some folks carry things too far. But I think a dose of women's suffrage is probably a good thing. A little goes a long, long way."

"Do you hear those bells?" Mrs. Jacobs asked. "They're so festive! Feels like Christmas already." She reached up to give Tanner a pat on the shoulder. "You did a fine job, son."

"Thank you, Mama."

Alanna hardly had time to think about things. The bells continued to peal and the suffragettes approached, singing their hearts out. "'Jingle bells, jingle bells, jingle all the way!'"

As the jingling sleighs came into view, loaded with the boisterous Sleigh Belles, the song rang out louder than ever. Tanner's laughter rang out, as well, and all the more as the girls passed by and waved.

"What is it, son?" his mother asked as they disappeared from view, the sound of the petal bells resounding as they went. "Why are you laughing?"

"Oh, just thinking about what they're singing. Hope they don't send the wrong message to folks."

"That has always been my concern." Alanna pulled the quilt up over her shoulders to counteract the cold drifting in from the cracked window. Once again her joints felt stiff and sore. Would she ever adapt to this frigid environment?

"Yes, only this time I'm worried they're going to make people think they're a bunch of ding-dongs." Tanner grinned. "That's just what they're going to look like, parading through town with those bells clanging like that. No telling what sort of write-up this is going to get in the paper."

"Oh, I've heard all about it from Katie, trust me," Mrs.

Jacobs said. "She's convinced that Ellie will do a counter piece in *The Modern Suffragette*, so I doubt the women will pay much mind to whatever turns up in the newspaper. They rarely do." Her brow wrinkled. "Though I do wonder how Ellie can write anything at all right now, to be honest. I heard from the doctor myself that she's not expected to hold on much longer. She's been very ill, you know."

"Yes, I heard." Alanna shook her head. "I wonder what the rest of the girls will do if they lose their good friend."

"I'm sure it will take the wind out of their sails a bit," Mrs. Jacobs said. "Or, I should say, it will take the ring out of their bells." This, of course, brought a chuckle from everyone in the vehicle, even Tanner, who looked more relaxed than he had in days.

Alanna glanced down the street, mesmerized by the crowd. "I never expected to see this many people. Did you?"

Tanner shook his head. "Nope."

"At least the merchants will be happy," Margaret said. "The shops in town have been so empty of late. This demonstration has brought a lot more folks to town in the middle of winter."

"Well, then, we will have to do a bit of shopping when the rally ends," Mama said. "I'm always looking for an excuse to shop."

"Should we get out of the car and go to the town square so that we can hear our congresswoman's speech?" Mrs. Jacobs asked.

"I have no interest in hearing that woman speak," Tanner said. "I thought perhaps Alanna and I could use the opportunity to do a bit of window-shopping." He turned to face her. "If you would like that."

"Very much." She offered him a warm smile, which turned out to be the last warm thing available. Once they stepped outside of the car the shivering began. Chivalrously, he slipped his arm around her shoulder and braced her from the wind.

"This is what a Southern gentleman would do. True?" he asked.

Her teeth chattered as she responded. "I have n–no i–idea. In S–S–Savannah it never gets this c–c–cold!"

"Well, let's pretend, then."

After their mothers headed off to hear Jeanette Rankin's speech, Tanner pointed Alanna in the direction of the department store. "Are you in the mood to shop?"

"Always."

A few steps down the sidewalk, Alanna found herself enjoying Tanner's closeness. Still, one thing bothered her, and she'd best address it so that it could be corrected quickly. Pausing, she turned to face him. "Tanner, you should trade places with me."

"Beg pardon?"

"Trade places. You should walk on the street side of the sidewalk."

He stopped altogether and gave her a pensive look. "I'm walking wrong?"

"Well, not wrong, exactly. Perhaps here in Montana a fella can walk on the side closest to the buildings, but it's a common courtesy—one all gentlemen in the South understand—that a woman is at less risk when she's on the inside, not the street side."

Tanner let out a whistle then slapped himself in the head. "Is there some sort of rule book with all this written down? I'm never going to remember it all." He slipped into the spot on the street side with a sour look on his face.

"Sure you will." She took his proffered arm and gave him a comforting smile.

"Well, boy howdy, a fella could get fouled up in a hurry if he mixes the rules. What if I accidentally walk on my hands and not my feet? Then what?"

Alanna giggled and leaned in close to enjoy the warmth of his nearness. "You're just being silly now."

"Is silly allowed? I daresay I could get kicked out of genteel society if I let my silliness get in the way."

"Likely."

They took a few more steps and then he paused to gaze up at the sky overhead. She squinted and looked up as well, trying to figure out what fascinated him so.

"High, wide, and handsome," he whispered.

"Beg your pardon?"

He glanced her way with a smile. "Oh, that's what folks call Montana. High, wide, and handsome. Kind of like me." He grinned. "Only, I'm not wide."

"Hardly."

His brow wrinkled. "Do you think I'm too thin? Katie is always trying to put pounds on me."

"No, I wouldn't say you're thin." Alanna scrutinized him. "I'd say you're just about right." She clamped a hand over her mouth, her face now blazing.

"Well, thank you." He grinned. "It's been a long time since anyone has flattered me in such a way. I accept your compliment."

"We...well, we should go shopping."

Alanna turned toward the department store but stopped when she found herself within kissing distance of Tanner. His brows arched and a mischievous look came over him. Her heart began to race, and she found it difficult to keep her breathing steady.

They continued to gaze into each other's eyes. She wanted to throw her arms around his neck and give him a kiss square on the mouth.

Her cheeks heated up at the very idea. They provided an interesting contrast to the rest of her body, which, by now, felt like a frozen block of ice.

Still, Tanner must be thinking the same thing, judging from the twinkle in his eyes. Instead, he marched to the door of the store, swung it wide, and led the way inside. This gave her heart time to slow to its usual pace. Oh, but how she wanted to stand close to him, to feel that peculiar sensation in her stomach and heart all over again.

Stay focused, Alanna.

She browsed the store but didn't find much of interest until she came upon several tiny sculpted bears that lined one of the shelves. "Ohh, I have to buy one of these." Picking one up, she examined it with a keen eye. "I just love artwork."

"Do you now? Well, there's a gallery nearby. Want to take a look?"

"As soon as I pay for this little fella." She visited with the clerk as she paid for her little treasure and even answered a few of his questions about her supposed accent. Strange, how people in Montana thought she talked funny. Stranger still because they all did but didn't seem to realize it.

After purchasing the little bear, Alanna and Tanner continued their trek down Main Street, enjoying an easy conversation. She couldn't recall feeling this comfortable around a fella in a long time, but she did her best to guard her heart. No point in thinking about the impossible, after all. Still, as he slipped his arm around her shoulders to keep her warm, Alanna couldn't help but grow in her respect for him. He did have a gentlemanly way about him.

She paused as they came upon a store window with a magnificent oil painting in the window. "Oh my goodness. Is this the art gallery you were talking about?"

He nodded. "Yep. One of my favorites."

She stopped, nearly losing her breath as she gazed upon the vivid colors in the painting. Everything about it felt familiar, from the brushstrokes to the vivid colors. It reminded her for all the world of the painting in Papa's study.

"Has to be," she whispered.

"What is it?" Tanner asked. "What has you so mesmerized?"

"This painting. I've seen a marvelous piece by this artist before. I'm sure of it."

"Oh?" He leaned forward and put his nose close to the glass to give it another look.

"Yes. I know you're not going to believe it, but there's a painting in my father's office that resembles this one in nearly every respect. Margaret sent it to us last Christmas."

He nodded. "Yes, well, this artist has garnered some acclaim in this area."

"I can see why. The colors are vibrant and lifelike. And he's captured the brilliant features of the flowers with such majestic colors. The brushstrokes are heavier than most, which I really like. You can see the texture of the oils. It's magnificent."

"You think?"

"Yes." She paused. "This might sound odd, but the painting in my papa's office reminds me of…well…you."

"Me?" Tanner's right brow elevated. "You have a painting that looks like me?"

"Yes. Funny, isn't it? As soon as Mama and Tessa and I saw you—in person, I mean—we felt as if we'd already met you because of the painting. It took us a moment to realize that you just resembled the cowboy in the painting." Alanna laughed. "But then again, I suppose all cowboys would look alike to me. In Georgia we don't see a lot of them."

"No cowboys in Savannah, eh?" He chuckled.

"Hardly. When we refer to men in hats, we're talking about bowlers, not Stetsons. And the idea of a fella in Savannah showing up at a social event with a gun strapped to his side is laughable."

"I see."

She gazed at the painting in front of her. "There's something about this one that seems familiar. Such beautiful countryside."

"It's the Bitterroot mountain range in the spring, when the wildflowers are in full bloom. You should see it in the spring-time." As always, when Tanner spoke about Montana, she could sense the zeal behind his words. He really loved his home. No doubt about that.

"I feel like I already have seen it in the springtime just by looking at this painting. This is lovely. So pretty, in fact, that I might just have to talk Mama into buying it and taking it home as a gift for Papa. Or maybe I could purchase it myself so that I have a lasting memory of my time in Montana."

At this, she sighed and gazed into Tanner's eyes, the weight of her words bringing an unexpected sadness. For, while she had once dreaded coming to Montana, she now dreaded leaving. And no painting—even one this beautiful—could fill the empty spot in her heart whenever she thought about it.

* * * * *

As ALANNA SPOKE THE WORDS "lasting memory of Montana," Tanner's heart lurched. In just a few months, the beautiful woman on his arm would be gone, back to Savannah. Sure, she would carry with her a painting with vivid reminders of her time here— a painting he'd spent weeks perfecting, no less—but that would never be enough to satisfy him. Not when his heart desperately ached for more.

FOURTEEN

As I ponder my legacy—what I will leave behind when I soar from this earth—I am aware of how important every word can be. For, when this frail body is no more, my words will live on through these articles. How, then, can I do them justice, knowing that they will be scrutinized once I've crossed over to Glory's golden shore? I must simply trust that they have been penned with the right heart, the right spirit. And I must repent for the overzealous words that have stirred more action than intended. All things in balance, ladies. All things in balance.

—Ellie Cannady, editor of *The Modern Suffragette*

* * * * *

ALANNA ENJOYED HER TIME WITH Tanner far more than she cared to admit. When the rally came to an end, they wound their way through the crowd to find their family members. Katie and Tessa remained close to the center of the activity, of course, practically clinging to the congresswoman's skirts. Not that Alanna really blamed them. There seemed to be an amazing energy in the crowd, one she'd never sensed before. It had little to do with the cold weather and everything to do with the zeal exuding from those in attendance.

"Have you seen Mama and Margaret?" Alanna called out to Tessa, to be heard above the crowd.

Her sister pointed to the stage, where Mama and Mrs. Jacobs stood alongside Margaret, chatting with the pastor's wife. Very interesting, indeed. Surely the pastor and his wife did not agree with the congresswoman's philosophies, did they? Still, why else would Mrs. Sullivan attend the rally? Perhaps to keep on eye on this. Yes, surely she planned to report back to her husband about the women's shenanigans.

Katie finished her conversation with Jeanette Rankin and faced Alanna. "Well, this has been a glorious day in every respect. What did you think of the bells?"

"They sounded like a grand cathedral choir singing out God's praises."

"Oh, I thought so too." Katie's eyes glistened with moisture. "It was a spiritual experience, to be sure. Floating along over the snow with those bells ringing madly...I enjoyed every minute."

"As did I." Tessa took hold of Katie's arm. "How can I ever thank you for including me?"

"Happy to have you." Katie slipped an arm around Tessa's shoulders and gave her a squeeze. "We are soul sisters, are we not? Kindred spirits in every regard."

"We are." Tessa's beaming face left no questions about her feelings on the matter.

The crowd thinned, and Katie gazed up at the now-empty stage. "I do have one regret, and it's a big one. I'm just so heartbroken that Ellie couldn't be here. But we've done this in her honor. And if, God forbid, she doesn't linger many more days on this earth, we can rest easy, knowing we've given her this special gift."

"So, the rally was meant to honor Ellie?" Alanna pulled her coat tighter to brace herself against the wind.

"Yes, and to thank Jeanette Rankin for her brave stance on our behalf as the country's first female congresswoman. One can scarcely imagine the taunting she must receive on Capitol Hill. I shudder to think about it."

Alanna shuddered too, but not for the same reason. The idea of a woman serving in Congress still felt rather odd to her. She wouldn't say so, however. Not today, with everyone in such a jovial mood.

"You look troubled, Alanna." Katie took her arm. "Is everything all right?"

"I suppose."

"Let me ask you a question." Katie paused and gave her a pensive look. "You've stated that you will challenge this woman's movement with every ounce of strength in you. Is that right?"

"Well, I..."

"How is your disagreement with those of us who believe in women's rights any different from our fight to gain equality?"

"I beg your pardon?"

"You are willing to go to battle to prove a point—the point that we are wrong. But in marching up to the front of the battle lines to state your case, you are only showing us what a strong woman you are, which proves my point quite clearly. Women are tough…even Southern women. You're made for bigger things than simply baking bread and washing dishes."

"Well, I…" Alanna paused, realizing that anything she said from that point on would come across as an argument. And an argument, no matter how she tried to fancy it up, would only make her look like the tough, determined female Katie had just described.

Strange, she certainly didn't feel tough right now. No, indeed. As she looked between Tanner and Katie, she suddenly felt like a puddle of melted snow. And, just for the record, she'd never baked a loaf of bread in her life.

* * * * *

STANDING IN THE MIDST OF the town square, Tanner found himself surrounded by females. Ordinarily, this would not have frustrated him, but on a day like today—when he only had eyes for one—he longed to spend more time alone with her, not encompassed about by so many zealous suffragettes.

He'd hardly had time to think, though, when Katie drew near. Fine lines formed on her brow. "Tanner, I need to ask a favor."

"You need more bells?"

"Hardly." She laughed. "I'm worn out and freezing cold. So is Tessa. Would you mind terribly if we went back home in the car with Mama and Mrs. Lessing? Maybe you and Alanna could go back in the sleigh? The horse is kicking up his heels, ready to go."

He glanced Alanna's way, and she threw in her two cents' worth. "Sounds lovely."

It did sound like the ideal situation, though he had to wonder if perhaps Mama and Mrs. Lessing had put Katie up to this. Their matchmaking skills were in full swing these days. Not that he minded, of course. After all, spending more time alone with Alanna was exactly what he'd been hoping for.

Minutes later he waved good-bye to his sister and the other ladies then turned to face the woman who'd held his thoughts captive all morning. "You ready to become a Sleigh Belle?"

The rolled eyes clued him in as to her answer. "Hardly."

"Looks like you have little choice. That sleigh is covered in bells and I don't have the time or the inclination to remove them right now."

"Oh, I'm keen on riding in the sleigh, just not keen on being called a Sleigh Belle." She laughed. "Regardless, please don't remove the bells. I love the way they sound. They put me in the mood for Christmas. In fact"—she gestured to the snow-packed fields off in the distance—"all of this puts me in the mood for Christmas."

"Then let me help you aboard."

They settled in, and the horse kicked up his heels and took off across the snow. Tanner drank in the sites around him, particularly the beautiful woman to his right. Being here with her on this crisp, white day felt incredible, the ideal way to usher in the Christmas season with the perfect gift at his side.

"I can see now why you love Montana so much." Alanna gave him a winsome smile. "Though, of course, I hate to admit it. This is the most beautiful winter scene I've ever witnessed. Truly, we have nothing to compare."

Tanner thought about her words. "I love it here, Alanna. Always have. It sets my imagination on fire. The landscapes are unlike any you'll find elsewhere. You can look across vast fields of white that stretch you in every conceivable way." *And stretch your paintbrush too.* "Gives you courage to try things you've never tried before. I find it so relaxing—and thrilling at the same time."

"I can see why, though I can't believe I'm confessing it aloud." Her cheeks flushed pink—perhaps from the cold.

The sleigh moved with lithe grace across the snow, the jingling sound of the bells ringing out a symphony as the horse pulled them at a leisurely pace. Tanner passed an extra quilt Alanna's way then gestured with his head to the mountains in the distance. "Did you know that a field of diamonds appears every night at sunset?" *And did you know that I plan to paint that scene if I can capture the colors with my brush?*

"A field of diamonds?" she echoed.

"Yes. If I took you up in those hills and we gazed down at the town at night, you would see the lights from the houses twinkling like the facets of a diamond. It's breathtaking, really." Here, he paused. "But you have to be up high to see it all. I kind of think…" He hesitated, unsure of sharing too much of his heart.

"Think what?" She pulled the quilt up to her shoulders and shivered.

"Think that God, Himself, must've arranged it so that He would have something spectacular to view when He looks down on this part of the world. Of course, there are a thousand other things He could look at." Tanner turned his gaze to Alanna, losing himself in her eyes. Yes, there were certainly plenty of beautiful things to look at around here, especially now that Savannah had come to Montana.

He cleared his throat and focused on the road. "If you look closely, you'll find mountain goats tucked away in those craggy peaks. Ever seen a mountain goat, Alanna?" Tanner wanted to slap himself silly for saying something so unromantic, but it was too late to take it back. Instead, he just offered what he felt sure came across looking like a goofy grin, and he drummed his fingers on his knee instead.

"Of course not." The glow of her smile warmed his heart. "How you do go on."

Tightening his grip on the reins, he tugged and slowed the horse. This, of course, also slowed the jingling of the bells. Not that he minded their softening. It helped to clear his thinking. "How can I not go on about the place I love? I've lived in Montana all my life and rarely dreamed of traveling elsewhere. Why would I want to, when everything a man—or woman—could ever need is right here?"

She shook her head. "There are a few things a woman would like to have that cannot be located in Missoula, Montana."

"Such as?"

Her eyes took on a dreamy look. "Fine restaurants. Lovely department stores with adequately supplied clothing areas. A millinery. Those sorts of things."

"I just took you inside a wonderful department store."

"Well, yes, but it falls woefully short compared to the shops back home…"

"…in the South." He finished the sentence for her. "But I'll betcha can't buy minnows and worms in those fancy shops back home like you can in our stores here. Or tackle."

"I can't figure out for the life of me why your stores sell such nonsensical things."

"Because the locals enjoy our rivers and lakes, that's why.

Have you seen the Snake River yet? It stretches for miles and miles, winding this way and that."

"Hence the name."

"Exactly, only longer. And as wild as a snake too. Many a man has flipped a canoe in those raging waters. When the snow melts in the spring, the river rushes like nothing you've ever seen. It's thrilling. And the fishing is the best anywhere. I can catch my fill of rainbow and bull trout."

"Bull trout? That's a fish?"

"You bet. Some of the best you've ever tasted. And cut-throat too."

"Sounds dangerous."

He laughed. "It's a kind of trout. I'm telling you, our rivers are teeming with the best fish in the country, and it's all there for the taking. So, I'm mighty glad the department store carries bait and tackle. Wouldn't be caught dead at a store that didn't."

She sighed.

With a tug of the reins, he slowed the horse's pace a bit more. By now, the bells had almost stopped jingling. "I can see that my conversation has not persuaded you to fall in love with our great state, but I'm not willing to give up that fight just yet. How do you feel about flowers?"

She gave him a hopeful look. "From a beau, they're quite lovely. I'm partial to roses."

"If I took you up that hill right there, I could show you wild-flowers guaranteed to take your breath away. In the springtime, of course." *But you won't be around in the spring, will you?* No, she would be leaving as soon as the winter snows thawed, headed back to a place where men put on airs and walked on the correct side of the sidewalk, shielding their ladies from possible harm. He swallowed hard. "From up there, I could show you alpine views through long, narrow stretches of trees and glorious waterfalls."

For the first time, he saw the look of interest in her eyes. But it faded quickly as she gave her response. "Brett told me to stay away from the mountains because of coyotes and bears."

"Ah. Bears." Tanner grinned. "Seen a few in my day, and not the little carved ones like you found in the store in town. Wolves too, but none like the fellas you probably know from home."

Her mouth flew open. "I'll have you know, the fellas from home are perfect gentlemen. I thought I'd already made that clear."

He snorted. "Then we have nothing to compare."

"That's a fact."

"We make up for it in other things, though. We have the most magnificent bald eagles you've ever witnessed take to flight." He closed his eyes briefly, envisioning it. "I think that's my favorite part of all." Tanner opened his eyes and focused on the road.

"The eagles are your favorite part?"

"No, the fact that they have a wide-open sky to soar across. Montana goes on and on."

"Kind of like its inhabitants." She snickered.

He chose to ignore her. "No, I mean, in Montana you have room to breathe."

"Unless some long-winded local draws all the breath out of you by talking so much."

He clamped his mouth shut, realizing just how long he'd let his glowing descriptions go on. "Well, I guess I know when to quit," he said, feeling more than a little embarrassed. How could he help himself, though? Montana inspired him, not only as an artist, but also as a man of faith. Where else could one find such majestic evidence of the Lord's creative powers?

Alanna grew quiet. After a couple of awkward moments, she put her hand on his arm. "I'm sorry, Tanner. That was rude. Your description of Montana was beautiful. And I know every word is true. Just this morning I saw a white-tailed deer, and Brett pointed out a flock of Canadian geese flying overhead." A pause followed. "I think I'm just tongue-tied because I have nothing to counter with. All the things you've said are wonderful. I loved every part of your description."

"Even the part about the wolves?"

"I've only met one, and he's tamer than I expected." She gave him a little wink, which set his heart to soaring.

"I hear they can be further tamed with kind words and hot chocolate. What do you say?"

"I say the house is right there." She pointed to Brett and Margaret's place, and he sighed. So much for a long, romantic ride. Why had he wasted such a wonderful opportunity talking about the scenery?

FIFTEEN

Much of the struggle between men and women comes down to one thing, I believe—communication. Our methods and modes of communicating are vastly different. Women may say one thing, but men hear another. The same is true in reverse. Many times I have listened to men clearly state their point only to be misunderstood by women. Ladies, the time has come to say what we mean and mean what we say. The time has also come to hear what's been spoken to us and not overreact. Our impulsive reactions can land us in a lot of hot water if we're not careful. Many of us are known by our passion but not our moderation. May our kindness be known to all.

—Ellie Cannady, editor of *The Modern Suffragette*

* * * * *

ALANNA DID HER BEST NOT to sigh aloud as Tanner went on about their surroundings. He seemed nervous today, which she found very odd. Perhaps it had something to do with the ever-present jingling of all those bells. Still, she had to wonder if he ever talked about anything other than the landscape. Glancing his way seemed to open the Pandora's box once again. Off he went on another tangent.

"It's too cold to fish now, of course, or to swim, but if you stay through the spring, you can take a boat down the Blackfoot or the Bitterroot. Both rivers converge in the valley." He flashed a boyish smile. "Do you like to swim?"

"Well, yes, but I certainly won't be staying through the spring. We will be headed out on the first train once the snows melt. We're just here long enough to…" *To talk some sense into my sister and to bring her home where she belongs.* "Anyway, we're only here through the winter."

"Then I'm praying for a long winter."

Her breath caught in her throat as she heard his words.

"The idea of you leaving makes me…" He paused, and for a moment she thought she saw a hint of pain in his eyes as he pulled the horse to a stop in front of the house.

"Happy?" she tried.

"No." The pain in his eyes was palpable.

"C'mon, admit it," she teased, fighting off the shivers that caused her teeth to chatter. "You'll miss our sparring."

"Well, yes, I'll definitely miss sparring with you." He reached to take her hand, as she relished the warm feelings that washed over her at his protective touch. "But it's more than that, Lana."

She resisted the urge to correct her name. Her heart now fluttered in her throat.

"I don't mind admitting that I'm a little jealous of those gentlemanly types in Savannah. They've captured your heart and your imagination."

Heat crept up her neck and into her face. "Heavens, you make it sound as if I've known dozens of beaux. I've only ever had my eye on one, and it wasn't serious. More of a passing fancy, really. Besides, despite my former thoughts on the matter, men in the South aren't really that different from the fellas up here."

"Likely you're right about that," he said. "From what I've figured out, men are men, no matter where they live. Sure, you can dress 'em in fancy duds and parade 'em around a room in a prissy waltz, but inside they're still aching to be sitting by a river with a fishing pole in hand."

"I daresay Daniel wouldn't even know how to bait his hook." Alanna clamped her free hand over her mouth and groaned inwardly.

A spark of jealousy flashed in Tanner's eyes. "Daniel? Who's that?"

Why in the world had she mentioned Daniel's name? "Oh, just a young man I know from school." She shifted her gaze to the mountains. "Nobody important."

"If he's nobody important, why are you red in the face talking about him?"

"Am I?" Her hands went to her cheeks at once. "Strange. Maybe I'm just warm."

"It's thirty degrees outside."

"Is it?" She fussed with the quilt, determined to stay focused. "Well, in that case, I must be cold. And to respond to your original statement, I truly don't think the men up here are all that different from our gentlemen back home, in spite of my earlier predictions."

"So, this Daniel...is he your beau?"

She fought to come up with the right words so as not to make this any more awkward than necessary. "I wouldn't say that, though many a person has told me that we make a handsome couple." Her nervous giggle echoed through the air. "It's just silly, isn't it? Anyway, he would never be the sort to go fishing. He's far more settled into his life in law school."

"Still. You said he doesn't know how to bait a hook? I'd say, based on the color of your face when you mention his name, that he's more skilled at it than you know."

"What do you mean?"

"I mean, he's snagged you. Grabbed you with the hook and held on tight. He's reeled you in closer to shore than you realize."

"Oh, posh. He doesn't interest me."

"Doesn't he?"

"No." Alanna shivered. "Don't be silly."

"Well, then, I can stop worrying about Daniel." Tanner teased her with his twinkling eyes. "But let's say you *were* looking for a beau. What traits would you be watching for?"

"Oh, that's easy." She calmed down a bit. "Any future beau would have to be polite and charming."

"I always say please and thank you."

"And, of course, it wouldn't hurt if he happened to be moderately handsome."

"Just moderately?" Tanner squared his shoulders and puffed out his chest.

Alanna stifled a laugh. "Most of all, though, he would have to have a soft spot in his heart for my family and a firm walk with the Lord. I can't imagine giving my heart to a fella who hasn't already given his to the Lord."

This time his expression grew more serious than she expected. "I walked the aisle of the church at age eight and meant it with my whole heart. And you can see that I have a soft spot for family. Why else would I have let Katie talk me into making these bells?"

"Tanner, stop." She smacked him in the arm. "When are you going to stop flirting with me?"

"As soon as you see that I don't need to transform into anything—or anyone—other than myself to be eligible."

"E-eligible?"

He reached over to take her hand and gave it a squeeze. "For a place in your affections."

He might as well have squeezed her heart. Alanna flinched and pulled her hand away. "Tanner, I..." In spite of her feelings to the contrary, she wanted to explain that she couldn't possibly give her heart to someone who lived so far away from her home. A little harmless flirtation might be fun, but in the end they both had to acknowledge the truth—they were worlds apart in every conceivable way.

Still, how did one go about letting someone down without hurting him, especially someone this ideal?

"You're a wonderful fella," she managed. "Probably one of the most wonderful I've ever known." The horse stamped his foot and let out a whinny, likely unhappy with standing still in the cold for so long. The bells jingled merrily as a rush of cold air blew by, but the familiar sound did nothing to ease the strange gripping sensation around her heart.

His eyes narrowed. "But?"

She hesitated, tears suddenly covering her lashes as she

thought about her words. "But you're from Montana, and I'm from Savannah." Her words came out as a hoarse whisper.

He stepped down from the sleigh and gestured for her to join him. She rose and leaned forward, allowing him to encircle her waist with his hands. Tanner lifted her from the sleigh and they stood in silence, face-to-face.

His voice now lowered to a whisper as his lips brushed across the wisps of hair framing her cheek. "I don't know about you, but I think that has a lovely ring to it. It rhymes and everything."

Her breath caught in her throat, and she could hardly speak. "Y–yes, but a rhyme doesn't make for a romance."

"Want to bet?" There were touches of humor around his eyes. He paused and appeared to be thinking and then blurted out, "There once was a guy from Montana, who fell for a girl named Alanna. They wed in the spring, their hearts on a string, and named their first offspring..." He paused then snapped his fingers. "Banana?"

She would have laughed, but the serious expression on his face, coupled with the finger he ran down her cheek, caused her to think twice.

Unfortunately—or perhaps fortunately—the moment ended there. Brett approached from a distance with a wide smile on his face. He patted the horse on the neck and grinned. "We could hear you two coming from miles away. That's what I call making an entrance."

Tanner took a step back from Alanna and turned to his brother. "I know it's annoying, but Katie would have a fit if I removed those bells. And with Christmas coming, it didn't make much sense to take them off anyway." He raked his fingers through his hair, looking like a cat caught with its nose in the cream.

And Alanna? Well, she felt more like a mouse caught in a trap. With her heart in her throat, she turned and sprinted across the snow.

* * * * *

TANNER WATCHED AS ALANNA TOOK off toward the house. He didn't even try to hide the sigh that arose. Brett slapped him on the back. "Tanner, I can see you're in a world of trouble."

"Trouble?"

"Yep. She's snagged a piece of your heart, hasn't she?"

He glanced after Alanna once more, watching as she disappeared into the house. "Mm-hmm."

"Watch yourself, my boy." Brett chuckled. "Southern women thrive on being snagged. Once a gentleman takes an interest, it is the woman's role to drag him along and make him think he stands a chance, even if he doesn't. And trust me when I say that she's aching for more attention from you even if she's not voicing it. You can take it to the bank. Now, what she'll do with that attention, I'm not sure. But she's enjoying every bit of it."

"Sounds cruel. You think she's going to break my heart in the end?"

"I'm not saying that. I'm just cautioning you. She's only here for a season. How do you plan to court her from afar once she's gone?"

"You told me that God could use this to shape and mold me."

"But I didn't say you would come out with a girl on your arm." Brett's brow furrowed. "I'm not saying God can't work a miracle here, Tanner. Just that these ladies—Ma included—are setting you up. So take the good and toss the bad. Give Alanna the attention and see how she responds, but don't be surprised if it's just a ploy to string you along."

"I've given her attention, but she's acting skittish."

"Playing hard to get, likely. It's part of their strategy."

"Strategy?"

"Yep. But they always want the attention, regardless."

Tanner didn't have an answer to that, but he was certainly willing to give it some thought. In the meantime, it looked as if he needed to come up with a solid plan where Alanna was concerned. Either she cared for him or she didn't. Either she wanted his attentions or she didn't. Time would tell, in either case.

SIXTEEN

Christmas is nearly upon us, sisters. The Lord has been gracious to allow me more time with my friends and family. For that, I am extremely grateful. During this beautiful, holy season I would encourage you to focus not on our platform or our resounding message to political leaders, but rather on those you love. Remember the true meaning of the holiday. Enjoy some time gathered around the table with loved ones, all arguments and dissension aside. There will come a day to fight for our rights. This is not that day.

—Ellie Cannady, editor of *The Modern Suffragette*

* * * * *

ON THE MORNING OF CHRISTMAS Eve, Alanna awoke to the smell of bacon cooking downstairs. She rolled over in the bed and smiled as she saw Tessa's peaceful face. In spite of the rustic feel of the place, they had all been sleeping much better here. Must have had something to do with the heavy quilts and cozy feather pillows.

Tessa stirred and came awake slowly. She gave Alanna a peaceful grin, followed by a "Merry Christmas Eve!" before sitting up in bed.

Alanna sighed as an unexpected heaviness came over her. "I find myself missing Papa today. He's always been such an integral part of our Christmas celebrations."

"Me too. I've been feeling that way for days." Tessa yawned and stretched. "I know he would be tickled to see Mama looking so happy and healthy. I believe Montana has made her more..."

"Robust?"

"Yes, that's the word. She has definitely changed."

Changed might be a bit of an understatement, actually. No longer the fragile flower, her mother now worked alongside Margaret in the kitchen, preparing meals and laughing constantly. So much for her weak constitution. It had disappeared, replaced with a newfound zeal and sense of purpose.

"What do you suppose has gotten into her?" Tessa asked.

"I have no idea." Alanna shook her head. "Did you notice that she offered to help Brett in the barn the other day? Trudged all the way through the snow. Why, at home she would call for Papa and the runabout and ask for a ride to the barn!"

"Brett said she talked the whole way. He hardly knew what to make of her chatty demeanor. Said he hardly managed to get a word in edgewise."

"Very, very odd." Alanna could barely make sense of it, in fact. She'd expected Mama to struggle to fit in during their time in Montana. Instead, she appeared to be thriving.

"I'd be willing to bet she's the one who's downstairs cooking right now," Tessa said. "Have you ever seen her cook before?

I mean, honestly, it's so refreshing. And yummy, too."

"True. I've rarely seen this side of her." Alanna swung her legs over the side of the bed and shivered. "Back home she hardly goes into the kitchen except to fetch a glass of water for her aspirin powders."

"Or to tell Cook how to prepare the ham for the Easter party."

"I know. It's certainly out of character, but I'm enjoying watching her."

"Me too." Tessa lowered her voice. "I couldn't believe that fried chicken she made the other night. It was better than any back home."

"Can you get over the fact that she was on her feet for so long with Tanner and Katie's mother, baking up a storm? I think she enjoyed it, don't you?"

"Very much."

"I've never seen so many sweets. And those dumplings Mama made for dinner last night were wonderful. I think she's tickled to help Margaret in her time of need."

"Poor Margaret. She looks just miserable." Tessa rose and reached for her dressing gown. "I can't imagine being in such a delicate condition in the middle of winter."

"She rarely complains, but I know her feet were aching last night. She could barely get them into her shoes. And I could see that her back was really bothering her as well, though she wouldn't dare complain."

Tessa wrinkled her nose. "I wish I could help her, but Katie needs me today. We're putting together a plan for the upcoming New Year's Eve party for the suffragettes."

Alanna did her best not to sigh aloud. Still, she could

hardly help herself. "Do you plan to keep this up when we get back to Savannah?"

Tessa offered an enthusiastic nod. "Oh, yes. Katie is training me well. She's already come up with a name for the group I'm going to start when I get back home. We can't be the Sleigh Belles, of course, so she has suggested the Liberty Belles. We'll champion the rights of liberty for women all across the state of Georgia. It's going to be marvelous. She's even suggested that I offer to write a column in our local paper."

At this, Alanna couldn't hold back the groan. "You will make our family the laughingstock of Savannah if you write for the *Daily Morning News*. Promise me you won't do it."

The expression on Tessa's face shifted from enthusiasm to defeat. Her shoulders slumped as she responded. "Oh. Well, I thought you would be happy. I felt sure by now you would be in agreement with the principles these women stand for. They are worlds apart from us, Alanna, and I like their world. Very much, in fact. And I respect them too. They are brave and strong."

Alanna had to admit that she enjoyed the women she'd met in Montana too. Even envied them a little. They had a confidence about them that she'd not seen before. Still, she could hardly voice this opinion aloud, now could she? Not after being so vocal in her stance against the suffrage movement.

"If we could stay on in Montana instead of going back home, I feel sure you could be won over to our way of thinking," Tessa said. "But I know we have to leave in a couple of months."

"Stay on in Montana?" Alanna's heart quickened. "Is that what you're secretly wishing?"

Tessa shrugged. "Maybe."

"Well, remember what Papa always says: if ifs and buts were candy and nuts, every day would be Christmas."

"Around here, every day *is* Christmas." With a springy bounce Tessa sashayed to the window, where she pulled back the curtain and revealed a winter wonderland. "It's prettier than a picture-postcard. Just feels so perfect."

Mama's voice called out from the bottom of the stairs, and Alanna rushed to get dressed. The smell of breakfast lured her as never before. She found Mama at the stove with Margaret seated at the table, her feet propped on a chair.

"Are you all right?" Alanna rushed to her sister's side.

Wrinkles creased Margaret's brow as she shrugged. "Just feeling a little under the weather today. But I'm sure it's to be expected."

A rap sounded at the door, and Tanner stuck his head inside. "Mind if I come in?"

"Do we ever?" Margaret chuckled. "You know you're always welcome, Tanner."

He stood in the doorway and shook the snow from his jacket, then took a few tentative steps inside after pulling off his icy boots. "Brett told me my presence was requested this morning to help put up the tree. Is that right?"

Margaret nodded. "Yes. He chopped down a fine one last night and left it in the barn. Would you mind bringing it in?"

"After breakfast," Mama chimed in, turning from her work at the stove. "Come on in and have some flapjacks and bacon, Tanner."

Flapjacks? Since when did Mama use words like *flapjacks*? Alanna stifled a laugh. Seemed odd to see her mother so content with a spatula in her hand, but the truth of it was evident.

She glanced Tanner's way, her defenses melting at his winsome smile and sock-covered feet. Her mind raced to the conversation they had shared in the sleigh, and heat rose to her cheeks as she remember the touch of his hand. Whatever would she do with these conflicting feelings? For now, she had little choice but to press them away and forget about them. No point in stirring embers to encourage a flame that should never have been lit in the first place.

"Tanner, can you take me back to your place when you're ready to go?" Tessa asked. "I need to help Katie today."

"Might be awhile. Have you looked outside?" He gestured to the window. "It's colder than usual out there."

Tessa moved that direction and then looked back, her mouth rounding into an O. "The snow is really coming down."

"Yep. Had a doozy of a time getting over here this morning. But it should stop soon. That's my prediction, anyway."

"Oh, but I don't want it to stop. How lovely it would be, to have snow on Christmas." Tessa twirled around, her voice animated.

"That would certainly be a first for my girls," Mama chimed in.

Alanna went to work, helping her mother get the table ready, and then joined the others for breakfast. Brett filled everyone in on the new calf, and before long they were laughing and talking about Christmas. After filling up on two plates of food, Tanner left them and headed to the barn alongside Brett to fetch the tree. They reappeared minutes later and made quick work of setting up the beautiful fir in the parlor just in front of the window.

"You chose a fine one, Brett." Tanner gave the expansive tree an admiring look after bracing it. "I think it's nicer than the one

I cut down for our place, though I hate to admit it."

"Oh, no. Yours is perfect. I saw it yesterday." Tessa gave him a flirtatious smile, which rankled Alanna more than a little bit, especially after her younger sister's earlier comments about staying in Montana. Clearly Tessa had set her sights on Tanner. Was he to be her ticket for staying here?

A shiver ran down Alanna's spine, but she hardly had time to think it through before Tanner glanced her way with a broad smile. "How do you ladies celebrate Christmas in Savannah? I'm guessing things are a mite different than they are here."

"Oh my." Alanna glanced at the tree and found herself missing Papa more than ever as memories flooded over her. "You are right to say that things are different. We begin decorating in early December. Then usually around the second week, we have a lovely party." She paused, deep in thought about the many festive events she had hosted over the years. Certainly they were different than the rustic Montana approach to Christmas, but they had been fun. Mostly. "My calendar is pretty full during December, to be quite honest."

"So you enjoy a wide circle of friends?"

She paused to think about his question. "I suppose you could put it like that. I know a lot of people."

Mama entered the parlor, wiping her hands on her apron. "It's very different here," she said as she walked over to the tree. "You know fewer people, but it seems as if you know—and care—about each other more." A little shrug followed. "I've never known the kind of intimate friendships you Missoulans enjoy."

He shrugged. "It's easier in a small setting, I suppose. Not so many people vying for attention. And in a smaller group you really learn to pay attention to the particular needs of people."

"I just love the folks here." This time Tessa chimed in. "Everyone works together in Montana. Back home, it always seems to be each man—or woman—to himself." She giggled. "Or herself. You get the idea."

Alanna had to admit, her sister's words held considerable weight. Back in Savannah, she enjoyed a healthy competition with her friends to see who could outdo whom with the finest dresses, hairstyles, and parties. Here, folks worked together to accomplish mutual goals. It felt good to merge forces, even in something as simple as decorating a Christmas tree.

Margaret's voice came from the kitchen, startling her. "Tessa? Alanna? Would you help me with the popcorn? We need to get it started if we're going to get it strung before lunch."

They headed off to join her in the kitchen, and their joyful laughter resounded as they shared story after story, memory after memory. The ever-present sound of the corn kernels tinging and pinging against the sides of the pan filled Alanna with happiness. She loved that sound. It took her back to a childhood Christmas where she and her sisters had helped Cook make sticky popcorn balls. She could almost taste them now, their gooey goodness flooding over her and sweeping her back to that delicious place.

Seconds later the most tantalizing aroma filled the air as the popped corn was transferred from the pan to a bowl. Fluffy bits of white tempted the eye, and she grabbed a couple and pressed them into her mouth.

"I've always loved that smell." Tessa closed her eyes and grinned. "Heavenly."

"We never get much strung on the first batch," Margaret said.

"Most of it gets eaten." With Brett's help, she began a second batch, and before long the room was filled with the sound of popping kernels once again.

At this point, the real work began. Alanna could hardly call it work, however, because she enjoyed herself so much. At the kitchen table, Tessa and Mama made a quick task of stringing the popcorn. With Tanner at her side, Alanna peeled apples and oranges and got the wassail started. Its pungent aroma filled the room like a fruity stream of goodness laced with hints of cinnamon.

By the time she served up mugs of the spicy wassail, the work was more than half done. At one point Tanner offered to help the other women, but he ended up eating more than he threaded, so Alanna set him to work making a colorful paper-chain garland for the tree instead. When Brett headed to the barn to fetch the turkey for tomorrow's meal, Margaret excused herself to take a nap, but Alanna didn't mind. She rather enjoyed being the one in charge as they placed the homemade decorations on the tree minutes later.

As they worked alongside one another, she thought about all the expensive ornaments on their tree back in Savannah. Odd how a strand of popcorn and a few homemade garlands could make Margaret's tree even lovelier. In fact, the finished product was, Alanna had to admit, the prettiest tree she'd ever laid eyes on.

* * * * *

AFTER HELPING WITH THE TREE, Tanner made his way to the barn to check on Prissy's newborn calf. He found himself more conflicted about Alanna than ever before. In spite of her strange reaction to him in the sleigh, she now laughed and conversed as if nothing had ever happened. Had she changed her mind, perhaps? Or, was she, as Brett suggested, just stringing him along like a strand of popcorn, trying to get his attentions? Was this all part of some master plan to make him look like a fool in the end? If so, he would best her at that game. Yes, indeed. Tanner chuckled, just thinking about it.

Once inside the barn, he visited the calf, which appeared to be doing well in spite of the plummeting temperatures. The tiny babe struggled to stand, falling and then rising again, triumphant. Tanner gave him a pat on the backside. "For a sissy little thing, you sure have a lot of gumption."

"I can only hope you're talking to the calf and not to me."

He turned to find Alanna standing behind him, holding a pot of coffee in one hand and a mug in the other. He grinned and stretched out his hand for the empty mug, which she filled in short order. "Well, now, you are a girl, and most—my sister excluded—run on the sissy side. But I'd have to say I've seen a tough side of you too. Not that I've figured you out, exactly. There are plenty of things that still elude me about you so-called Southern belles."

"Whatever do you mean?" She set the coffeepot down and took a seat on a bale of hay.

"I mean, for such a small gal, you're loaded with gumption. You might claim to be the gentler sex, but there's more power in the wave of your fan than you're willing to admit."

"I don't have a clue what you mean." Her eyelashes took to

batting again, convincing him that Brett had, indeed, been right. She was stringing him along. Well, two could play at that game, now couldn't they?

"See? There you go again. You Southern women say you don't believe in the suffrage movement, but you still have your ways."

"My...ways?" She brushed an imaginary speck from her coat.

"Yes. Your ways of getting what you want." Courage rose within him as he continued. "You might not march with placards or sleigh bells, and you probably don't write articles for the paper. But I've determined that your methods of swaying the menfolk are far more powerful than all that." His thoughts shifted to their conversation in the sleigh—how she had snatched a piece of his heart and then left him standing alone, empty-handed. Surely, as Brett said, she meant to tease him. The whole thing must be a ruse, a way to garner even more attention. Well, he would give it to her.

She stared up at him, her brow creased. "I can't imagine what you mean."

"Can't you?" He forced back the chuckle. "Aw, c'mon, Lana."

"That's A–lanna."

"Alanna. You sweep in here all Southern charm and gentility and turn everything upside down in my world."

"I've done no such thing." She gestured to the barn. "Everything is just as it was."

"Hardly." He took a seat next to her and slipped an arm around her shoulders then fingered a loose tendril of hair on her cheek.

"Tanner." She appeared to flinch as she gazed into his eyes. "Release your hold on me at once."

"Nope. Can't." He ran his fingertip along her cheek, waiting for her to melt in his arms like butter. Wasn't that the idea all along?

"I insist." Her expression hardened, and he felt her stiffen in his arms. "I fear all of my hard work to turn you into a Southern gentleman has been in vain."

"Trust me, your work has not been in vain." He planted a tiny kiss on her cheek. "Not at all. Neither has its real purpose eluded me. I've been keen on your plan from the beginning."

"My plan?"

Cupping her chin, he searched her upturned face. "To get me to kiss you. Isn't that what we're working up to here?"

Her face turned red and she pulled herself from his grasp. "Hardly. And if that's what you're thinkin', let me set you straight immediately. I don't want or need a kiss from the likes of you."

"I see." He grinned. "Then I guess you're more liberated than I thought because I felt sure you were fishing for a kiss."

She crossed her arms over her chest in a defiant gesture. "I can assure you, this was no fishing expedition. And just because I don't require your kisses doesn't mean I'm liberated. I'm just waiting for the right fella, one who understands me."

"You'll be waiting a mighty long time. I've never yet met a man who understood a woman."

"That is beside the point." She brushed her tears away with the swipe of a hand. "Never mind. I don't expect you to understand. You've never understood me."

"I—I guess I haven't." His heart plummeted to his toes as the realization set in. "So you don't really want me to kiss you?"

Her eyes spoke one answer, her lips another. "No. I don't." She bent her head forward and studied her hands. When she raised her head, tears streamed down her cheeks.

Tanner's heart felt like lead. "I've misunderstood your intentions?"

"Completely." Again the expression did not match the answer. But what could he do? He'd already made a fool of himself. No point in making matters worse. Tanner rose and walked over to the calf, giving him a gentle pat on the side. "Well, then, I'd say I've just made an idiot of myself. For both our sakes, I'm extremely sorry."

She sighed. "It's not all your fault, Tanner. I've probably been leading you astray by spending so much time being focused on changing you. I do hope you will forgive me for that. It seems so silly now."

"If you will forgive me for trying to kiss you."

"It wasn't a very gentlemanly thing to do." Her eyelashes batted again, nearly driving him out of his mind. Why, oh, why did she continue to tease him if not to win his affections? Was this whole thing a ploy of some sort? Just part of her game to convert him into a Southern gentleman?

"You've tried—with no great success, I might add—to turn me into a gentleman," he said after awhile.

"And have failed miserably," she added.

"Perhaps. As my papa always says, 'You can't make a silk purse out of a sow's ear.' But in spite of my misunderstanding, I think it's time the tables were turned."

"W–what do you mean?"

"I mean, all is fair in love and war—at least that's what I hear.

I bided my time while you worked to convert me into your idea of what a man from the South would look—and act—like. It's about time you let me show you a little something about what is expected of a Montana woman."

"I—I beg your pardon?" She swept a tendril away from her face.

"Stop fussing with your hair. That's number one on my list."

She rolled her eyes. "You don't have a list."

"Don't I?" He reached into his pocket and came out with a piece of paper that contained scribblings from top to bottom. Alanna looked as if she might be ill as she glanced over it. "You've actually been thinking about this?"

"Of course. You put thought into your list for me. I put equal thought into my list for you." He glanced down at the paper. "Now, a real Western lady knows how to ride a horse."

"R–ride a horse?" She paled. "That's first on your list?"

"If you like, we could jump ahead to roping cattle."

"No, no." Alanna shook her head. "Let's go back to the horse."

"Let's skip the horses and talk about cooking." He referred to his list once again, then looked her way. "A western woman knows how to cook over an open fire."

"I don't even know how to cook on a kitchen stove. Back home in Savannah we have a cook. She handles all the meals for us."

"All the better. You can learn the proper way, unhindered by habit or convention."

She winced. "What else?"

"A Western woman knows how to doctor folks when they're sick."

"I don't have a medical degree," she argued. "So that one is impossible."

"A Western woman doesn't use the word *impossible*. She learns to make do in any situation."

"But, I—" Alanna didn't have much time to think it through, however. The door to the barn swung wide and Tessa raced inside, wide-eyed and breathless.

"Tanner."

Just one word, but she spoke it with such trembling that Tanner realized its seriousness. He turned to face Alanna's near-frantic sister and felt the quickening of his pulse. "What is it?"

Tessa looked as if she might be ill on the spot but finally managed to spit out the rest. "Margaret—Margaret's having the baby."

SEVENTEEN

Ladies, I have often shared on the topic of working together to accomplish a goal. I've seen men do this too, of course, but no one knows how to rush to the rescue of a brother or sister like a kind-hearted woman. I've seen the ladies in our community tend to the needs of others, even putting their own wants and wishes aside to do so. This is an example of the Christmas spirit, is it not—giving without any expectation of receiving in return? This year, as you look after one another, ask yourself, "How can I bless a sister in need today?" Then, go forth and serve with all of your heart. The Lord will honor your efforts, I assure you.

—Ellie Cannady, editor of *The Modern Suffragette*

* * * * *

ALANNA BOLTED TOWARD THE HOUSE behind Tessa. As she reached the door, she turned back to Tanner, who followed on her heels. "Tanner, you have to go after Katie and your mother. Margaret will need them."

He shook his head and pointed to the car, which was covered in snow. "It's a real blizzard out there. Might take me a while to get there and back if the roads are snowed under."

Alanna stopped to stomp the snow off her boots before entering the house, her thoughts now shifting to Tanner's safety. Once inside, she turned back to him. "I've got the perfect solution. You can borrow Brett's sleigh. You'll be there and back in no time."

"It's still covered in bells."

"That's perfect." Tessa grinned and then sprinted toward the stairs, adding, "Katie will hear you coming and know that something has happened."

Alanna placed a hand on Tanner's arm, all former misgivings erased in a moment. "Go, Tanner. Please."

"I'll do my best." He glanced through the window, worry lines now creasing his forehead. "Though, to be honest, I'm worried about bringing them out in this. I just hope we make it back in time."

"What can be done if you don't?" Alanna paced the room, her heart in her throat. After a couple of minutes she pursed her lips and released a slow, steady breath. "There is no choice. Mama and I will have to deliver the baby."

Mama entered the room carrying a handful of blankets and towels. "We will keep her calm and steady, Lana. Don't fret. I've been through this before, you know."

"I—I won't fret." Alanna spoke the words but didn't mean them. Her gaze shifted back to Tanner, who bolted toward the door. He turned back to gaze at her with piercing eyes. In them, she read a thousand things—an apology for what had happened in the barn. Empathy for the situation with Margaret. And…love. She read love in his eyes as clearly as anything she'd ever seen.

For a moment, anyway. Just as quickly, he disappeared out of the door. A short time later, after bounding up the stairs to her sister's room, Alanna heard the jingling of bells and peeked out the window. She watched as the sleigh sailed away from the house and then turned her attention back to Margaret, who sat propped up in the bed with a pained expression on her face.

"Is—is he going after Katie and his mother?" Margaret blew out a few short breaths and leaned back against the stack of pillows Mama placed behind her.

"Yes. Shouldn't take too long on the sleigh."

"Those bells." Margaret's eyes flew open. "Hope they don't summon every woman in the county."

"What do you mean?"

Tessa looked up from her spot on the edge of the bed and grinned. "It's a signal, silly. The suffragettes all know to pay attention when they hear the bells. They're to follow the sound."

"So, you're telling me that every woman in the county might follow Tanner back here?" Mama paled. "If so, we'll need to get ready for them."

"We've got wassail made and all those sweets you baked with Mrs. Jacobs. The foods for tomorrow's Christmas celebration are ready to be cooked, as well." Margaret released several pants then squeezed her eyes shut. "Ooh, that was a hard one."

"I do hope Katie gets back in time." Tessa rose and paced the room.

Brett popped his head through the doorway. "Anything I can do?"

"Yes." Margaret nodded, and Alanna could almost see the relief in her eyes. "I need you to prepare the turkey and the ham and get them into the oven right away."

"I—I beg your pardon?" He gripped the door and stared at her, eyes narrowing in bewilderment. "We're cooking Christmas dinner? I thought we were having a baby."

"We're..." Margaret paused to puff out a few quick breaths. "We're doing both. Please, Brett. Put the turkey on. Company's coming."

"Well, sure." He pointed at her belly. "Company's coming, but I don't think he—or she—will be up to eating a big meal right away."

Margaret swatted at the air. "Not the baby, silly. The neighbors. They're coming, I guarantee you, and we need to be ready for them."

"Darlin', I'm sure they'll understand if we're not." He looked as if he wanted to say something else. Instead, he nodded and turned to go down the stairs.

"He will forgive me later." Margaret managed a weak smile. "But you know me. I can't abide the idea that folks might stop by on Christmas Eve and not have anything to eat."

"We've got cookies and pies aplenty," Mama said with the wave of a hand. "So don't fret. Your guests won't go hungry."

Alanna felt her frustrations mounting. "I cannot believe we're having this conversation. Here you are, having a baby, and you're worried about your neighbors. It's...ludicrous."

At this, Margaret erupted in laughter. "I know you're right. What's wrong with me?"

"Nothing is wrong with you. You're just always thinking of others." Alanna sat on the edge of the bed and reached for her sister's hand. "But this is your day. You must focus on yourself and on this baby. Promise me that's all you'll think about."

"I'll try." Margaret's weak smile twisted into a grimace as another pain set in. She squeezed her eyes shut and counted "One, two, three, four...twenty-six, twenty-seven." Her eyes popped open, and she rubbed her belly. "They're getting longer."

Alanna, gave her a warm smile, one she hoped would bring encouragement. "You're so strong, Margaret. Truly, you amaze me."

"Me? Strong?" Margaret laughed then winced in pain. "Right now I feel anything but. I don't mind admitting that I feel weaker right now than I've ever felt."

"With good reason," Mama chimed in.

Margaret's face contorted. "I'm a firm believer that we have to come to the Lord admitting our weakness so that He can do the work of strengthening." Here she began to puff and pant. "How many times I've tried to strike out on my own without depending on Him."

"You?" Alanna could hardly believe it.

"Yes, me." Margaret released a few slow breaths as the contraction appeared to ease. "I set off to Montana—so flippant in the way I left all of you behind—and felt sure I could make it for the sake of my husband. I put my head up and squared my shoulders and made the journey. But somewhere along the way I had to admit that my strength—what looked like strength, anyway—was nothing more than pretense. Inside, I was broken and lonely and confused."

"Oh, Margaret." Tessa rose and Alanna wrapped her arms around her sister. "I had no idea."

Mama and Tessa joined them on the bed, and before long a lone tear trickled down Margaret's cheek. "Some of us pretend to be strong when we're not, and some of us pretend to be weak when we're not," Margaret said. "There's really no difference."

"We simply have to acknowledge that all strength is found in Him and that we're capable of great things when we allow Him to work in our lives," Mama said quietly.

"That's what I want," Alanna whispered. "For God to work in my life."

"Me too." Margaret offered a weak smile. "And in the life of this little baby, too."

Her face twisted in pain again, and Alanna rose and walked to the window, praying that Tanner would arrive soon. She whispered a prayer for their safety and an extra one pleading with the Lord to bring them before the baby arrived.

She continued to pace the room and make light conversation, even as the banging and clanging of dishes from downstairs interrupted their reverie.

"What do you suppose Brett is doing down there?" Margaret swung her legs over the edge of the bed, but Mama signaled for her to stay put.

"I'll go down and check," their mother said. "Don't fret, Margaret. You have enough to do without worrying about Brett."

"He's never been at home in the kitchen." Margaret blew out a few short breaths, her brow knitted. "Though...not...for...lack... of trying." A long, slow breath followed, and then her pained expression eased into a peaceful one. "He has such a good heart, but his cooking skills are for the birds."

Alanna fought against rolling her eyes. "I cannot believe we're having this conversation right now, of all things. This is not the day to worry about who does the cooking. Just let the man put the turkey in the oven."

Margaret giggled. "Listen to yourself, Alanna. You're actually advocating a man doing the cooking."

"On a day like today, with you giving birth? I daresay, he can put the turkey in the oven."

"Yes, but can he actually cook it without burning the house down?" Margaret offered a weak smile. "That is the real question."

"Never fear, Mama is here." Their mother rose and made her way to the door. "If you can do without me for a few minutes, Margaret, I will help him get the meats started. And I will peel the potatoes, as well. Heaven knows we'll need them once the ladies start showing up." She disappeared through the doorway.

Alanna shook her head as she turned back to her sister. "You don't honestly think the women will come just because they hear those bells, do you? Because..." Her words drifted off as the jingling of bells sounded from outside. She rushed to the window.

"W–who is it?" Margaret panted. "Is Tanner back?"

"No." Alanna wiped the frost off the window and squinted to get a better look. "I think it's Mrs. Sullivan." She blew warm breath on the window and then wiped the pane with her sleeve. An unladylike gesture, for sure, but desperate times called for desperate measures. "Yes. It's definitely the Sullivans."

"She brought her husband?" Margaret groaned.

"And their son."

"Hope the men aren't hungry."

"Don't worry about that. Just…"

Alanna gazed at her sister as she counted, "One, two, three… twenty-nine, thirty." The contractions were definitely intensifying.

Downstairs a knock sounded at the door, and before long, Alanna could hear voices rising in excitement. Moments later, Mrs. Sullivan bounded into the room, her hands clasped together and her eyes dancing with delight.

"We're having a baby!" she exclaimed.

"Indeed." Margaret gave several quick pants. "We are."

"Well, don't fret. I know just what to do. I've helped with many deliveries over the years." Mrs. Sullivan rolled up her sleeves and went about the business of checking on Margaret's progress, something Alanna had never witnessed before and hoped to never see again. "There now. Looks like it could be any minute now. Just breathe slow and steady, my dear."

Another long contraction followed, and Margaret winced in pain.

"It's all right to cry out, honey," Mrs. Sullivan said with a half smile. "No point in trying to be heroic."

Margaret's face twisted. "I–I'm just worried about scaring the men."

"There she goes, thinking about others again." Alanna plopped down on the side of the bed, feeling a little woozy herself. "Next thing you know, she'll be up baking a cake for them."

"Such a good-hearted soul, your sister." Mrs. Sullivan gave Alanna a warm smile. "Must be her Southern upbringing."

Just then Margaret let out a string of near curses, startling them all. She gripped her belly and doubled over, wailing.

"Nothing to be ashamed of." Mrs. Sullivan put up her hands and grinned. "Happens to the best of us."

Off in the distance the jingling of bells rang out. Alanna raced to the window to discover another sleigh arriving. It did not carry Tanner and Katie, however. Instead, a group of young women emerged and ran toward the house. Minutes later another sleigh arrived. And then another.

From the bed, Margaret remained focused and steady, though she occasionally cried out as she panted. The room began to fill with women young and old. Mama came first, followed by Tessa, and then all the Sleigh Belles poured in. Margaret, in her usual fashion, extended a hand of welcome before counting, "One, two, three...thirty-one, thirty-two."

Only when she hit thirty-three did Alanna realize the time had come. With the help of nearly a dozen feisty Sleigh Belles, Margaret pushed a baby girl out into Alanna's waiting arms.

* * * * *

TANNER SNAPPED THE REINS, HURRYING the horse along. Katie sat to his right in the sleigh, her nerves showing as she babbled nonsensically about the weather. Mama sat to his left, her eyes wide with excitement. Moments later, Brett and Margaret's house came into view, though it was not as he'd left it, by any stretch of the imagination.

"Oh my goodness. Look at that, will you." Katie pointed to

the sleighs—probably six or seven of them in total, all covered with bells. "The Sleigh Belles have come to the rescue."

"I knew they would come." Mama grinned. "You can always count on the women in these parts to rush to lend a hand."

"Looks like they've come in force." Tanner chuckled. "Hope Margaret and Brett were ready for them."

"I'm just glad to see others here," Katie said as their sleigh came to a halt in front of the house. She scrambled down from her perch and took off running. Mama followed on her heels, moving at a slightly slower pace.

"You left your bag." Tanner held up Katie's bag then bolted from the sleigh, following on her heels. She turned, and he pitched it her way before tending to the horse.

When he arrived at the barn, he found nearly a dozen other horses inside, including the pastor's two palominos and a variety of others. He made sure they were all warm and fed and then headed to the house.

No sooner had he arrived inside than a flurry of activity met him. He wasn't sure which had him more discombobulated—the smell of burning piecrust or the voices of nearly a dozen women as they shared the story of Margaret's new baby girl.

Finally, breaking through the cacophony of sounds, a clear, angelic sound emerged. An infant's cry.

In that second, everything else came a halt. The spirit of Christmas took over, and his heart was filled with a hopefulness he had never before known.

Now, to find Alanna, so that he could share this blissful moment with her.

EIGHTEEN

Ladies, I will open my heart to share a special message this Christmas season. Rarely do I find myself more vulnerable than when I look into the eyes of a newborn babe, particularly a girl-child. For, in that moment, I see all the potential for her life—twenty, thirty, even fifty years from now. Our daughters, granddaughters, and great-granddaughters will have glorious, productive lives, thanks to the work we have done on their behalf. They may not pause to thank us. Many won't even realize the inroads we've made. But we will know, and that is all that matters.

—Ellie Cannady, editor of *The Modern Suffragette*

* * * * *

A WAVE OF EMOTION WASHED over Alanna as she gazed into the eyes of the beautiful infant. Joyous love exuded for the little girl with pink cherub cheeks and golden wisps of hair now wrapped in her mother's arms.

"Oh, Margaret." Alanna eased her way down onto the edge

of the bed, tears streaming. "I've never seen anything more precious." With the tip of her index finger she caressed the darling little cheek.

"My tiny Christmas present." Margaret did not lift her gaze from the babe's face, but the emotion in her voice left little to the imagination. She was smitten. Less than ten minutes old and the baby had stolen the hearts of all in attendance. And there were more than a few in attendance, though most had ventured downstairs to help with the cooking.

Margaret gestured for Brett to join them on the bed, and he came over, eyes misty. "This is the happiest day of my life." He snuggled up next to Margaret and gazed into his daughter's face. Alanna looked on at the three of them and thought they looked very much like a Christmas painting. All that was missing was the stable and the hay. Of course, Brett's cowboy boots looked a little out of place hanging off the edge of the bed, but never mind that.

"I'm sorry I had you working so hard downstairs," Margaret said. She gave him a little shrug.

"I daresay you were working harder up here." Brett leaned over and gave her a kiss on the cheek. "I was tending to a turkey and ham. You were tending to something a little more important."

"Yes." Every eye in the room shifted to the babe.

For a few seconds, anyway. Katie came bursting through the door, pulling off her hat, coat, and gloves and letting them fall to the floor. She took one look at the baby and erupted into tears. "Oh, I'm too late." The new auntie shook her head and sank onto the edge of the bed. "Forgive me?"

"Forgive you? Why, you're just in time." Margaret gestured

to the babe. "What do you think of our little Christmas present?"

"I think she's—" Katie leaned over to look at her. "I think she's the most beautiful little doll I've ever seen. The perfect gift." After she got control of herself, she took another peek. "What will you call her?"

Margaret stroked her finger along the baby's cheek. "We will have to think on that."

Brett rose and paced the room. "She's definitely a gift from above, so we need to give her an appropriate name. Something that speaks to the season, of course."

Margaret nodded. "At first I thought about *Noel*, but I think perhaps we should call her *Given* instead."

"Given?" Alanna asked, just to be sure she'd heard correctly.

"Yes." Margaret cradled the infant close to her breast. "Because she was given to us. What do you think?"

The child began to coo—truly, a heavenly sound coming from one so small—and Alanna's eyes filled with tears. "I think you're absolutely right, Margaret. She is a gift we will all cherish for years to come."

"What a precious bundle," Margaret whispered. "All wrapped up with ribbons and bows."

"No bows just yet." Alanna pointed to the infant's scant wisps and chuckled. "But one day soon."

Her thoughts reeled to Savannah. Home. Back home, this little doll would be dressed in frills from the get-go, donned only in the finest for all of society to see. Here, she lay in her mother's arms, wrapped in a homespun blanket.

Kind of like that babe in the manger.

Alanna felt the breath go out of her as she thought it through. Yes, very much like the babe in the manger. He came with no fanfare. No ribbons and bows. And yet was He not the greatest gift given to mankind?

She gazed once again into little Given's face. Her apple-dumpling cheeks. Her tiny little chin. Those perfectly formed ears. They spoke of perfection. And grace. And hope for better days ahead.

"You will have a wonderful life, little darling," Alanna whispered into the infant's ear. "Your mama and papa will see to that."

"Yes, indeed." Margaret gave the little darling several soft kisses on the brow. "You have changed your mommy's life forever, baby girl. Nothing will be the same now that you're here."

Alanna wondered at her sister's words. Would things really be different? If so, what did that mean? Had giving birth changed Margaret's thoughts on women's rights, or was she referring to something else?

Brett leaned in close to his wife and daughter, his face awash with joy. Alanna quietly left the room. She'd barely made it out the door when she bumped into Tanner. As she gazed into his eyes, her heart raced.

"You frightened me."

"Sorry. Just wanted to make sure everything's all right. "

"More than all right." She sighed and gestured through the open door at the scene before them.

"The baby...she's fine?" Tanner whispered.

"Oh, she's more than fine. She's...miraculous." Alanna pulled the door closed behind her.

"All babies are. Or so I hear."

"Oh, but this one really is! And to come on Christmas Eve—what a gift." Alanna reached for his hand and gave it a squeeze. "They're calling her *Given*."

"Given?"

"Because God has given her to them. Isn't that precious?"

He smiled. "I like it. No one has a name like that, at least around these parts. She'll be one of a kind."

"She will. And she will grow into a lovely young woman, ready to face any challenges life might bring her."

"Hopefully not too many."

"No. But she will be strong-spirited like her mama, I'm sure."

"No doubt."

"And like all the women who helped bring her into the world." Alanna chuckled. "I've never seen so many ladies gathered in one room before. To think, they all came out on such a wintery day to help. That really touches me." A lump filled her throat, and tears followed.

"Are you all right?" Tanner took her by the arm and led her to the top of the stairs, where he gestured for her to sit.

"More than all right. I feel as if I'm forever changed." After she settled into place, he joined her, slipping an arm around her shoulders. She leaned in close, her heart spilling over with a thousand emotions at once. "I'm transformed," she whispered. "I know that Christmas has the power to do that to a person, but this time it's not just the usual things about the holiday that are affecting me. It's not the snow or the ornaments on the tree or the gifts. It's not even the food, which is going to be wonderful, of course."

He chuckled. "More wonderful than you know. All those

ladies are working together downstairs to create a meal unlike anything I've ever seen before."

"It's going to be marvelous." Alanna's heart swelled with anticipation. "But this Christmas, something extra-special has happened inside me, something that transcends all that." She swallowed hard. "Watching Given come into the world takes me back to the faith I had as a youngster. I can't begin to tell you what a majestic faith it was."

"Oh?" He pulled her a bit closer, and she rested her head on his shoulder. Gone were the concerns about the future. Gone was the frustration about his lack of gentlemanly skills. All that remained was this moment, these thoughts.

"Yes." Tears flowed in a steady stream as she wondered how to make him understand. "I had faith to believe the Lord for anything and everything I asked for. Especially at Christmas. It always seemed He extended a supernatural amount of faith at that very special time of year."

"What would you ask Him for this year, if you really could have any Christmas gift in the world?"

A lump rose in her throat, and she did her best to speak around it. "I've already got it, now that the baby has come. She's by far the sweetest gift I've ever seen, and with the perfect name too."

"But besides the baby?" He peered into her eyes. "What else would you ask the Lord for?"

Her heart thumped wildly as she contemplated his reason for asking. Was he fishing for an answer? His eyes searched hers, and she felt more vulnerable than before. In spite of her earlier statements to the contrary, she felt completely at home in

Tanner's arms. Should she wish for this possibility to continue through the spring?

Oh, but what of her secret desire to coax Margaret and Brett into coming back to Savannah? Yes, that should surely be her wish for this season, shouldn't it? But saying it aloud—voicing it as a Christmas wish—suddenly made her feel selfish. And very, very wrong. Yes, she'd been wrong on every level. They didn't belong in Savannah. They belonged right here, at home in Missoula.

"Still thinking?" Tanner teased.

Alanna nodded. "Yes." She offered an answer sure to pacify him but also one that would not give away too much of her heart. "I think I would ask for God's peace to reign in all of our hearts." After thinking further, she added. "A far different kind of gift than I would have asked for as a child, to be sure."

"A far greater one," Tanner said. "And long-lasting too."

From behind them, Alanna heard someone sniffling. She looked up to see a misty-eyed Katie.

Alanna heart raced. "What is it, Katie? Has something happened to the baby?"

"No, no." She smiled weakly. "The baby's perfect. Absolutely perfect. Never seen anything like her, in fact."

"Then what's happened?" Tanner rose and gestured for his sister to take his spot on the step.

Katie plopped down next to Alanna and sniffled again. "She's just so innocent. So pure."

"Well, of course." Tanner grinned. "Aren't all babies?"

"Yes, but when I look into her face, I see such peacefulness. It's God-breathed. Honest." Katie began to cry in earnest now.

"I'm still not sure I understand why this upsets you." Alanna reached for Katie's hand. "What has you so troubled?"

"Don't you see, Alanna? I'm *always* troubled. Every day of my life. I live with so much internal turmoil because I'm always seeking change. In my life. In the lives of others. In the political scene. In the suffrage movement. I'm never satisfied."

"Ah." Now they were getting somewhere.

Katie reached into her pocket and came out with a hankie, which she used to dab her eyes. "I've always felt that I could bring about peace in the hearts of the women in our little circle. If I worked hard enough. If we changed the law so that women could have equal rights. If everything fell into place just so."

"So you've been working to produce peace? Is that what you're saying?" Tanner gazed down at her, creases forming between his eyes.

Katie nodded. "Yes. Only, now, when I look at Given, I'm not so sure I needed to be working so hard. I see that peacefulness—real peacefulness—is something we're born with. The cares of life try to steal it from us and we can replace it with all sorts of things—good deeds, included—but in the end, we still come up feeling empty."

"What's really troubling you, Katie?" Tanner asked. "I have a feeling there's more to it than that. I know you. You're going to go on working, no matter what. You'll keep on going until you see the results you want."

"Even if it kills me." Katie sighed.

"What do you mean?" Alanna gave Katie's hand a squeeze.

"I've been giving great thought to something you said the last time we spoke, Alanna." Katie turned and gazed into her eyes with such intensity that Alanna felt a cold chill run down her spine. "You told me that only God can bring about change. Well, you were right, though I always hate to admit when others are right."

"That's a fact." Tanner grinned.

Katie sighed. "I'm not saying He won't use us along the way, but it does relieve my mind to know that I don't have to work so hard to accomplish His goals, if that makes sense."

"It makes perfect sense." Alanna slipped an arm around Katie's shoulders. "More than you know. I have my struggles too, you know. It's been hard to trust the Lord with the finer points of my life."

"Oh?"

"I mean, I've always trusted Him for the little things, like making sure I get invited to the best parties and attend the finest schools. But I've rarely trusted Him with the things that really count. In the grand scheme of things, does it really matter if Sally Nelson invites you to her latest soiree or whether Peter Jamison adds you to the list of guests to spend Saturday afternoon on his father's yacht?"

Katie grinned. "What a life."

"Yes, what a life, indeed. I was raised to make much of little and little of much. I've cared too much about things that mean nothing at all and not enough about the things that really matter."

"We're opposites and yet we're alike, as well." Katie gave her a warm smile. "When it comes right down to it, we're both working, working, working toward a goal." She sighed. "I can't speak for you, of course, but in all of my working, I've worked myself right out of the kind of peace you were referring to earlier. It eludes me when I'm angry and frustrated at folks who deliberately rile me up—like Tanner, for instance."

"Who, me?" Tanner pursed his lips.

"He just does it to get your goat," Alanna said, stifling a giggle. "Trust me. I know him pretty well by now. He thrives on such banter."

"Get my goat?" Katie laughed through her tears. "There you go again, Alanna. You always bring a smile to my face with your expressions."

"Happy to be of service." Alanna grinned, no longer insulted by Katie's teasing.

"But what I want to say is quite serious." Katie's expression shifted. "The most important thing God has shown me through our friendship—the thing I've had a hard time confessing until now—is that I'm not meant to be in control. I have such a hard time releasing my hold on things, especially things that I care deeply about."

Alanna sighed. "Me too." Indeed. Hadn't she struggled to give this whole situation to the Lord also?

Katie rose and brushed off her skirt. "I can't help thinking about one thing, though. It torments me, in fact."

"What's that?" Alanna stood alongside her.

"You know me. I claim to be a pacifist, but I most assuredly go to battle over the things I believe in." Katie gazed at her with such intensity that Alanna could feel the emotion driving the wrinkled nose and furrowed brow. "That's how passionate I am. But what if we get everything we hope for and it's still not enough? What if this was never about our rights in the first place?"

Alanna didn't say anything right away, realizing that Katie needed time to think this through and come up with an answer for herself.

Tanner cleared his throat and extended an arm in Katie's direction. "I can promise you, the only one in our midst with any rights worth worrying about is that baby. She has the right to a blissful first day of life, free from strife." A delicious aroma wafted up the stairs. Smelled like pumpkin and nutmeg. "And because I rode in that ridiculous sleigh all the way home and back again, I have the right to get first dibs on the pumpkin pie."

"Oh no, you don't." Katie said. "There are more than a dozen other people here, Tanner. You need to let the ladies go first."

He sighed. "I guess it is the gentlemanly thing to do." A quick wink followed as he looked Alanna's way. "And we all know I thrive on being a gentleman."

"Just don't become a dandy." Katie dried her eyes and offered a weak smile. "I don't think I could take it if you get too citified."

"Trust me, that will never happen."

All three of them laughed in unison. The tantalizing scents from downstairs were too much to refuse, so Tanner led the way down the steps. As they neared the bottom, he turned back to look at Alanna, who didn't even try to hold back the coy smile. Why, oh, why, had she rejected his kisses in the barn? Why had she feigned disinterest? Was that really just this morning? Oh, how she longed for those kisses now that she could see everything in the proper light.

Yes, whether he knew it or not, Tanner Jacobs had stolen a piece of her heart. Not that she wanted it back. Oh no. She would much prefer to tie it up with a ribbon and a bow and offer it to him once and for all—the perfect gift for the perfect day.

NINETEEN

Christmas is behind us, ladies. Rarely have I been this reflective at the onset of a new year, but with the possibility of war hovering over us, I cannot help but look ahead. Those who know me can attest to the fact that I am opposed to war. However, that does not mean I have no empathy for those who will serve our country. On the contrary—my thoughts and prayers are with them. I may never see a literal battlefield, but I know what it is to fight in the spirit. With this new year, I recommit myself to enter that battle afresh... on my knees.

—Ellie Cannady, editor of *The Modern Suffragette*

* * * * *

LESS THAN A WEEK AFTER Christmas, Tanner left his post at Fort Missoula with a heavy heart. His visit with the company doctor had not gone as he had hoped. In spite of his zealous attempts to convince Doc Keller that he should be allowed to fight for his country, the answer was a resounding no. Thanks to a childhood illness he could scarcely remember, Tanner would never serve his country on the battlefield, at least according to the doctor. Now he must find a way to aid in the war effort from home.

These feelings of conflict that rose inside of him could not be squelched, though he fought to convince himself it was for the best. He was needed at home. This, he'd been reminded of, time and time again. But with the ever-present realization that Alanna would be leaving to go back to Savannah as soon as the snows melted, he could no longer abide the idea of staying in Montana.

Somehow, he must reconcile the feelings warring within him, and he must do so in a quiet way so that Alanna would be none the wiser. Not to mention Mama. As much as he'd hoped to fight for his country, the idea of leaving the ranch caused all sorts of conflicting feelings to arise. Would they ever subside?

After leaving the fort, he headed into town to the mercantile to pick up supplies before going back to the ranch. He stopped in front of the art gallery with his heart in his throat as he realized that his painting in the front window had gone missing. Not that it really mattered. In his current frame of mind, Tanner didn't want to think about his paintings. Maybe he would never paint again. Not until after the war, anyway. Stepping away from the canvas and brush would be his silent rebellion for not getting to do the one thing he felt most called to do—fight.

As he stared through the glass at the empty spot where the beautiful landscape had been, Tanner was reminded of his sister's words: "I do wonder why it is that men are happiest when they're fighting."

He shook off the frustrations that rose up at the reminder

then turned his attentions to loading his purchases into the car. No point in fretting over what could never be. If he couldn't cross the globe to tend to the needs of his country, he could at the very least take care of things at home.

* * * * *

IN THE WEEKS AFTER GIVEN'S birth, Alanna grew increasingly more concerned about Margaret's mood. Things grew to a frightening point on a Saturday morning after Brett headed out to tend to the cattle. Margaret lay in the bed, weeping and unable—or unwilling—to hold the baby. Alanna took over the responsibility of Given's care as the tears flowed on Margaret's end. She eased her way out of the bedroom, babe in hand, to give her sister some privacy.

"I don't know what to make of it," she said to Mama a few minutes later as they met in the parlor. Gazing into the infant's beautiful eyes, she sighed. "Your mama's struggling, little one."

"It's not uncommon after giving birth," Mama said. "Happened to me when Tessa was born, remember?"

Alanna tried to recount the memory but could not. "What is the cause of it?"

Mama released a little sigh as she reached down to take baby Given from Alanna's arms. "I can't say why it happens, but the doctor called it the blues. Said it's common among women who've just given birth." She gave the infant several light kisses on her brow.

"Very odd. How long does it last?"

"No idea, though I did know a lady once who suffered terribly for months."

A gripping sensation seized Alanna's heart. "You don't think that will happen to Margaret, do you?"

"Surely not." Mama shrugged off the idea as she laid Given down on the edge of the sofa and began the task of changing her diaper. "She's a strong, sturdy girl. We all know that. She'll snap out of this soon enough, I daresay."

"I hope so."

"And in the meantime, I'll send Tanner for the doctor. Margaret will just think he's following up on the birth of the baby. We can ask for his advice."

"Good idea. I would feel better."

As her mother handed off the freshly diapered baby and disappeared into the kitchen, Alanna fought to keep her focus on the matter at hand. She couldn't help but think of all those speeches Margaret had given about women's equality. It seemed in the past couple of weeks, she'd climbed into a hole of her own choosing—one that left her vulnerable, weepy, and somewhat irrational. Not at all the strong, liberated soul she'd once been.

But what could be done about it?

Alanna could only think of one thing—prayer. She would offer up a plea to the Almighty to spare her sister from whatever anguish she might be facing.

She headed back up to Margaret's room and found her sister sleeping. With little else to do, Alanna paced the room, keeping a watchful eye on baby Given, finally placing her in the cradle as she dozed. Of course, watching a sleeping infant took very little effort.

Minutes later the babe let out a cry, and Margaret startled awake. She sat up in the bed, a wild-eyed look coming over her. "Is that the baby?"

"Yes." Alanna peeked into the cradle, happy to find the infant had settled down. "But she's gone back to sleep. You should do the same."

"I feel as if I sleep all the time now." Margaret rested her head against the pillow. "So much for saying I'm a pillar of strength."

"You've just had a baby. It takes time to recover. Besides, you were up half the night. I heard you pacing the floor in between feedings."

"My schedule is off-kilter. I don't know night from day anymore. And when I am awake, I feel as if I have no energy at all." Margaret shifted her position. "I've never been one to take to my bed, even in the worst of circumstances." Her eyes filled with moisture and she shook her head. "I don't know what's come over me. I really don't."

"Try not to fret, Margaret. Please."

"There's just so much to think about, now that Given's here."

"Like what?"

Margaret propped herself up and sighed. "I'm starting to think that you were right all along."

"About what?"

"About going back home to Savannah."

Alanna's heart twisted. "Do you really mean that?"

"I—I don't know. I just know that life here is difficult. When I look into Given's precious face, when I see those tiny hands and beautiful eyes, I wonder if she's going to be strong enough to last in these surroundings. I wish she had a proper layette, one like we had as girls. I can't give her anything like that here. She will never have a fancy cradle or delicate clothes." Margaret buried her face into her pillow. A muffled, "What was I thinking?" followed.

Alanna stroked her sister's hair. "You were thinking it would be wonderful to spend your life in a new place with a man who loves you more than life itself."

Margaret lifted her teary face and sniffled. "Y–yes."

"And you were thinking it would be lovely to have your daughter share in the adventure of growing up in a place where she can experience new and wonderful things with a freedom women in the South cannot."

"Yes." A half smile lit Margaret's face. "You always know just what to say to cheer me up, Lana."

"Usually it's the other way around, but I will accept the compliment. Just promise me you will rest easy. You need to stay strong for the baby, and that's not going to happen if you're exhausted."

Margaret yawned. "I will. I promise. And in case I haven't said it before, thank you."

"For what?"

"For coming all this way to be with me." Tears covered her lashes. "It means the world to me, Lana. Having my sisters here is such a blessing."

"I'm the one who's blessed."

"That makes two of us, then." Margaret's eyes fluttered closed, and before long her gentle breathing eased into a soft snore.

Alanna's thoughts shifted to Tanner. She couldn't help but feel some concern, knowing he planned to see the doctor this morning.

A shiver ran down her spine, and she whispered a prayer for the Lord's will to be done. Every time she envisioned him heading off to some strange place to fight for his country, her heart felt as if it would break in two. Then again, every time she thought about going back home to Savannah, her heart felt equally as heavy. Still, the inevitable road stretched out before her, beckoning her home.

Determined to shake off her uneasiness, Alanna headed downstairs to brew some tea. Perhaps it would warm her from the inside out and remove the never-ending chill that seemed to grip her heart when she thought about leaving.

She found Katie in the kitchen with Mama and Tessa and greeted her with a warm hug. "How are you doing, Katie?"

"Doing quite well, thank you. I've just had the most glorious news. Ellie Cannady is doing a bit better."

"That's wonderful news."

"I'm headed to her house now for a visit. Just stopped by to invite Tessa along, but she's keen on staying here with the baby. Would you like to join me instead?"

"You want me to meet Ellie? In person?" Alanna set the kettle to brew and considered Katie's suggestion. "I'm still not convinced that we would get along, to be quite honest. I find her writings thought-provoking, especially these past few weeks, but they do not move me to change my opinion on the matter at hand."

"I'm not trying to persuade you to change, Alanna," Katie said. "That is not my goal. You've had the benefit of a college education—not something many can boast. I simply thought you would enjoy meeting another woman with a similar background."

"Similar background?"

"Yes. Ellie was raised in the South as well. She attended Sweet Briar, in Virginia. Her sister is Patricia Cannady of the Amherst Cannadys."

"Are you serious?"

"Very. She's a well-bred Southern woman. In fact, she's only lived in the Northwest for a few years. She came because her husband wanted to chase after his dream to own a ranch."

"She's...married?"

"Well, not anymore. But her husband was quite well-known in these parts as an excellent rancher. I daresay he garnered more acclaim than she has, and that's really saying something, since she works so hard on behalf of women."

"I see."

Only, she didn't. Why did Katie say that Ellie was once married but was married no more? Had her liberal ways driven away her husband?

A shiver ran down Alanna's spine. This speculation was the only thing that made sense. Strong women like these suffragettes were apt to drive away men who could not tolerate their aggressive side. Surely this Ellie Cannady, whoever she was, must've ruled her roost with an iron fist for her husband to bolt out the door.

"What do you say, Alanna?" Katie gave her a curious look. "Would you like to meet her?"

"You should go, honey," her mother said. "And don't worry about Margaret and the baby. Tessa and I are happy to stay here and tend to them. Besides, it might be fun to visit with someone who hails from our neck of the woods. You never know—you and Ellie could end up being fast friends."

"I rather doubt it," Alanna said. She turned back to Katie. "But you've piqued my curiosity, for sure. I think it might be an interesting way to spend an afternoon, as long as you're sure she's up to having guests."

"As for how she's feeling, the doctor says her recovery has been nothing short of a miracle. From the day we held our Sleigh Belles rally, her health has improved. Isn't that remarkable?"

"Very."

"I do wonder how to go about spreading the word that she's doing better." Katie said. "Many of our Sleigh Belles from across the state have been planning to come to Missoula for her funeral, you see."

"Might be a problem, should she choose to live." Alanna suppressed a smile.

"A happy problem, to be sure. Still, I have to wonder what we'll do with so many women from across the state, should they descend on us at once."

"Surely they won't come unless..." Alanna didn't complete her sentence. "Well, you know."

"Hope not. But you know how these women can be. They're a little impulsive at times."

"So I've noticed." Alanna quirked a brow, and Katie laughed.

"I probably deserved that, after all I've put you through." Her expression brightened. "So, what do you say, Alanna? Ready to meet the woman behind the words? The one who's penned so many wonderful articles on our behalf?"

"As ready as I'll ever be," Alanna said. She reached for her coat, wondering how in the world she'd been tricked into going.

Surely this was all a ploy to win her over to the suffragette way of thinking. She wouldn't play into their hands. No, sir.

She would, however, enjoy a ride in the sleigh across fields of creamy white snow. And she would meet the infamous Ellie Cannady, if for no other reason than to say she'd finally done so. Perhaps in doing so, she could accomplish two things at once: first, figure out what sort of woman was behind this suffragette nonsense, and second, use her Southern charm to persuade Ellie Cannady to lay down her arms once and for all.

TWENTY

Folks who meet me face-to-face are often surprised to find such a spitfire wrapped up in a tiny little package. I can attest to the fact that tenacity has nothing to do with size or age. Or health, for that matter, though I must confess that my ability to fight fire with fire has diminished greatly as I've undergone physical challenges in recent months. Still, the spirit is strong, though the flesh is weak. Lest you think I'm giving up—or giving in—think again. I will rise from the ashes and live to fight another day. Of this, you can be quite sure.

—Ellie Cannady, editor of *The Modern Suffragette*

* * * * *

THE JOURNEY TO ELLIE'S HOUSE took longer than Alanna expected. She shivered beneath the quilts as the sleigh jingled its way across the snowpacked roads; her back was stiff and her lips numb. "My g–goodness." Her teeth chattered so hard, she could barely get the words out. "She l–lives a long w–way from t–town."

"Yes, she is rather secluded. Her ranch is near the base of the mountains. But she likes it that way." Katie snapped the reins, urging the horse along. This, of course, only served to intensify the sound of the bells.

"She lives on a ranch?" Alanna raised her voice to be heard above the bells.

"Well, it belonged to her husband's family," Katie countered.

"I'm not sure I understand." *Did she acquire it in the divorce?*

Katie pointed to a vast expanse of land up ahead. "We're almost to Ellie's place. I think you're going to love her ranch. And you'll love Ellie too, I just know it."

The ranch, as Katie described it, turned out to be a large spread seated upon a beautiful mountainous backdrop. Covered in glistening mounds of snow, the expansive barn drew her eye at once. What really took her breath away, however, was the house. A true ranch-style beauty, it sat atop a hill overlooking the acreage, which glistened white underneath a cloudless sky.

Katie pulled the sleigh up to the house and made quick work of tending to the horse, getting him settled underneath warm blankets.

"Are you ready?" She turned to Alanna, who nodded. They made their way to the front door of the house and Katie knocked before calling out a "Yoo-hoo!"

The door creaked open after a few moments of waiting. Alanna tried not to gasp aloud as she laid eyes on Ellie Cannady for the first time. A frail, slightly hunched woman—probably not more than four foot eleven—greeted them at the door. Wisps of silvery-white hair sat thin upon her pink scalp, and blue-gray eyes twinkled with mischief as she looked their way. Her soft, wrinkled cheeks spread into a buttery smile as she saw Katie.

"Oh, you darling girl." Ellie extended her arms and gestured for a hug, her hands and voice trembling. "You've come for a visit. I heard the bells and my heart took to flight. What a wonderful surprise."

"So happy to be here." Katie swept the older woman into her arms and pressed a couple of kisses into her hair. "And you look to be in fine shape, Ellie. After giving us such a scare." She gave her a scolding look. "Shame on you for worrying us."

Ellie waved her trembling hand and ushered them inside the warmth of the house.. "Well, worry no more. I'm alive and well." A pause followed. "It's your doing. All of you, I mean." Her expression grew more serious. "I've sensed your prayers, Katie Ann. You've been lifting me up to the throne room, haven't you?"

"I have." Katie grinned. "And so have the other Sleigh Belles. We've had a prayer vigil going for some time."

"Well, don't stop now. Doc Keller came by a couple of days ago and told me I'm nothing short of a living, breathing miracle. I owe it in part to you wonderful girls. I must also give credit to the good doctor. His treatment of my weakened lungs has proven effective in holding the lupus at bay. Such a terrible disease, this is. But, as I said, the whole thing is rather miraculous. Most folks in my condition would have succumbed."

"I've always enjoyed a good miracle." Katie grinned. "Particularly one of biblical proportions such as this."

"Me too. Especially one that gives me extra time on this earth with lovely young friends like you." Ellie gave Katie another hug then turned her attention to Alanna, the wrinkles around her eyes deepening as she took her in. "Whom have we here?"

Katie gave Alanna a little nudge forward. "I've brought a friend, Ellie. This is Alanna Lessing."

"Alanna." Ellie spoke her name with great tenderness, as if they were old friends parted by time and space. "I've heard so much about you from your sister."

"Y–you've met Tessa?" Alanna could hardly believe it. Why, Tessa had never mentioned meeting Ellie Cannady in person.

"Met her?" Ellie chuckled. "Well, of course. She and Katie brought me meals on at least three different occasions when I was at my worst. What a blessed girl she is. Those oatmeal cookies were by far my favorite. Ate every last one of them." She grinned. "Well, what my great-grandbabies didn't steal, anyway."

"I will tell Mama. She and Mrs. Jacobs baked them." *And to think I suspected Tessa of stealing those cookies.*

"Come and give me a hug."

She took a couple of tentative steps toward Ellie, wondering if a hug might injure the poor woman. How could this petite little thing, hardly big enough to handle a pot of stew, corral hundreds of women to action? Perhaps her strength came from inside, not out.

"Don't be shy now." Ellie wrapped her in a surprisingly tight embrace. "In spite of appearances, I won't break, sweet girl. Of that, you can be sure."

"All right, then." Alanna returned the embrace. Afterward, she stepped back and smiled, finally shaking off the bitter cold that had gripped her all the way over in the sleigh. "Thank you for having me in your home, Ellie. It's lovely." She glanced around, taking in the beautiful needlework pieces on the walls. "Did you stitch these yourself?"

"Certainly did." Ellie took a few hunched steps to an exquisite needlework piece on the wall to their right. "I've enjoyed needlework from the time I was a young girl. Back in those days, we spent hours developing our handiwork so the fellas would think us talented." A frail but sweet ripple of laughter followed from Ellie. "These days I can't see well enough to thread the needle. But if I could, I would stitch just to rest my mind. There's something so precious about creating a thing of beauty. And driving the needle in and out of the cloth repetitively brings a certain sense of calm."

Alanna wanted to ask the obvious question: "Don't suffragettes find such work menial?" but refrained. Instead, she smiled and said, "They're lovely. Truly."

"Thank you." Ellie paused and gazed at her. "Where are you from, Alanna? You have the most wonderful Southern accent. I would guess you hail from my home state of Virginia."

"Georgia, actually. I'm from Savannah."

"So happy to meet a Southern sister." Ellie reached over to give her hand a squeeze. "Your lovely accent tickles my ears and makes me wish I had the energy to travel home to see my younger sister." A lingering sigh followed. "Perhaps one day she will come here to see me. One can hope, anyway."

"Oh, I wish you could visit Savannah," Alanna said. "It's a glorious city, filled with every good thing."

"I've seen it firsthand. Visited a few years back." Hunched and moving at a snail's pace, Ellie made her way over to the sofa, where she gestured for the girls to take a seat. "Made a trip down to support a good friend just after my dear husband passed on. Perhaps you know her. Her name is Juliette Low."

"Juliette Low?" Alanna could hardly believe her ears. "The woman who founded the scouting organization for girls?"

"Yes." With a pained expression on her face, Ellie settled into the rocking chair across from the sofa. "She lives in Savannah."

"I know. Of course. She's quite well-known and certainly well-loved. I've met her at several social functions. Juliette is a lovely lady, admired by all."

Ellie pulled an afghan over her knees, and Katie rose to help her tuck it in around the edges. The elderly woman lovingly gazed at the younger. "Would you mind tending to the fire, Katie? You always do a better job than I do."

"I would be happy to." Katie crossed to the woodstove, where she stoked the fire.

Ellie continued to share, her voice a bit more animated. "Do you know Juliette's personal story?"

"Not at all." Alanna rested against the sofa, her gaze traveling between Ellie and Katie, the latter continuing to fuss over Ellie's well-being.

"She was married for many years to a man who did not love her or treat her well. He repeatedly asked her for a divorce, but she would not acquiesce. Then, one day, she arrived home to find him with his mistress."

"Oh no." Alanna brought her hand to her mouth as she absorbed this news. Why, in all her social interactions with

Juliette, she'd never heard this story. "That poor woman."

"Yes. Juliette finally agreed to give the man the divorce he sought, but in the end, he passed away before it was final. Quite a tragic tale."

"I had no idea."

"You see, Alanna, even in the South, women are impacted by the issues we have fought so hard for in the Northwest."

Heaviness settled into Alanna's heart as she realized the purpose of this conversation. Why were these crazy suffragettes so intent on winning her over? "What do you mean?"

"It's a sobering truth, but if you must know, Juliette's husband—that scoundrel—left everything he owned to his mistress, not his wife."

Alanna gasped. "Surely you jest."

"No. Not at all. He made an allowance for Juliette, but it had to pass through the hands of the mistress first."

Her thoughts tumbled as she tried to absorb this news. "That's the most horrible thing I've ever heard."

"One of the most horrible, to be sure. But justice prevailed. Juliette appealed to the courts, and they granted her the widow's portion."

"Thank goodness."

"Yes, thank goodness. It was, of course, the right thing to do. But what thrills my soul when I think of sweet Juliette is this—she did not let what happened to her stop her from moving forward and founding the organization you mentioned earlier."

"The Girl Scouts?"

"Indeed." Ellie paused and drew several labored breaths.

"Just a few years back she met a wonderful man—Robert Baden-Powell, the founder of the Boy Scouts. He and his wife Olave encouraged her to reach out to girls in much the same way he was reaching out to boys—to teach those youngsters how to be strong and develop character so that they could thrive and give back to their communities."

"I see."

"Do you, Alanna? Do you see the primary purpose we women serve? The Lord put us here to serve—not as slaves, but as women who can hold our heads up high and make a difference in our circle of influence. That's where Juliette excels even to this day. She holds her head up. She doesn't allow what happened to her to stop her from impacting the lives of others."

"What a wonderful story. The next time I see her at a function in Savannah, I will see her in an entirely new light."

Odd...as soon as Alanna spoke the words "in Savannah," the strangest pain pierced her heart. For, while she longed for the comfort of the South, her heart—at least for the moment—remained rooted in Missoula.

When had that happened?

Katie drew near. "Alanna, are you all right? You're not looking well."

"Oh, I–I'm fine." She forced a smile and kept talking. "I only wish I'd known about Juliette earlier so I could have lent her my support. I've contributed to her cause, of course, but would have given even more if I'd known."

"And isn't that the point?" Ellie's eyes misted over. "Women caring about other women? Women making sure that no one is overlooked or left out? That's truly what the suffrage movement is about. We care about those who are suffering, plain and simple."

"I—I never really thought about it like that before."

"No doubt you envisioned us a wild pack, despising men and demanding our rights. Is that it?" Ellie leaned back against her chair, looking more exhausted than before.

"I suppose you're right. That has been the picture in my head."

"One you gleaned from newspaper headlines, no doubt."

"I suppose."

"Well, then, I challenge you to visit with Juliette firsthand when you return to Savannah for a closer look at a woman who's changing the landscape of society for other women. Perhaps you Southern belles just need an example to follow. She's a fine one."

"She is, indeed."

"You know, I think some women have it wrong. They think that the suffrage movement is self-focused. Nothing could be further from the truth. Our primary calling is to care for the needs of others—just as Katie and Tessa have done for me over the past several weeks, and just as many of our local women did after my precious husband passed on. Plain and simple, it's a matter of seeing a need in a sister and doing what you can to meet it."

"The Golden Rule," Alanna whispered.

"Yes. And the story of the Good Samaritan, all rolled into one." A lovely smile lit Ellie's face as she turned to face Katie. "Which reminds me—I really must thank you, Katie."

"For what, Ellie?"

"I've been so energized by the news of all the recent activity from our local ladies. The Sleigh Belles' rally was a tremendous success. I understand that you raised a lot of money for the cause." Her eyes misted over, and she brushed away the tears.

"Yes. And women, came from all over the region to participate. I think you would have been proud of the Sleigh Belles, Ellie."

"Oh, I am. It just brings my heart such joy to know that women are realizing their God-given potential. When I look around, I see gals who used to think so little of themselves. Now they're working in the community, caring for the poor, reaching out to the widows...truly, all the things the Bible calls us to do. To give of oneself is the most liberating thing of all."

"I do believe you're right." Katie's broad smile shared her feelings on the matter.

Over the next hour or so Alanna listened in as Ellie continued to share her thoughts on the women's movement. Her version sounded very much like a sermon one would hear in church, not a hard-fisted political speech. By the end of it, Alanna could almost see herself joining in the ranks of women to care for those less fortunate.

By the time they parted ways, her thoughts on Ellie—and on all things related to the suffrage movement—had changed significantly.

Only when she found herself alone in the sleigh with Katie, however, did she feel comfortable asking the question that had tormented her all day. "Why didn't you tell me?"

"Tell you what?" Katie glanced her way.

"That Ellie Cannady was elderly. That she has great-grandchildren."

Katie looked perplexed by the question. "I'm sorry. I thought you knew."

"Not at all. I knew she had been ill, of course, but I never imagined her to be elderly. After reading her articles, I envisioned her to be my age—militant in voice and strong in stature. The woman I met today was—"

"Anything but."

"Yes."

Katie gave her a compassionate look. "Alanna, maybe you've had an incorrect view of the suffrage movement overall. There are a few who get carried away at times, but we usually repent. We're passionate, of course, as most people are about the causes they support. But, honestly, most are just ordinary women striving for better lives for themselves and others, primarily their own daughters."

"I see that now."

"I'm glad. And like Ellie said, one of our key purposes is to tend to the needs of the widows and the orphans, as the Bible instructs. In order to be freed up to do that, we have to raise awareness in the political arena. Here in Montana we're already blessed to have the right to vote. Not all states have afforded women such a privilege."

Alanna shook her head as she thought it through. "I daresay it will be a long time in coming for our fair state of Georgia. Folks don't seem to grasp the idea the same way they do here."

"For the very reason you were once so opposed, I would imagine. An incorrect perception of what we are trying to do. But we can turn that perception around in a hurry if we care for the needs of others before our own. Then people will see what we're really all about."

Alanna shifted her gaze from the gorgeous mountains in the

distance to the shimmer in Katie's tear-filled eyes. "I'm finally seeing it, Katie. And I think I'm finally seeing you for the first time too."

"I'm glad." Katie reached over and gave Alanna's hand a squeeze. "I know I've come across as a fool at times. I do hope you will forgive me for that."

"Silly girl. As you said, you were—or, rather, are—very passionate. But when I think about the widows and orphans, I get passionate too. It's the role of the church to care for folks in need. We don't always do the best job, so it's probably good that the suffragettes have made the less-fortunate their mission as well."

"We've always cared about those less fortunate, Alanna. Perhaps I've just been been so zealous about the political end of things that you couldn't see the forest for the trees."

Alanna didn't respond because her thoughts were elsewhere. Had she really misjudged these women? Were their motives somewhat different than she had imagined? How could she fault Katie and Tessa, who so clearly excelled in the area of caring for others?

Alanna's thoughts shifted back to that day on the train when she'd watched her sister care for the little ones in need of food. Tessa had given up her own dessert—even handed over her daily fruit portions to the children she met. Perhaps she'd always been a suffragette.

Maybe she's just been Christlike all along and I didn't see it.

"If this is what it means to be a suffragette—caring for those in need—I suppose I've been a supporter of the women's movement all along. I just never understood it till now. Why, back in Savannah, I always championed causes to care for women and children in need. Just last year I hosted a fund-raiser to provide indoor plumbing at the orphan's home."

Katie urged the horse forward through the snow then turned to face her with a crooked grin. "You've been one of us all along, sister."

Alanna swallowed hard as Katie used the word "sister." For whatever reason, she thought of Tanner, of his impulsive marriage proposal. He hadn't meant it, of course. But if he had—if the whole thing hadn't been a joke—Katie might've been her sister after all.

Of course, that could never really happen. In just a few short weeks, she would be going back to Savannah—for good.

Katie dove into a lengthy speech about all the wonderful things Alanna could do for the suffrage movement once she arrived home, but Alanna scarcely heard a word of it. Her heart lodged in her throat, making it impossible to speak. For while she wanted to think of serving women and children in need back in Savannah, she had to realize the truth of it. Her heart wasn't in Savannah at all.

It was right here—in Montana.

TWENTY-ONE

The onset of a new year is the perfect time to speak to the issue of passion. Passion drives us. Fuels us. Gives us the energy we need to get things done even when we don't feel like doing them. It can spill over onto others and catch fire, not unlike the great wildfires we have witnessed here in Montana in years past. But passion can also be misunderstood or misread. In our zeal, we must not deliberately offend or paint others as our enemies. Instead, we should seek the heart of God and ask Him daily: "Lord, fill me with Your passion for others so that I might better serve them and, in doing so, serve You."

—Ellie Cannady, editor of *The Modern Suffragette*

* * * * *

TANNER READ ELLIE CANNADY'S ARTICLE one last time, bothered by what he'd read. Not that he disagreed with Mrs. Cannady's thoughts. No, for weeks now he'd found himself reading her articles with greater interest than before, finding them almost—familiar.

A little too familiar, in fact.

It didn't take long to come to a conclusion on the matter: while he believed these to be the thoughts of Ellie Cannady, they were most assuredly the words of his younger sister, Katie. How many times had he heard her use the expression "paint others as our enemies?" And hadn't she just told him three days ago, after coming down from an hour of hiding away in her room with her writing tablet, that she needed to repent for being overly zealous? Those words had been followed by a comment about serving God by serving others.

Yep. She'd definitely written this week's article, at the very least.

He paced the kitchen, taking adequate time to think this through. Perhaps the situation with Ellie was worse than he'd feared. Maybe she had passed away and the Sleigh Belles were keeping the news from the community. Or, perhaps her health had deteriorated to such a point that she needed someone else to take over her column permanently, someone who could convey her thoughts in a similar voice and style. Katie would be the logical candidate, of course. He shivered as the word *candidate* slipped through his mind. Next thing he knew, his younger sister would be running for Congress and challenging Jeanette Rankin for her seat.

He willed his thoughts to slow down and then walked to the foot of the stairs. "Katie?" He called out her name, ready to get this conversation behind them. "Can you come downstairs for a minute?"

She appeared at the top of the stairs, dressed in her hat and coat.

"What is it, Tanner? I'm about to leave for Margaret's place. I'm taking a meal for the family. Margaret's still not well, you know."

"Yes, I know. But what I have to say needs to be said here, in the house. Once we get in that sleigh I'll be addlepated from all the bell-ringing."

"All right." She perched on the sofa and removed her hat. "What has you troubled? I see the worry lines between your eyes. What have I done this time? I will repent right away, I assure you. I'm a changed woman."

"Yes, well, this is not an accusation, mind you. I'm just curious about something."

"What is that?"

He paused and then blurted out the question. "When did you begin writing Ellie Cannady's articles for her?"

"W–what?" Katie paled and fussed with the ribbons on her hat.

"All along, you've said that Ellie Cannady has been writing them."

"It's, well, it's her column, for sure." Katie offered what appeared to be a forced smile. "She's been writing it for years, you know."

"Yes, but from what I understand, during the last few weeks the tone of her pieces has changed slightly. Some would say the words don't even sound like hers."

"Oh?" Katie's gaze shifted to the ground. "Well, she hasn't been well."

"Katie."

She didn't respond, so he tried again.

"Katie."

This time she looked his way, chewing on her lower lip. "Yes?"

"When did you take over for Ellie?"

"I, um—"

He raised his index finger, convinced he already knew the answer. "I'm guessing about three months ago. That sounds about right. That's when you started disappearing into your room for hours on end with your writing tablet. You were in there crafting articles."

Katie's mouth closed—always a sign that she had something to hide. "Is there something specific that makes you think I've been writing her columns?"

"C'mon, now. That last bit about passion being like a wildfire? That didn't sound a bit like Ellie Cannady. And didn't we just have a conversation to that effect last week?"

With a wave of the hand, Katie appeared to dismiss that idea. "Well, that's just silly. Ellie has many facets to her. I'm sure she's witnessed a few wildfires in her day."

"But she's also been very ill, which makes me wonder how she could possibly produce such beautifully written articles while in poor health."

"You think they're beautifully written?" Katie perked up at this news, her smile a little too bright.

"Very." If nothing else, he would win Katie over with flattery. "They're getting better by the week, in fact."

"Do you really think so?" She pursed her lips and giggled. Just as quickly, she snapped to attention, donned her hat, and stood. "Well, for your information, Ellie is feeling much better. If you don't believe me, ask Alanna. We went to see her last week. She can tell you that the Lord has been gracious and is doing a fine job of bringing our fearless leader back around."

While he was relieved to hear this news, Tanner still knew that Ellie had not written those articles—at least not the most recent ones.

"I'm grateful she's on the mend. Still, I can't help but notice how the tone of her articles has changed substantially over the past few months. It's not that she's softening, per se. It's something else, as well."

"Oh?" Katie gazed off into the distance. Just as quickly, she looked back with astonishment on her face. "Wait a minute. Since when do you read *The Modern Suffragette*?"

"Since the very first time you asked me to help you with one of your projects. Don't think for a minute that I would contribute to a cause unless I researched it."

"Well, yes, but you've always acted as though the women's movement was wrong in every conceivable way. If you've been reading the articles…"

"Then likely I have softened in my stance." He gave her a compassionate look. "Though I have a feeling it has little to do with Ellie, as I said, and more to do with you. So answer me plain, Katie. Have you been writing those pieces?"

She released a puff of air, and her shoulders slumped forward. "Maybe one or two."

"Mm-hmm. And who wrote the others?"

Katie gave him a hopeful look. "You aren't going to ask which two I wrote?"

"Don't have to. You wrote the one on the merging of the two suffrage associations, and I'm convinced you penned this week's offering on passion."

"Yep. You know me well. And if you must know, Margaret

wrote the one on taxation without representation. The one about the role of the sexes was Tessa."

"Tessa is writing for Ellie now too? Does her mama know?"

"Does she know?" Katie laughed. "Tanner, you don't know women at all, do you? Her mama helped her craft the article. Even told her to add the tribute to Jeanette Rankin." Katie paused and gave him a pensive look. "But just so you know, Ellie has been writing them too, even in her hour of need. She's penned some beautiful pieces, weakened condition or not. Did you read the one about leaving a legacy? And the article about physical challenges? She wrote both of those, though terribly ill at the time."

"I see." He shook his head and chuckled. "But it boggles the mind that you ladies have done this and managed to keep it a secret."

"For months, just as you guessed." Her eyes twinkled as she adjusted her hat. "Speaking of secrets, I'm not the only one who's good at keeping them. You're pretty good at it as well."

"What do you mean?"

Katie's eyes glistened. "Have you told Alanna about the paintings yet?"

"I thought we agreed not to discuss that."

"You agreed. I did not."

His heart quickened. "Katie, let's stick to the subject. When the time is right, I will tell Alanna about the paintings. But there's a specific reason I brought up the articles today. There's a rumor going around town that Ellie hasn't been writing them, and I'm afraid it's gathering momentum as we speak."

Katie paled and sat once again. "Really?"

"Yes. You know how Douglas Cain is, over at the *Missoulian*.

He's been out to get Ellie from the get-go. I have no doubt he will use this as fodder for his upcoming political satires. He will say that you ladies took advantage of the other women by putting words in Ellie's mouth, and he will say that you were deceptive in penning the articles under her name."

"Pooh on that. Someone had to do it. Ellie wasn't able to. And besides, she's shared her heart with us so many times that we knew what to say. Perhaps we didn't say it using exactly her words, but our motives were pure and our hearts in the right place."

"Only, you let people believe they were Ellie's articles. Douglas will say that you did so deliberately to lead people astray."

Katie looked at him as if he'd grown two heads. "I don't like to repeat myself, Tanner, but you leave me no choice. She's been terribly ill. And our thoughts on paper were really hers, anyway. Ellie has mentored us for years. We know her backward and forward."

"So you were just her mouthpiece?"

"Ugh! How you put things. Can't you just admit that what we did for Ellie was nice? It was a kind gesture on our part to keep her column going when she was ill. Besides, the ladies wouldn't care even if they did know."

"All right. So then tell them."

"W–what?"

"Tell them. In the next article, tell the truth. Let folks know what you've been doing—and why."

"I—I wouldn't dare."

"This is going to come back to haunt you if you don't get it out into the open. Trust me. I've already heard from Brett, who spoke with Douglas yesterday morning. Douglas is convinced something is amiss with Ellie's columns. He and Ellie have been at odds for years, you know, and he would like nothing more than to bring her—and the whole movement—down."

"Yes, I know. That's the primary reason we kept the column going, so that he wouldn't feel he'd backed her into a corner or somehow convinced her to give up the fight."

"Well, go on fighting, but do so in an open and honest way. The women will forgive you for leading them on if you explain. See if you can get a quote from Ellie to add to the next column. Or do an 'as told to' piece."

"Tanner, that's a wonderful idea." Katie reached up to give him a peck on the cheek. "Thank you, thank you!"

"You're welcome."

She took a few steps toward the door then turned back. "If you don't mind my asking, why in the world are you helping me fix this? I thought you were opposed to the suffrage movement. Has your opinion really changed that much?"

"Like any issue, it's always harder to resist when it hits closer to home." Tanner's expression tightened. "I don't want to see you hurt. If he runs an exposé or some sort of satire piece, it won't just wound Ellie; it will likely scar you as well."

"I'm beyond scarring. You know how tough I am."

"Yes, but his words are read all across this great state. Words have power. So why tempt him? Just handle it and all will be well."

"Yes, all will be well." She flashed a smile so bright, he almost believed it would be.

* * * * *

ALANNA PACED THE UPSTAIRS HALLWAY, more troubled than she'd been in days. She turned to face her mother and released a slow, methodical breath. "Mama, what are we going to do? I'm so concerned about Margaret's frame of mind."

"We're going to go in there like we did yesterday and the day before that and do our best to encourage her to get up out of bed and into a pretty dress. Then we will smile and act as if everything is fine."

"When it's really not." Alanna swallowed the lump in her throat, rapped on Margaret's bedroom door with the toe of her shoe, and then entered with the breakfast tray in hand and Mama following directly on her heels.

True to form, she found Margaret curled up in bed, sound asleep. The baby slept in her cradle nearby, blissfully unaware that her poor mother still battled "the blues."

As Alanna set the tray on the bedside table, Margaret startled awake. She rubbed her eyes, then sat up in the bed. "W–what time is it?"

"Ten-fifteen."

"It's late. I've slept in again." Margaret glanced over at the cradle. As if on cue, baby Given began to cry. Alanna walked over to her and picked her up then handed the little doll to her mother. Cradling her, Margaret's tense expression softened. "I know things have been out of sorts of late, but I believe I've come up with the perfect solution."

"Oh?" Alanna took a seat on the edge of the bed, curious.

Margaret's face lit into the first smile in weeks. "I've spoken to Brett," she said after a few seconds. "He thinks he can get the renters to agree to vacate our home in Savannah."

Alanna's heart skipped to double time as she pondered her sister's words. "Are—are you saying that you and Brett are coming home?"

Margaret offered a slow nod, and a lone tear began to trickle down her cheek. "Every time I think about doing this without you and Mama and Tessa, I can't bear it." Her tears fell in earnest now. "It will destroy me to raise this sweet baby girl apart from all of you. And if we come back home, well, just think of all the wonderful things we can do together."

"Well, yes," Alanna said. "That's true."

She should be celebrating this news, of course, but couldn't find it in herself to do so. No, something niggled at her. She forced a smile and then backed out of the room, leaving Margaret and Mama alone to chat. When she arrived downstairs, she found Tessa in the kitchen entertaining Katie and Tanner, who looked to be in the middle of some sort of debate. Nothing new there, of course.

"Alanna, maybe you can help us settle an issue." Tessa turned to face her with arms crossed.

"And what would that be?"

"Tanner thinks we should let the readers of *The Modern Suffragette* know that we've been writing the articles in Ellie's column. What do you think?"

"I beg your pardon. You've been doing what?"

"Writing Ellie's articles." Tanner drew near, his fists planted on his hips as he stared at Tessa. "It's been going on for a while now. And Katie's not the only one involved."

Alanna listened as he explained then looked back and forth

between Tessa and Katie as they threw in their two cents' worth. By the time they finished, her thoughts whirled madly, especially the part about Tessa's involvement. And Mama? Had she really helped them as well? "I hardly know what to say. What will the women think once they know?"

"They will think we are heroines, rushing in to save the day for our fearless leader." Katie grinned.

Tessa did not look convinced. "I daresay, coming clean carries a risk. I would just as soon let folks think Ellie's been penning those articles. It's certainly easier. Besides, now that she's getting better, she'll take over the task again and no one will be any the wiser."

"Honesty is always the best policy," Tanner threw in. "And as someone who has spent the last several weeks pretending to be a Southern gentleman when he's really not, I can attest to the fact that coming clean is for the best." Tanner's lopsided grin charmed Alanna at once—and made her feel a little badly about trying to convert him in the first place.

She offered a little sigh then turned to Katie. "Your brother thinks I'm due for a comeuppance for trying to convert him into a gentleman."

"What else do you say on this subject, Tanner?" Katie asked.

"Fair play is turnabout." He quirked a brow and Alanna groaned.

"He says it's my time to be converted. He wants to turn me into a woman of the West. Can you imagine?"

"Actually, I can." Katie giggled. "You should learn to tend to the animals. Or better yet, let him teach you how to ride."

Alanna stared at her. "I told Tanner to put that ridiculous

notion right out of his head. I can't believe he told you."

"Told me what?" Creases appeared between Katie's eyes.

"Told you that he's trying to talk me into riding his palomino."

Tanner put his hands up in mock defeat. "I didn't say a word. Honest."

"I had no idea." Katie clasped her hands together. "But I would give my eyeteeth to see you riding across the range on Casey's back. He's a fine horse and perfect for the job. So gentle."

"Oh no. I'll tell you the same thing I told Tanner. It's out of the question, especially with the weather. My back gets really stiff in the cold, so I can't possibly—"

"I'm not saying you should do it now," Katie interrupted, "but one day before you leave to go back to Savannah? Please?"

Alanna chuckled at the very thought of it. "I don't imagine the horse would take kindly to a Southern belle seated on his back. No telling what sort of rider I would be."

"Only one way to find out. Promise me you will ride before you go head home. That's only a couple of months away."

Alanna paused, her heart quickening at the idea of going back to Savannah. "I can't make a promise, but I will think about it."

Katie's eyes narrowed into slits. "Well, this is the time and the place, no doubt about it. It's a new year, and you're a new woman." She paused and appeared to be thinking. "But if you're really going to be converted to a woman of the West, we need someone specific to use as an example. Someone from history." She snapped her fingers. "Oh, I know! Sacagawea."

Alanna's nose wrinkled. "Sacaga–who–wa?"

"Sacagawea, the Indian woman who carried her baby on her

back as she guided the explorers Lewis and Clark all across the Northwest."

Carried a baby on her back? Alanna felt a little faint at this proposition. "Isn't there someone else I could emulate?"

"Of course." Katie paused for a moment or two before blurting out, "Charley Parkhurst."

"Charley? Isn't that a man's name?"

"Only in this case, Charley was a woman," Tanner chimed in. "She drove a stagecoach for thirty years without anyone catching on to the fact that she wasn't a man."

"I can't even imagine what she was wearing."

Katie rolled her eyes. "Don't get so distracted by the clothing, Alanna. Women up here have to be more rugged, or they'd never survive." She paused. "Oh, I know another. Annie Oakley. She wasn't really from the West, of course, but she appeared in all those Wild West shows. Folks equate her with the West."

"If you're asking me to ride bareback or shoot a pistol, I'm afraid I'm going to disappoint you with my response."

Katie clasped her hands together. "Oh, but don't you see, Alanna? A real woman of the West is a gal who isn't afraid to get her hands dirty. She tends babies, slaves over a hot stove, and medicates a gash in the horse's leg when necessary. On top of all that, she braves the elements, fights her enemies with the gun her husband taught her to shoot, and even digs a few graves if the need calls for it."

Alanna suddenly felt weak. She turned to face Tanner. "If this is what you expect of me, you can keep right on wishing. I will never be such a woman."

As she gazed into his teasing blue eyes, she realized his words about turning her into a Western woman were nothing but a ruse—a way to get her riled up. Oh, but how she suddenly longed to become all he wanted her to be. Maybe turnabout really was fair play. And maybe, just maybe, this Southern belle could try her hand at becoming a real woman of the West. Perhaps in doing so, she could ride off into the sunset on the back of a palomino, forgetting about the troubles that were sweeping in around her like a Montana wildfire.

TWENTY-TWO

There's a wonderful Scripture in the first book of Timothy. Young Timothy is looking to Paul, his mentor, for wisdom and courage. Paul encourages his young prodigy to stir up the gift that is inside of him. Ladies, this is the message many of us would like to leave with you today—we who have followed in the footsteps of our fearless leader, Ellie Cannady, who has faced death and lived to tell about it. We, who have penned articles on her behalf during her hour of need, using our gifts to stir your hearts in her absence. What gift has the Lord placed inside of you? How can it be best utilized—not just to spread the word about women's rights, but as mothers, sisters, daughters? We encourage you today to stir up your gifts. Don't let them sink to the bottom of the soup pot. Give them a good stir and watch the Lord work through you.

—Missoula's own Sleigh Belles,
writing for *The Modern Suffragette*

* * * * *

Tanner listened to the back-and-forth conversation with the ladies, happy to hear them settle on the obvious choice: they would make an announcement in The Modern Suffragette so that their readers would know the truth—about everything. Their words would be vague and discreet, yet truthful.

He paid particular attention as they penned the article—together—and smiled at the outcome. Surely this explanation would satisfy Douglas at the *Missoulian*. How could he fault the women for banding together in Ellie's time of need?

Content that they had things under control, Tanner headed out to the barn to check on Brett, who had looked anything but happy as he passed through the kitchen on his way out to feed the animals. Yes, something was surely amiss, and Tanner would get to the bottom of it.

He found his older brother in the barn, as was so often the case, tending to the cows and horses. Only this time, Brett muttered under his breath as he worked, and his body was tense.

"Brett?"

His brother turned his way, face tight. "Sorry, Tanner. Didn't know you were there."

"Clearly." He paused, not wanting to interfere and yet sensing the trouble in his brother's heart. "How can I help?"

Brett scooped up a bale of hay and tossed it into the first pen. "Convince my wife she should stay put in Montana. She's practically got our bags packed."

Tanner felt the air go out of his lungs. "What do you mean?"

"I mean, she's got me sending wires back and forth to Savannah to see if our home there is available. She's ready to hit the trail the minute the snows melt. Or sooner, if the train can get out before then. We'll be leaving with her family to go back to Savannah, at any rate."

"No." Just one word, but it seemed to be the only one Tanner could muster. "Surely you jest."

Brett's eyebrows drew together in an agonized expression. "Does this look like the face of a man who's joking? I can assure you, I'm not. Margaret has finally succumbed to the months of emotional tugging on Alanna's part. She's now convinced we need to live near her family." He sat on a bale of hay and raked his fingers through his messy hair. "And frankly, considering the condition Margaret's in, I have little choice but to go along with this. It's clear she's in a bad way. I don't want my daughter to suffer just because I'm stubborn and feel that she should be raised in Montana."

"But, Brett, Margaret loves it here."

"'Loved' it here. Until her sister started filling her head with all sorts of nonsense about how much better life is in the South."

"I'm ready to admit I was wrong, Brett." Alanna's voice rang out from behind them. Tanner turned to find her standing there, looking ready to cry. "It was wrong of me to try to woo her back. My motives were pure, I assure you. But it's clear I'm the one who has caused all of this, and I'm terribly sorry. If it makes you feel any better, I haven't worked to convince her of this in recent weeks. My—well, my thoughts on the matter have changed significantly."

Tanner perked up at this proclamation.

Brett released a lingering breath. "You didn't cause her medical condition, Alanna. I know that. And I know that you love her, so I don't fault you. It's just that she's very vulnerable right now." He rose and came nearer. "Honestly, I think we've run out of options. She's convinced herself that raising Given in Montana is out of the question, that the child deserves the kind of upbringing she had."

"Then we'll just have to convince her otherwise." Alanna's weak smile lifted Tanner's spirits and gave him hope.

"Yes, that's right." He patted his brother on the back. "If she can be convinced to leave, she can be convinced to stay. If we all work together, that is."

Brett shook his head. "I'm tired of trying to convince my wife that my way of life is better than hers was. She's been very good to go along with me all this time. And she's been the rock in our relationship, I don't mind admitting. But that rock is crumbling, and it's time for me to be the husband and father God intended. If that means picking up and moving to Georgia, then so be it. I will do whatever needs to be done to see my wife and daughter healthy and happy."

Tanner felt the fight go out of him at Brett's statement. How could this be mended? In just a few short weeks, they would all be gone—Brett, Margaret, Given...and Alanna. Out of the corner of his eye, he caught a glimpse of the beautiful Southern belle. Her face was awash with tears. Surely not even a beautifully crafted article in the paper could mend this. What they needed was a good old-fashioned miracle.

Thank goodness he knew where to go to find one.

* * * * *

ALANNA'S HEART FELT LIKE LEAD as she paced the length of the barn. Convinced she could fix this, she put her hands on her hips, released a slow breath, and faced Brett. "I don't want you to give up just yet. Promise me you will pray about this."

"I have been, and it's the only solution that comes to mind."

"Let's give the Lord time to move. After all, nothing can be done until the snows melt anyway."

"It's just a matter of weeks before the train will begin running again," he said. "That doesn't give us as much time as you might think. Just enough to settle issues related to the ranch." He walked farther into the barn, tossed another bale of hay into one of the pens, and shrugged. "I'll manage."

Alanna had a feeling he was happy for the excuse not to look her way. Who could blame him? After all, he was being asked to leave his home, his friends, his way of life—to trade it in for a life he would truly abhor but one he would tolerate to make his wife happy.

"Will you sell the ranch?" she whispered.

He pursed his lips and muttered something she couldn't quite understand. She did make out, "I'm sure Tanner would be happy to take over my property. Maybe this is how it was meant to be."

"You know better than that." The anger lines around Tanner's eyes shared his view on the matter.

Alanna grimaced, realizing the position this put Tanner in. "No, Brett," she said. "This isn't how it was meant to be. You are supposed to be here in Montana, working the land and raising a brood of rough-and-tumble little girls who will probably end up marrying some fellas who love this part of the country even more than you do."

His face broadened in a smile...for a moment. "Can't envision Given ever getting married, so I'd rather not think about that, if you don't mind."

Tanner gave his brother a slap on the back. "It's inevitable. And I agree with Alanna. You're meant to stay here and raise a passel of daughters who will run around with messy hair and torn dresses, climbing trees and riding horses."

Alanna didn't even shiver at this news. To think, just a few weeks ago, the idea of girls being raised in such a rustic environment would've sent her reeling. Now it sounded...ideal.

Brett released a lingering sigh. "Don't you two understand? I've had my turn. Margaret has given up everything she ever knew and loved to be here in Montana with me. Now it's my turn. I have made up my mind to have a happy wife."

"And a happy life—for all involved?" Alanna asked.

"If she's happy, I'm happy."

She snapped her fingers as another idea came to mind. "Brett, I have it! It's the perfect thing to lift Margaret's spirits. I'll contact Papa and get him to come here for a few weeks. I know she's missing him terribly. That's half of the problem, I think—her desire to have more time with family."

A hopeful glint lit Brett's eyes. "Not a bad idea, though it will be awhile before the train can make it through, as I said."

She thought about the situation Papa would face at the university, should he vacate his position for more than a few days. "It will take him some time to figure out a plan on his end, as well, but perhaps it can be done. In fact..." Another idea set in. "Maybe we can convince him to come when the snows melt and stay on through the end of the summer. That way we could all spend more time with, well, all of you." She set her gaze on Tanner, whose smile shared his thoughts on that suggestion.

"Do you really think he would come?" Brett asked.

"He indicated as much in his last letter. He's weary of being in Savannah without us. And you know Papa, Brett. He's an adventurous soul. It nearly killed him to put us on the train, knowing he had to stay behind. Maybe he could use a trip to the Wild West as material for his students."

"Could be."

She continued to ramble on about the possibilities but figured Brett didn't hear a word of it. He rushed through the process of feeding the animals then turned back toward the house, ready to spend more time with the baby. This left Alanna alone with Tanner. Not that she minded one bit. In fact, she'd looked forward to this very opportunity.

* * * * *

TANNER'S HEART RACED AS HE found himself alone with Alanna. The conversation with Brett had given him the courage to speak his heart.

"Will you come for a walk with me?" He extended his hand, and she took it, a delightful smile on her face. Tanner led her out to the yard and over to the fence. Leaning against a post, he gestured to the mountain range in the distance. "I hope you will bear with me as I share something."

"Of course." She pulled her scarf a bit tighter around her

neck and pressed her hands into her coat pockets.

"Missoula is a place of convergence."

"Convergence?" Her nose wrinkled, making her tiny freckles more pronounced.

"Yes." He pointed off in the distance. "Over that way are the Bitterroot Mountains. And over there is the Sapphire Range."

"Ah." She gave a little shrug, no doubt underwhelmed by his conversation about their surroundings. Only, this time he had a point.

"Now this way…" He pointed to the east. "That's the Garnet Range. You'll notice a theme here."

"Jewels?"

"Right. But not all of them. We've got the Rattlesnake Mountains and the Reservation Divide too. All those mighty mountains converge here, in the valley that is known as Missoula."

"Fascinating." She still looked a bit perplexed.

He took her hand. "Yes, but you're missing my point. How many times have you said that being from the South makes you different? Alanna, I believe that the Lord brought you to Missoula—not just to tend to your sister while having a baby, but so that we could meet."

Her eyes widened. "What do you mean?"

He slipped his arm around her shoulders and pulled her close, planting tiny kisses in her hair. "God doesn't see those various mountain ranges as separate," Tanner whispered. "He sees them as one. One brisk sweep of his fingertip shaped them all."

"That's a lovely image, Tanner." She relaxed in his arms. "I can almost see it happening right in front of my eyes."

"Me too. But here's what I'm getting at." Tanner turned to face her and took her hands in his. "When he sees the two of us, He doesn't see a girl from Savannah and a fella from Montana. He sees two people converging—coming together. Linking hands and hearts."

At the word *hearts*, his own heart began to do a strange little dance, one he'd never experienced before. He reached out and rested his palm on her cheek; her skin was cold beneath his fingertips. Tanner left it there until she cradled her face into it and her eyes fluttered closed. She leaned lightly into him, tilting that beautiful face up toward his, and opened those green eyes wide. Tanner's hands slipped around her waist in a comfortable embrace.

"It's time to stop thinking about how different we are." He whispered the words, his breath soft against her ear. "I might be the Rattlesnake Mountains and you might be the Sapphire Range, but in the end, we're just two people standing in the valley, wondering how—or if—we can take two separate worlds and merge them into one."

She gazed up at him, her eyes sparkling like gems at this proclamation, which gave him the courage to do the one thing he'd been dying to do all along. The boy from Montana wrapped his arms around the girl from Savannah and gave her a kiss that merged their two worlds once and for all.

TWENTY-THREE

Only one thing can bring down barriers. It's an age-old solution, one advocated thousands of years ago in the book of First Corinthians: "And now abideth faith, hope, charity, these three; but the greatest of these is charity." When I speak of charity, I do not mean the sort one might imagine. I speak of love, the kind that forgives offenses and extends grace. Yes, love is the only true mountain-mover. It pulls down walls, replacing them with hope. As our cold Montana winter gives way to the tiny buds of spring, may hard hearts thaw and may love rule the day.

—Ellie Cannady, editor of *The Modern Suffragette*

* * * * *

ALANNA'S HEART FELT NEAR-TO-BURSTING AS Tanner leaned down to kiss her. In that moment, every barrier between them was swept away, leaving behind only the blissful knowledge that God had, indeed, brought her here for a greater purpose. She wanted to sing, to dance, to proclaim the intense joy that could be found when one surrendered to God's ultimate plan.

Instead, she gazed up into Tanner's eyes and giggled.

And giggled.

And giggled some more.

While she wanted to behave like a lady, she could not. Everything inside her fought against it. Tossing her Southern sensibilities aside, she wrapped her arms around his neck and kissed him all over again, not just once, but twice.

Er, three times.

Afterward, he gazed at her, eyes sparkling. "Well, now, that was certainly worth waiting for."

"Mm-hmm." She sighed and leaned into him. "I can't believe I spent so much time fighting the inevitable."

"It was inevitable, wasn't it?" He brushed his hands through her hair, finally bringing them to rest on her shoulders. "God brought you a long, long way to meet me."

"To a place that once terrified me." She shook her head, remembering. "I feel so foolish now."

"Why foolish?"

"Because, back home, I jokingly called Montana 'the Great Unknown.'" She paused to think about how far she'd come. "I think maybe I was just afraid of what I couldn't see. Or touch."

"Or understand." He shrugged. "Montana is vastly different from Savannah."

"Vastly."

"And we are as different as night and day, after all."

On this point she had to disagree. "Actually, I think we're more alike than either of us have been willing to admit. We're not just alike in ideology and beliefs, but in our love for family and our desire to see good things come to those we love."

"True." He placed several more tender kisses along her hairline, sending a shiver down her spine. "And just for the record, I'm glad Montana isn't the Great Unknown any longer."

"It's becoming more familiar by the moment." Another girlish giggle threatened to escape, but she quickly brought it under control as his lips met hers. She thought about the first time she'd seen snowcapped mountains—how heaven and earth seemed to kiss. She now understood what that felt like. Her heart sailed heavenward as she gave herself over to the joyous moment.

When the kiss ended, she sighed. "I don't mind admitting, I was wrong—about everything."

"Everything?" His eyebrows elevated mischievously. "Have those crazy Sleigh Belles converted you to their way of thinking after all?"

She shrugged, unsure how to answer. For, while she did not agree with all their principles, she did find value in their desire to care for those less fortunate.

He gave her a funny look as she hesitated. "Don't tell me you're going to hang bells around your neck and go prancing through town. If so, I might just have to run for cover."

"No. You won't see me doing that." She felt her pulse quicken as the truth set in. "But I am praying about whether or not my staunch opposition to their ideals was entirely correct. I must confess, I do see some good in what they're doing." She paused and gave him a sheepish look. "Not all, mind you. I see the need for balance. But I think it makes sense that women should be protected when it comes to their right to own property and that sort of thing."

He chuckled. "All right, then. But I still think you would look silly marching through town wearing a placard or ringing dozens of bells. Can't even imagine it, in fact."

"Me either. A Southern belle would never do such a thing." She ran her index finger along his cheek, enjoying the smile it coaxed out of him.

"But a sleigh belle would." He paused and gave her a pensive look. "So which are you?"

"I'm just me. Alanna. From Savannah. In Montana." She laughed. "And apparently quite good with rhyme, though I never realized it till now."

"You're good at a lot of things."

"Oh?"

"Yes. You're good at taking a fella's heart and twisting it inside out. You're wonderful at caring for your sister's new baby. Your ability to handle Katie in a moment of crisis is admirable. And I bet you'll be good at horseback riding too, if we can ever get you on my palomino. Casey's rarin' to go."

"Horseback riding?" At this she pulled away from him and crossed her arms. "Back to that, are we?"

"Well, you've already become a woman of the West in so many other ways. Figured that one last issue needed to be addressed."

"I see."

She didn't, of course, but this wasn't the time to argue. No, when Tanner wrapped her in his strong arms once more, she decided that arguments were highly overrated.

* * * * *

As Tanner held Alanna close, he could literally feel their hearts beating in tandem. So much for the things that had once divided them. Right now, in this moment, no barriers remained. No conflicts. No problems.

Other than the obvious one, of course. Unless the Lord stirred Mr. Lessing's heart, Alanna would be leaving for Savannah in a few weeks, and all of this—the joy, the hopefulness, the comfort of her embrace—would come to an end.

He forced himself not to think about the inevitable, focusing instead on this moment. Holding her close felt so natural, so comfortable, that he knew he could trust her with every facet of his life, even the one thing he'd kept from her.

Tanner cleared his throat; he knew it was time. "Alanna, I need to tell you something." He paused and glanced at the mountain range in the distance. "No doubt you've noticed I'm very fond of the scenery."

"To say the least." She chuckled. "I would have to be blind not to notice. I've never met anyone so infatuated, in fact."

"It's breathtaking, but there's more to it than that." He paused, ready to share his heart. "The beauty that surrounds me is my inspiration to do the one thing I feel most strongly about."

"And that would be?"

"Paint."

"Paint?" Her brow wrinkled. "You mean painting the barn? Brett told me you planned to do that, come spring."

"No." He couldn't help the grin that followed. "Painting in oils on a canvas. Creating works of art."

"Art?"

"Mm-hmm."

"Wait…" She paused and took a step back, her mouth widening into an O. "You're an artist?" When he nodded, she clamped a hand over her mouth. Pulling it away, she whispered, "Oh, Tanner. Are you telling me—?"

He nodded again. "Yep. The painting at the gallery, that's the overlook from the top of the Bitterroot Range. I painted it last spring on a particularly hot day. Had a lot of trouble with the oils because of the heat and humidity."

"Oh. My. Goodness." Alanna gasped. "I—I bought it."

"You what?"

"I bought that painting. I went into town less than a week after the rally and purchased it."

He couldn't help the smile that followed.

Alanna's eyes filled with tears. "It's so realistic. So familiar. I figured it would be the best reminder of my time in Missoula. Looking at it is the closest thing to actually being here. It's in my room, packed for the trip home."

"Home." As he spoke the word, his heart felt as heavy as lead.

"Yes." Her eyes filled with tears. "I never dreamed you'd painted it, Tanner, but I always felt drawn to it, just as I felt drawn to the painting in my father's study." Her hand covered her mouth once again. "Oh. My. Goodness."

"Yes. That one was painted a long, long time ago. Brett and Margaret bought it at an auction last year." He smiled, remembering. "I had no idea she planned to send it to her family in Savannah until last Christmas when she told me she'd already sent it to your father. I understand he's always been very fond of the West and has longed to visit. She thought perhaps it might inspire him to make the trip."

"I had no idea."

"Seems a little odd, when I think about it. I never set out to do a self-portrait, but that's what I ended up doing. To be honest, I'd only painted landscapes until then. Thought I might practice painting real people by starting with myself."

"You did a marvelous job. It's very lifelike."

"Thank you. I wasn't particularly proud of it, at least not at first. When I finished painting it, I hid it in the barn, but Katie found it."

"What was she doing in the barn? I thought she was scared of the cows."

He laughed. "Yes, but she overcame her fear temporarily when Snowball had puppies. I'd hidden the painting in the loft, and Katie stumbled across it while looking for a blanket for the dog. She showed it to Mama, who showed it to Brett, who showed it to Margaret. And then..." He sighed. "You know what a softy I am where Katie's concerned, right?"

"Right."

"Well, she and Margaret were hosting an auction to raise money."

"For the suffragettes?"

"Yes." He groaned. "Now you see. I gave her the painting, never thinking it would sell. But Margaret purchased it—paid a pretty penny for it, in fact—and the rest is history."

"I can't believe I got to meet not only the cowboy in the painting, but the one who painted it, as well." Alanna shook her head. "This is remarkable. No wonder I felt as if I knew you all along. I'd been staring at that painting for months, completely mesmerized."

"I think it's true, what they say—that a piece of the artist's soul is left on the canvas." He paused, realizing just how right those words were.

"I should have known. Everything about the paintings reminds me of you. Of course they're yours."

"So, you had a little foretaste of Montana."

"And of you." She gave him a little kiss on the cheek. "We've been kindred spirits all along."

"Yes, we have." He pulled her into a tight embrace and planted a tiny kiss in her hair.

Her brow furrowed. "I just have one question. That day in town when we saw the painting in the gallery—why didn't you tell me then?"

He chuckled. "I tried to on the way home. Remember how I went on and on about the scenery?"

"As if I could forget."

"I was really trying to give you a hint, I guess. Thought maybe if you could see how much I loved the countryside, you would put two and two together and come up with four."

"I've never been very good at math."

He gave her another little kiss. "Well, don't worry about that. I can add and subtract well enough for the both of us. But I do feel I owe you an apology. Ever since you arrived, you've had to put up with my glowing descriptions of Montana."

"Now I see why. As you said, it's your inspiration." The admiring look on her face shared her thoughts on that matter. "But there's got to be more to this story, Tanner. What else have you painted?"

"What else?"

"Yes, besides the cowboy and the one landscape at the gallery. Surely there's more."

His face grew warm. "Well, I suppose there are a few paintings I've not shown anyone."

"Will you show me?"

"Are you sure you really want to see them? They're not very good."

"Let me be the judge of that."

He led the way to the base of the loft. "You're not afraid to climb, are you?" he asked when they reached the ladder.

She shook her head. "Not at all."

"Well, c'mon, then." He led the way up the steps. Once they arrived, his secret was unfurled once and for all.

Alanna gasped as she took in the paintings, nearly a dozen in total. "Tanner! Why, this is a regular studio."

"Yes. My studio, in fact." He grimaced. "Brett offered me the space, knowing that I could work here without Katie or Mama finding out. Not that I'm ashamed, mind you, but they have a way of nosing in and making themselves at home. It helps to have my own creative space."

"Well, of course. And this explains why you spend so much time out here." She chuckled. "And all this time I thought you were fond of Prissy and the rest of the cows."

"Well, I am fond of them." He pointed to a canvas in the corner where he'd painted the new calf's portrait.

"Oh, Tanner." She made her way across the loft, beyond several bales of hay, to the painting. "This is so lifelike. Why, it looks just like the sweet little fella."

"I thought I might give it to you as a present when you go."

As he spoke the word "go," his heart lurched once more.

Alanna continued to stare at it. "I still can't believe Margaret didn't tell me. She's known all along and didn't say a word."

"I asked her not to."

"But, Tanner, look at all this. You could sell these and make a fortune."

"That was never the idea. I've always just loved to paint. From the time I was a boy, in fact. I love taking things and shaping them with my paintbrush."

"We have that in common, as well."

"What do you mean?"

"I tried to shape you into my image. Oh, not with a paintbrush, but I certainly did a fair job of trying to make you into something you were not. I tried to take a perfectly good cowboy and paint him into a Southern dandy." She sighed. "I do hope you will forgive me for that. The only one who needs to be shaping anyone into His image is the Lord, and I'm the one He needs to be working on, not you."

Tanner chuckled. "I hope you're not saying I'll never make it as a Southern gentleman."

Her expression grew more serious. "Tanner, you're more of a gentleman than any of those fellas back home. In fact, you're the most gentlemanly gentleman I've ever met. When I see what you've done on your sister's behalf, I can tell that your heart is as big as the sky over Montana. So don't ever doubt yourself. I'm sorry if I made you feel anything less than the gentleman you already were. Will you forgive me?"

"Forgive you?" He chuckled. "I learned a lot, thank you very much."

"Most of it pure foolishness."

"Maybe a little, but not all. You were right to remind me that God never intended men to plow over the women in their lives. We can all stand a bit of refinement. And in case you haven't noticed, I've been working on my manners. Had to change a few of them to impress you."

"Well, don't change too much, Tanner. I daresay I liked you just the way you were all along."

"Oh, you did, eh?" He couldn't help the happy grin that followed. "Well, that's encouraging news. I guess this would be the right time to tell you that I liked you just as you were too. Southern accent and all."

"Accent?" She stared at him, perplexed. "What do you mean?"

"Come on, now. You know."

She shrugged. "I haven't the faintest clue what you're referring to."

"Mm-hmm." He chuckled. "Anyway, I love it. But I'm stunned to confess that I hardly even notice it anymore, as strange as that might sound. I also love the funny lessons on social graces, the silly way you get mad at me when I mess up, and I love..."

"Y–yes?"

He couldn't help the words that followed. They were true, after all.

"I love you."

TWENTY-FOUR

Over the past several months, I have faced death and lived to tell about it. Because of this, my perspective on life has changed. I will continue to focus on the things that I can do to ease the burdens of women across this great land, but I will spend even more time keeping my eyes on eternal things. For, while we will not always be at home in this world—while troubles abound and answers elude—we will most assuredly thrive in the next. In that blessed place, all fears will be erased. All pain lifted. All struggles gone. Until that time, may hearts expand with love and grace.

—Ellie Cannady, editor of *The Modern Suffragette*

* * * * *

ON THE FIRST SATURDAY IN March, Alanna awoke to blue, cloudless skies. She peered out of the bedroom window, delighted to find that the snows had, for the most part, anyway, melted. The mountains still glistened with their usual white caps, but the fields, browned by winter's heavy weight, spread out before her, clear and anxious for spring. What a perfect day to surprise Margaret with a gift she wouldn't soon forget.

Alanna dressed much faster than usual, with Tessa babbling in excitement the whole time. Mama greeted them in the kitchen, fed everyone a hearty breakfast, then gave Alanna a wink.

"Are you ready to go?"

She nodded and glanced at Margaret, who sat with baby Given in her arms.

"What are you up to?" Margaret asked. "You've got something up your sleeve."

"We do." The twinkle in Mama's eyes nearly gave them away. "But you'll just have to trust us. Can you do without us for a couple of hours? We need to go into town."

"Of course." Margaret still looked perplexed. "But, why?"

"It's a secret." Tessa put a finger to her lips then giggled.

"How will you get there?"

"Tanner is taking us. He should be here any minute, in fact." Alanna scurried about, anxious to see him as always.

"I daresay he's been coming around here more than ever." Margaret's brows elevated. "He's become a permanent fixture."

Alanna didn't answer for fear her heart would give her away. Thank goodness, Margaret changed the subject.

"So you're all going into town but won't tell me why. My curiosity is piqued, for sure."

"That's the idea." Tessa took to giggling, and Alanna gave her a warning look. No point in spilling the beans.

Tanner arrived shortly with the car. He greeted her with a broad smile and a light in his eyes, one borne of anticipation, no doubt. A half hour later, Alanna stood at the train station alongside

Mama, Tessa, and Tanner, her nerves dancing. She paced back and forth, counting down the minutes until Papa's train arrived.

"Isn't this the perfect plan?" Mama's hands trembled as she took hold of Alanna's arm. "Once your papa arrives, everything will be set aright. Margaret will so enjoy having him here. I will too." Her eyes filled with tears. "I've missed him terribly."

Alanna's heart twisted. "So have I. It's been so hard without him."

"Don't make me cry." Tessa shook her head and dabbed at her eyes. "I want to look my best when he arrives."

"I think this will be just the ticket to seeing Margaret come around once and for all," Mama said. "She will get better once she sees your father."

"She seems stronger today than she was yesterday," Tanner chimed in. "Don't you agree?"

"Definitely." Mama grinned. "I've noticed a gradual change in her attitude and overall health."

"Yes, but having Papa here will be the icing on the cake." Alanna grinned, just thinking about it.

"Speaking of cake, that German chocolate one you made last night has tempted me beyond anything I've ever endured." Tessa sighed. "Now that your cooking skills have grown, I'll likely put on ten pounds."

"Hardly." Mama chuckled. "I don't know if you've noticed, Tessa, but you've lost a great deal of weight since we arrived in Montana."

"I know my dresses are looser. Must be all the hard work I'm doing with Katie and the other ladies. And I enjoy helping Brett on the ranch too."

Tanner nodded. "Katie has enjoyed your company for sure, Tessa. I don't know when she's had a better friend. And Brett told me that you make quite the cowgirl. You're not afraid of anything."

"Except snakes." Tessa shuddered. "We killed one out in the field just yesterday. Not sure I'll ever get used to those."

"Oh, even a snake won't get the best of you." Alanna took a deep breath and worked up the courage to share something personal with her sister. "Tessa, being here at the train station has reminded me of our journey from Georgia to Montana."

"What a trip that was." Tessa chuckled. "It felt like it would never end."

"Well, I want to tell you something about that trip, something I should have said a long time ago. I remember watching you on the train."

Tessa grinned. "Did I embarrass you in some way with my antics?"

Alanna shook her head, ashamed that her sister would make such an assumption. "No. Just the opposite, in fact. I watched you tend to the needs of the children and the mothers and felt such pride."

"You were proud of me?"

"I'm still proud of you, Tessa. You're a beautiful young woman with a heart for others. You've always had such a soft spot for the downtrodden."

"No doubt about that," Tanner added. "You've got the softest heart in town for people in need."

A beautiful smile came across Tessa's face. "I don't suppose I think of them as 'downtrodden.' I just see people and want to help. It would be impossible for me to pass by a hungry child and not feed him. If I had the power to do so, I mean. And I can't imagine walking past an elderly man or women in need and not offering a hand."

Alanna felt the sting of tears in her eyes. "That's exactly what

I mean. And I suppose that's a lesson I've learned about these suffragettes since meeting Ellie. I know that a few of them are overzealous in their approach, but most are just like you—simply women who want to help others."

Tessa reached for Alanna's hand and squeezed it. "Thank you for the kind words."

"You deserve that and so much more." Alanna felt a lump in her throat. She fought to speak around it. "When I see all of you working so hard, I feel…" She shook her head and dabbed away the moisture that now trimmed her lashes. "I feel so selfish. Most of my life, I've focused on myself—my possessions, my dresses, our lovely home…. I wanted the best of everything, and I wanted it all for me. If that's not selfishness, I don't know what is."

"Don't be so hard on yourself, Lana." Tessa slipped an arm around her waist and pulled her into a tight hug. "You're more giving than you know. You've passed down all those pretty dresses to me over the years, after all." She gave her a little wink.

Alanna's heart felt heavier at this proclamation. "That's not the same. I'm talking about the kind of giving that makes a genuine difference in the lives of people around us. When it comes to that sort of generosity, I've been woefully behind the times, and all because I couldn't see past my own wants and needs."

"Then perhaps this trip to Montana was meant to stir you awake to the needs of those around you." The words came from Tanner, who gazed at her with such an intensity that she felt her cheeks warm.

"I've been stirred, all right." Alanna gave a nervous chuckle. "And now that I have, I wonder if I'll ever be the same."

"Oh, you won't. I feel sure of that." The twinkle in his eyes let her know his feelings on the matter.

"Something about being here makes me feel…stronger. From the inside out, I mean."

"The Bible says we're to be strengthened in the inner man…er, woman." Tessa grinned. "Guess that applies to women, anyway."

"It most assuredly does," Mama said. "And don't ever doubt it."

"That aptly describes how I feel—strengthened in the inner woman." Alanna grinned. "Which makes me wonder why I'm getting all misty-eyed, if I'm suddenly feeling so strong."

Off in the distance, the shrill, piercing whistle of an incoming train sang out. Seconds later, black soot filled the air and the clacking of wheels against the track grew louder as the engine came into view. Alanna's heart danced as she anticipated seeing Papa again. He would, no doubt, find the females in his family remarkably changed. Hopefully the shifts in attitude and physique wouldn't alarm him.

Minutes later he emerged from the train, looking weary but happy. In that moment, every last woman—strengthened from within or not—melted into a puddle of tears.

* * * * *

TANNER FELT HIS HEART QUICKEN as he watched Alanna and her family reconnect after so many months apart. He prayed this reuniting would result in more than a brief visit from Mr. Lessing to the Missoula area. If everything went as planned, he could convince Alanna's father to consider a new life for them all in Montana. That conversation, of course, would have to wait for another day. For, while they had corresponded by letter several times over the last month or so, he had not ever met the man in person.

Alanna remedied that right away, introducing her father with a smile so broad, she looked as if she might take to dancing.

"Nice to meet you at last, sir." Tanner shook the older man's hand, noticing its softness.

"So, this is the fella who's put the smile on my Alanna's face, then." Mr. Lessing held his grip on Tanner's hand and gazed into his eyes with a hint of humor. "From the tone of her letters, I would say you've cast some sort of spell over her."

"It's Montana, Papa." Alanna gave her father a kiss on the cheek and then sighed. "This is the most wonderful place in the world."

"Ah." Her father looked back and forth between them. "So it has nothing to do with this fella, then?"

She giggled, and her cheeks turned a rosy hue. "Well, maybe a little."

More than a little, Tanner knew, but he wouldn't say so. That time would come later, or so he hoped. Right now he needed to stay focused on the matter at hand.

* * * * *

ALANNA LOOPED HER ARM THROUGH Tanner's, and they followed on Mama's and Papa's heels to the car. She listened in as her mother shared, words flowing like a river, about their months in Montana, going on about everything she'd fallen in love with—the baby, the food, the people, everything. By the time they found themselves in the car, Papa seemed tickled by Mama's chatter.

"You're a different woman, my dear." He gave her a kiss on the cheek.

"Am I?" Mama's cheeks flamed. "Well, not so different that you don't recognize me, I hope."

"Oh, I recognize you, all right." A sparkle lit his eyes. "You've got your spunk back."

Mama laughed. "I suppose you're right. Guess I lost it somewhere along the way."

A chuckle followed, and Papa's mustache twitched. "I think I rather like it."

"You do?" Mama did not look convinced.

"I do." He pulled her close and planted a kiss on the top of her head. "You have always been beautiful to me, but seeing you today, all riled up, with so much color in your face and that beautiful lilt in your voice, I see the same feisty female I married all those years ago."

Alanna could hardly believe such a thing possible. "Wait a minute. Mama used to be feisty?"

Her father laughed so hard, she wondered if the folks outside the car could hear. "Oh, the stories I could tell you. When I met her as a girl, she challenged me at every turn. She knew how to fight, no doubt about that. I still remember the day she nearly took my head off when I called her a tomboy."

"Mama, a tomboy?" Tessa giggled. "Impossible."

"Oh, no. Not impossible at all," Papa said.

"What changed, Mama?" Alanna asked.

Her mother's countenance shifted at once. Her gaze dropped to her hands, and she grew silent.

Papa cleared his throat. "I'm afraid my mother's to blame for that," he said. "Though she cared deeply about your mama, your grandmother Lessing had strong opinions about how women should be—especially society women. She and several of the other ladies in her circle made quick work of turning your mama into a Southern belle. Before I knew it, the tomboy faded to the background and a lovely, gracious woman took her place." His mustache twitched again as he looked Mama's way. "And just so we're clear, I adore the lady, but I've sorely missed the tomboy."

"I daresay she's back." Mama gave him a playful wink. "And she cooks too."

"Well, if that doesn't beat all. And the timing couldn't be better. I'm starved."

Alanna could scarcely believe it. To think that her grandmother had worked to convert Mama almost seemed laughable. Hadn't she done the same to Tanner? Well, at least now she knew where the trait came from.

They laughed and talked all the way back to the house. When they arrived, Papa took Alanna aside and gave her a hug. "I've missed you, Lana."

Tears sprang to her eyes again. "I've missed you too. So much that it hurt."

"You know, I said that your mama's changed, but she's not the only one." Papa looped his arm through hers. "Someone else around here seems different too."

"Me?" She grinned.

He nodded. "You've softened, Alanna. It looks good on you. But what has brought about this change?"

"You once told me that love makes people do strange and unpredictable things."

"Indeed it does."

"Have you ever known me to be unpredictable?"

"You?" Her father laughed. "Are you testing me in some way with this question?"

"Not at all. I just wonder if I'm the sort of girl that others might consider impulsive."

"You are the very opposite. Why, I've never known a female as steady and reliable as you. Now, please don't take this personally, Alanna, but you've almost been too set in your ways. You think everything through and reason it out in your head. You must get that from your mathematically minded father."

"Yes. Well, I guess you could say I've changed, then."

"Good. For once, I would love to see you throw caution to the wind and do something unexpected."

Her heart wanted to sing. For, while the Southern belle thrived on being steady and reliable, the Sleigh Belle longed to take to flight, to do something unexpected. Exciting. Fun.

Alanna knew just where to start. She would ride off into the mountains with the Montana wind in her hair and her cares whipping along behind her in the breeze.

If she could just figure out how to saddle up Tanner's palomino.

TWENTY-FIVE

Sometimes life surprises us. We think things are going to end one way and they end another. We expect to win a battle but land on our backs, defeated. We think we're the underdog and come out on top. Who can predict the conclusions to the scenes in our lives? Only the Lord knows, and He's not saying. One thing is for sure—you can trust Him with the details, large and small. He's a trustworthy God, one who has your very best interest at heart. So stop trying to fix everything. Rest easy in Him and know that He's probably got a surprise ending in store for you after all.

—Ellie Cannady, editor of *The Modern Suffragette*

* * * * *

EXACTLY ONE WEEK AFTER MR. Lessing's arrival in Missoula, Tanner paced the walkway outside Brett's house, trying to work up the courage to speak to the man privately. Tonight they would celebrate Alanna's twenty-first birthday in grand style. Folks from all over town would converge on Brett and Margaret's place for the celebration. Surely Alanna would be shocked by the surprise party. He hoped so, anyway.

But Tanner would prefer to celebrate something else, as well. If he could figure out how to approach Alanna's father and speak the words on his heart, this night would go down in history as one Alanna would never forget, birthday or not.

Sure, there were other details to be worked out. No doubt about that. But the Lord had already started the ball rolling, had He not? And whatever the Almighty started, He would surely finish.

Now, to distract Alanna for the afternoon. How would he go about that? Only one way—and Katie could help.

* * * * *

ALANNA FUSSED AROUND THE HOUSE all morning, helping Mama, Margaret, and Tessa tidy up. She'd never seen three women more interested in spring-cleaning. Not that she minded, of course. Seeing Margaret happy again made the day much more enjoyable. And sharing the time with Papa, who looked as happy as a lark, was the icing on the cake.

Speaking of cake, Mama had baked up a fine one for her birthday. Tonight after supper they would share it together. Nothing made her happier than sharing a birthday with her family.

She worked at a frenzied pace all morning and started up again after lunch. Somewhere around two in the afternoon Katie arrived, dressed in blue jeans and a button-up shirt. "I've come on a mission," she said. "Can you take a break from your work for the rest of the day?"

Mama and Margaret nodded their agreement, and before long Alanna headed out across the field toward the barn. "What are we doing?" she asked as they approached the first stall.

Katie pointed to a beautiful palomino adorned with sleigh bells. "Alanna, meet Casey. Casey, meet Alanna."

The horse let out a whinny, which caused the bells to jingle. Alanna flinched as the realization set in. "W–what's going on here?"

Katie reached inside a bag she'd been carrying and came out with a pair of men's blue jeans. "Alanna, it's time."

"Time?" Her heart quickened. "For what?"

"You know perfectly well. Have you forgotten that you once said you would learn to ride a horse?"

"I vaguely remember chatting about something like that. But I certainly never intended to do so on my birthday. Why, this is the last day on earth I would—"

The horse let out another whinny and nuzzled up against her.

"See? Casey wants to take you out on a special birthday ride. How can you turn him down? Besides, Tanner is the one who arranged all of this. He wants you to ride."

"If he arranged it, then why isn't he here?"

Katie's cheeks flushed. "Well, you know Tanner. Always busy with this and that. He'll come later, I promise. He told me to take you out to the foothills so that you could look down on the city."

"Oh, no." Alanna shook her head and took a couple of steps back. "There's no way."

"You've got nothing to worry about, I promise." Katie patted the horse on the neck. "Casey is sturdy and strong but not at all frisky. He will take good care of you. And I'll ride right alongside you on Ginger."

Somehow Alanna allowed herself to be talked into it. Moments later, dressed in men's jeans and wearing a shirt much too large, she watched as Katie saddled up Casey. As she led the horse out to the pasture, he seemed to come alive, shaking his head, stomping his foot, and whinnying with what appeared to be delight.

"See?" Katie said. "He's excited."

Wish I were.

Then the strangest mixture of dread and excitement flooded over her.

"Here's what I want you to do...." Katie gave instruction, asking Alanna to step up on the woodpile as the horse neared. "Grab ahold here..."—she pointed to something she called a "saddle horn"—"and swing your right leg over."

It took more than one try. And Alanna very nearly tumbled off the woodpile on the third attempt. But she finally managed to climb aboard on the fourth and set the sleigh bells jingling merrily. Relaxing into the saddle, she looked around the ranch, seeing it all in a new light. Suddenly the fields in front of her seemed as wide open as the skies. They beckoned to her.

Katie mounted Ginger and then, with the cluck of the tongue, urged her forward. Casey followed, and Alanna bounced up and down in the saddle, the bells ringing at will.

"Give him a tiny kick in the ribs with your heels," Katie instructed after they'd walked awhile.

"I—I don't want to hurt him."

"You won't. It's just your way of telling him to pick up the pace a bit."

Alanna gave the horse a tentative little kick, emphasis on *little*. His pace never changed. She tried again, this time a bit harder, and the palomino took off in a gallop, the bells now pealing madly.

Alanna let out a cry that echoed against the backdrop of the mountains in the distance. Just about that time, however, the horse's rhythm steadied and Katie rode up alongside her. In that moment, Alanna's fears disappeared. She felt a freedom she'd never known before. With the wind in her hair and the mountains in the distance, she felt as if she might be imagining this instead of experiencing it firsthand.

She leaned forward, grabbing hold of Casey's neck and enjoying the ride. Katie picked up the pace, and before long Ginger shot out ahead of them, her mane and tail flowing.

Minutes later, they came to a section of trees. Katie plowed ahead on her horse into a shaded area. Up ahead, just beyond a bend in the trail, Alanna saw something moving in the bushes. A deer darted across their path, startling the horses. Casey reared up and started running...straight for the mountain in front of her.

A scream rose from the back of Alanna's throat, but even it didn't drown out the pealing of those crazy bells. She tried to get control of the horse, but he would not be stopped. Instead, he ran with abandon, approaching the base of the mountain at lightning speed.

The faster he ran, the louder Alanna shouted—and all the more as her saddle worked its way loose, sliding down the horse's right side. She began to slip, slip, slip as the mountain drew closer. She cried out again, this time fighting to grab for the horse's mane. Perhaps fear caused her fingers to fumble. No matter how hard she tried, she couldn't seem to get a firm grip. In desperation, Alanna tried to work her arms around the horse's neck, but that failed as well. She found herself slipping down his side crazily.

"Katie!" she cried out. "Katie, help me!"

Unfortunately, Casey's frantic pace gave him the upper hand above Katie's horse. Casey galloped ever forward, chasing the elusive deer.

From behind her, Alanna heard Katie's voice cry out, "Jump off, Alanna! Jump!"

"No–o–o!"

Still, she had no other choice. Finally convinced that she could hang on no longer, Alanna made an attempt to leap from the horse. Even that, she managed to botch. Her foot got tangled up in the stirrup, and she found herself at the mercy of the horse—who continued to plow forward, his bells now ringing out the oddest cacophony of sounds against the wind in the trees.

Katie swept in alongside her and managed to get the horse to slow his pace just as Alanna pulled her foot free from the stirrup. She tumbled to the ground, landing solidly on her backside, then rolling a couple of times and bruising her shoulder.

"Ow!"

Katie scrambled down from Ginger and came running. Off in the distance, Casey continued to gallop toward the mountain, the bells jingling a strange, distant melody. Not that Alanna cared at the moment. Right now only one thing mattered—making sure nothing was broken. She trembled with such might that she could barely stand. When she finally managed it, she realized she'd injured her ankle in the stirrup incident.

Katie took one look at her ankle and remounted Ginger.

"I'm going for help," she called out. "Don't move, whatever you do!"

As if that were possible.

Still, as she sat amid the overgrown bushes, Alanna did have to question her sanity. How in the world had she landed in such a predicament? So much for feeling invincible. So much for the wind blowing through her hair.

"My hair!" She reached up to fuss with it and realized at once that she had brambles and grass in it. Oh, well. There would be plenty of time to deal with that back at the house.

The longer she sat, the more she realized that the situation with her ankle probably wasn't as bad as she'd feared. After a few minutes, she could actually wiggle it. Thank goodness. No bones broken. Still, it ached, and so did her shoulder, where she'd rolled after landing. And the pain in her backside beat all.

"Still, I'm alive." She attempted a weak smile. "And I rode a horse."

As if to taunt her, Casey reappeared, heading her way with his head down and the bells softly ringing.

"That's right, you silly horse. You should be ashamed. Look what you did to me."

He drew near and whinnied then took to nibbling the grass as if nothing unusual had happened—as if tossing a Southern belle to the ground happened every day.

Alanna sighed and leaned back on her elbows, trying not to let anxiety overtake her. A few minutes later, Katie arrived with Tanner riding in front of her on Ginger's back. Alanna took one look at him and burst into tears. She couldn't help herself.

He leaped from the back of the horse and ran to her, wild-eyed.

"Are you all right?" His breathless words shared his concern for her well-being.

"Bruised." She dabbed at her eyes and willed the emotion in her voice not to frighten him. "But I think my ego is more so." Alanna attempted a weak smile. "I thought I could do it, Tanner."

He gave her a kiss on the cheek. "Katie says you were doing a fine job. It's not your fault the horse got spooked. Happens to the best of us."

She felt a little better after hearing that. "I can't believe my first horse ride went so terribly wrong." A pause followed. "Oh, but it wasn't wrong at first. In fact, it was just as I'd imagine it to be—the feel of the wind in my hair, the view of the mountains getting closer, closer, closer."

Too close.

"About that hair…"

He ran his hand over her hair, and she grimaced. "It's a mess?"

He nodded and grinned. "That's one way of putting it."

"Are you making fun of me?" Moisture covered her lashes, and he kissed it away.

"Not at all. Just thinking how ironic this is."

"Ironic?"

"Yes." He chuckled and then pulled her close, planting tender kisses along her hairline. She relaxed in his arms. "You told me once that a real Southern belle would never show up for a social function in anything less than her finest."

Alanna sighed. "A social function?"

"Mm-hmm." He helped her stand, and she realized the pain in her ankle had eased a great deal. "What you don't know is this—this whole horse-riding venture was meant to get you away from the house for an hour or so, to give your guests time to arrive without your notice."

"My guests?" Her heart quickened.

"Mm-hmm." A boyish smile turned up the edges of his lips. "It's your birthday, you know."

"Well, yes, I know, but—"

"We're throwing a grand party, one a Southern belle would be proud of."

"Oh no." She brought her hand to her mouth as the reality set in. This whole thing had been a ruse meant to distract her? They'd done a fine job of it, no doubt—such a fine job that she wondered how, or if, she would be able to face her guests looking like something the cat dragged in.

* * * * *

TANNER COULDN'T HELP BUT CHUCKLE as he looked at Alanna— his beautiful, messy Alanna. No longer the prim, proper Southern belle, she now stood covered in grass and brambles, wearing a torn shirt with muddy blue jeans. Those long dark tresses were a tangled mess, but he'd never seen her look prettier.

"Now, I'm not saying you should go everywhere like this," he said, "but I think I rather like the look on you."

"You do?" She couldn't help the smile that followed.

"Yep. For once, you've let your hair down. Literally."

She reached up to straighten her messy hair but couldn't manage to tame it.

Tanner turned to Katie with a nod. "Do me a favor?"

"Of course."

"Go to the house and fetch her party dress. Take it and whatever else she might need to the barn. We'll meet you there and you can help her get ready, while I go back to the house to explain what's taking so long."

"Of course." Katie gave Ginger a nudge and they bolted in the direction of the house.

"Now, to get you back up on this horse." Tanner looked between Alanna and Casey.

She shook her head, eyes wide. "I—I can't, Tanner. Don't ask me to."

"Clearly you've never heard the age-old expression about falling off a horse and getting right back up again. It's critical, you know. If you don't do it now, you'll be scared for years to come."

He went to work, tightening Casey's saddle, then gave the horse a stern talking-to about his previous behavior. Turning to Alanna, Tanner smiled. "He promises to behave himself. Don't you, boy?" A pat on the neck produced a comforting whinny from Casey.

Though she protested, Tanner finally managed to get Alanna back up on the horse. He took the spot behind her, wrapping her in his arms as the horse plodded toward the barn. "Are you all right?" he whispered.

"I am now." She leaned back into him, and he felt her relax against him.

He hadn't planned to share his heart in this setting, this situation, but it felt right. Against the gentle jingling of the bells, he posed a question meant to ease his way into the conversation. "Why do you think I kept trying to get you on a horse?"

"To humiliate me?" She chuckled then turned to look at him.

"Of course not." With the cluck of a tongue, he urged the now-repentant horse along. "I knew you would excel at riding, by the way."

"You did? Why?"

"Because you excel at everything. Look at what a wonderful job you did turning me into a gentleman."

She laughed aloud. "I get your point. I'm terrible at both."

"Not my point at all. Have I not become a perfect gentleman? And are you not on the back of a horse at this very moment?"

"I suppose."

His heart raced as he got to the point. "And if you need any further proof that I have become a true Southern gentleman—one you can be proud of—just ask your father. He can tell you that I have passed the test."

"My father?" She sat up a little straighter. "What do you mean?"

A surge of joy rose inside Tanner as he held Alanna tighter. "I mean, I did the gentlemanly thing by asking him for your hand in marriage."

"What?" She turned so quickly, it almost threw him off-balance.

Steadying himself, Tanner chuckled. "He responded positively, I should add."

Alanna gasped and her eyes filled with tears. "W–when did you speak to Father? I've hardly been apart from him for a minute since he arrived."

Tanner urged the horse toward the barn as he answered. "I had a long chat with him this morning, but I must confess we've been corresponding for months."

"W–what? You've been corresponding?"

"Yes, by letter. For months." Arriving at the barn, Tanner dismounted before reaching to help Alanna down from the horse. They ended up face-to-face, her bruised cheek now apparent beneath the scratches and dirt.

"Your father is a great man, Lana. And he's an adventurous one too. For some time, I've felt that he might be a good fit to head the new mathematics department at State University of Montana. I've posed the question, and he has agreed to pray about it."

"You're serious?"

"Very. So you might consider adding your prayers to mine. And his."

"I will, of course." Alanna shook her head. "But it's all so remarkable. I never considered the fact that he might want to move to Montana." She grinned. "I never dreamed any of us would."

"I feel sure he will be a terrific asset to the school here, so I'm very hopeful."

"Yes, me too." Her cheeks flashed a rosy shade. "But let's go back to what you were saying about asking for my hand. Papa said yes?"

"He did." Joy flooded over Tanner as he gave her a kiss on the cheek. "I'll admit, I was a little nervous. He scarcely knows me."

"But he knows me." Her dazzling smile captivated him. "Papa certainly knows me well enough to recognize when I'm putting on a scene and when it's the real thing." She sighed and rested against him. "With you, I'm perfectly at ease. I'm myself, perhaps for the first time ever."

"Makes me wonder who you were before."

"I was a girl putting on airs. Trying to impress people with my manners and put-on social graces. And now—now I'm just a girl from Savannah in love with a boy from Montana." She grinned. "There I go again, making a rhyme."

"I love it," he whispered. "And what's more, I love you."

* * * * *

ALANNA'S HEART RACED WITH A joy she'd never known as the man she loved—the one she would soon marry—planted sweet kisses on her cheeks. Could this day possibly get any better? Sure, she was a mess on the outside, but on the inside, she'd never known such happiness.

From inside the house, she heard laughter and voices raised in song. A giggle rose as she thought about her friends and family throwing a surprise birthday party for her. "Sounds like they're having a lot of fun in there."

"They are, but no doubt they're wondering where you are. This was all for you, you know."

"Tell them I had to see a man about a horse." She offered a weak smile.

"That's what I love about you, Lana. Still maintaining your sense of humor even after taking a tumble. You're the epitome of grace."

"Yes, of course. Can't you tell? I'm such a lady." She gestured to her torn shirt and bruised cheek. "A real Southern belle."

"No, darlin'." He pressed a gentle kiss into her tangled hair. "With this horseback-riding adventure behind you, I think we can safely say you're a Southern belle no longer. As of today, you have officially joined the ranks of that illustrious group known round these here parts as the Sleigh Belles."

TWENTY-SIX

If there's one thing we Sleigh Belles know how to do, it's throw a party. So, ladies, come one, come all, to the celebration of the century held at the Missoula Community Church on the afternoon of Saturday, April seventh. Witness the "I do's" of two of Montana's favorites—Alanna Lessing, formerly of the Savannah Lessings, and Tanner Jacobs, brother of our organization's incoming president, Katie Jacobs. Many of you had planned to travel to this area to attend my funeral anyway, had you not? Fortunately, the Lord saw fit to heal me, and a wake is not necessary. So why not awaken to a new era instead, one filled with joy and celebration? Sounds like a lot more fun than a funeral any day. And what a fine opportunity to join hands, to celebrate as sisters. That's what we are, after all, dear ones—sisters.

—Ellie Cannady, editor of *The Sleigh Belles Sentinel*
(formerly known as *The Modern Suffragette*)

* * * * *

THE MORNING OF TANNER'S WEDDING day, he awoke to unexpected snow flurries fluttering outside his bedroom window. Within the hour, snow covered the ranch. His mother scurried about in the kitchen, fussing with the wedding cake—a true masterpiece. Still, he could scarcely think about anything except the obvious problem—the weather. He and Alanna had counted on a lovely springtime wedding, after all. Would this turn of events devastate her?

Katie arrived in the kitchen with the solution to his problems—the proclamation that she'd readied the sleigh. "The bells are in fine working order, just like they were at Christmas." She clasped her hands together and grinned, as if this whole thing had been some sort of heavenly plan.

He did his best not to groan aloud. "This isn't how I pictured my wedding day."

"Might as well make the most of it," Mama said with a grin. "You're getting married one way or the other."

"True."

"And you're getting the belle of the ball, no less." His mother gave him a wink that sent his heart soaring.

Less than an hour later, as he climbed aboard the sleigh, Tanner's thoughts shifted to Alanna. Suddenly nothing else mattered. Let the bells ring out! Let everyone in Missoula know! He would willingly soar across the snow, jingling all the way to the church, if it meant she would meet him there and merge her heart with his.

And as for playing the role of a gentleman? He would gladly do so for the rest of his life, as long as the belle of the ball continued to charm him with her feisty Western ways.

* * * * *

From the tiny classroom at the back of the church, Alanna looked out the window, her heart singing as she heard the familiar sound of guests arriving in sleighs covered with bells.

"I don't believe it." She released a giggle then turned to face her sisters. "Isn't it ironic?"

"Very," Margaret said as she held baby Given close. "But I love it. It's the icing on the cake, if you ask me."

"Speaking of cake, you should see the wedding cake Mrs. Jacobs just carried in." Tessa's eyes widened. "I'm going to gain five pounds just thinking about it."

Alanna laughed. "I can't wait."

The cake, of course, wasn't all she couldn't wait for. A shiver of anticipation ran down her spine as she thought about spending the rest of her life wrapped up in Tanner's arms. Whenever she thought about their future, she couldn't help but grin.

Of course, as the bride-to-be, she had a lot to look forward to, didn't she? And she wouldn't have to face the next several years without her family, either. Since Papa's announcement that he planned to take the job at the university, the whole family could stay together once and for all. The idea of having them close by filled Alanna with a contentment unlike any other.

She turned to face Tessa, who looked beautiful in her pink satin dress. "Remember that day you told me you would move halfway across the world to be with the man you loved?" Alanna asked.

Tessa pursed her lips. "Did I say that?"

"Yes. The very day I cooked up the plan to come to Montana

to fetch Margaret." Alanna grinned. "I find it ironic, on this, my wedding day, that you were the one willing to live on the opposite side of the country, if need be, and yet here I stand, ready to make a commitment to be a Montanan from this point on."

"We're all Montanans now," Tessa said with a wink. "You would have to haul me out of this state on a stretcher to get me to leave." Her eyes twinkled. "Have you noticed that James Sullivan has been trying to win my affections? Isn't he the most handsome fella you've ever seen in all your born days?"

"Well, it's hardly fitting for me to comment on such things on my wedding day," Alanna said. "Besides, I'd be hard-pressed to find a man more handsome than the one I'll be marrying today."

A knock sounded at the door, and Ellie Cannady peeked her head inside. "Safe to come in?"

"Yes, please." Alanna gestured for her dear friend to join them. "So glad you're here."

Ellie moved slowly into the room, still a bit stiff but smiling nonetheless. "I wouldn't have missed your big day for the world, sweet girl."

Alanna extended her hand. "How are you feeling?"

"Now that I see you dressed up in that beautiful white gown, better than ever." The elderly woman's eyes glistened as she drew near. "Wherever did you find that Battenberg lace? It's exquisite. I haven't seen anything like it in years."

"Mama had it shipped in from her favorite store in Savannah, of course. The satin too."

"And the veil? I've never seen anything so lovely."

Alanna fingered the hand-tatted edging along the eggshell

tulle veil and smiled. "It was Mama's. She wore it, as did Margaret. Now it's my turn."

"I'll wear it too," Tessa said, giving a sheepish grin. "Someday."

Ellie's eyes filled with tears. "You blessed girls. I pray you have long and happy marriages, all of you."

"You have no opposition to love and marriage, then?" Alanna asked.

"Opposition? Oh, precious, my husband and I would have been married fifty-seven years this spring." She dabbed at her eyes with a handkerchief. "I still miss him with such fierceness. They say it gets easier with time, but sometimes I wonder." Her tears gave way to a radiant smile. "It won't be much longer now till I see him again. We've got a lot of catching up to do."

"Well, don't go quite yet." Katie's voice rang out from the doorway. "We still need you too much, Ellie. There's a lot stirring, and I, for one, can't imagine any of it without you."

Ellie laughed and then turned to face her. "I'll do my best to hang on. I think I've given you all enough anxious moments already."

Alanna couldn't help the smile that followed. "On a happier front, look at the good that's come of it. All these wonderful Sleigh Belles have come to town for my wedding!"

"Yes." Ellie squeezed her hand. "What the enemy meant for evil in my life, the Lord has used for good." She chuckled. "Not that death would have been a negative. When you're my age, stepping through heaven's door sounds more like a blessing than a curse."

"I think you're the blessing, Ellie." Alanna gave the older

woman a smile. "You continue to motivate and encourage women in spite of all opposition."

A blissful look came over Ellie. "'For which cause we faint not,'" she whispered. "'But though our outward man perish, yet the inward man is renewed day by day.'"

"Amen," Katie whispered.

Ellie's eyes shone with great joy. "'For our light affliction, which is but for a moment, worketh for us a far more exceeding and eternal weight of glory; while we look not at the things which are seen, but at the things which are not seen: for the things which are seen are temporal; but the things which are not seen are eternal.'"

"I've always loved that verse," Alanna whispered. "But I didn't really understand it until recently." She bit back the giggle that threatened to erupt. "To think that, not so long ago, I considered my coming to Montana some sort of affliction, a burden I had to carry. Now I see that God has used it for His good and mine, as well."

"For all our good." Ellie gave her a soft kiss on the cheek then faced all of them. "We are thrilled to have you, Alanna. You're a true sister now."

From across the room, Katie began to sing, "'Jingle bells, jingle bells, jingle all the way,'" in joyful chorus.

Alanna felt the words on the tip of her tongue and joined in. "'Oh, what fun it is to ride—'"

"'In a one-horse open sleigh!'" Tessa and Ellie chimed in.

Within seconds, they were all laughing.

Mama popped her head in the door, her brow wrinkled.

"Someone singing Christmas carols in here?"

"Just celebrating a new season." Ellie extended a hand and Mama joined them, adding her voice to the fray.

Off in the distance, Alanna heard the church bells pealing.

"That's our signal," Tessa said, taking a couple of steps toward the door.

Papa met them and led Alanna into the church foyer. Her heart raced as she anticipated their walk down the aisle.

As they entered the sanctuary with her arm looped through her father's, she caught her first glimpse of Tanner standing at the front of the church. Gone were the blue jeans, the cowboy shirt, and the Stetson. The man she loved stood in proper wedding attire, looking very gentlemanly. She took one look at him and fought the instinct to bolt unladylike down the aisle. A Southern belle would never do such a thing, of course. Certainly not. Most assuredly not.

But a Sleigh Belle? Well, a Sleigh Belle just might.

Kicking up her heels, Savannah ran straight into the arms of Montana.

Award-winning author Janice Hanna, who also writes under the name Janice Thompson, has published nearly eighty books for the Christian market, crossing genre lines to write cozy mysteries, historicals, romances, nonfiction books, devotionals, children's books, and more.

Janice formerly served as vice president of the Christian Authors Network (christianauthorsnetwork.com) and was named the 2008 Mentor of the Year by the American Christian Fiction Writers organization. She is passionate about her faith and does all she can to share the joy of the Lord with others, which is why she particularly enjoys writing.

Janice lives in Spring, Texas, where she leads a rich life with her family, a host of writing friends, and two mischievous dachshunds. She does her best to keep the Lord at the center of it all.

www.janicehannathompson.com

AUTHOR'S NOTE

I could not write this story about the suffrage movement without mentioning my good friend Eleanor Clark, to whom the book is dedicated. Eleanor is an octogenarian, full of life and pizzazz. She is an author, a motivational speaker, and the matriarch of a large, vibrant family in Central Texas. Eleanor also happens to be a distant relative of Lord Baden Powell, founder of the Boy Scouts—hence the reference in this story.

Eleanor, who remains active in the political arena, has been a strong influence for Christian women, taking a stand for women's rights but carefully balancing them with her role as a wife and mother. Like the heroine in this story, she keeps her eye on the delicate line between the two and also understands the need to keep God at the forefront. She is truly the epitome of a modern-day suffragette, inspiring and filled with faith. Hats off to such a great example for today's Christian women! Eleanor, I love you! You continue to inspire me.